# THE DEVIL'S A FIGHTING

## Book two

## P and K Stoker

**Amazon**

*To our beautiful Charlie Bear xxx*

# CONTENTS

# THE DEVIL'S A FIGHTING

# CHAPTER ONE

**H**ell 3.0 and things are occurring…

*"Oh Bub, I'm dripping with sweat. Whew. I can't believe we did that. I'm not sure if I can manage anymore. That's the third one today, and I'm completely zonked. Done in."* Harry was mopping the back of her neck with her bandana and adjusting her damp clothing, whilst blowing her soaked hair from her forehead.

*"Harry, I never realised how unfit I was, that's completely wore me out. We need to call it a day. Oh, I'd pay good money for a shower, a cold beer, and some macaroni cheese. Mac with extra golden bubbling, melted cheese on top. Mmm, toasted garlic bread too. Lovely."* Bub was trying to stretch out his back, whilst taking the kinks out of his groaning neck and shoulders. His sleek muscles were glowing with sweat and his damp shirt was draped over a chair. That was some workout.

*"Off the floor you two lazybones, we have work to do. Hell 2.0 or is it Hell 3.0, won't fix itself? What did we agree to call it?"* Karen had slept then fumed then slept some more: for over ten years, so she was full of restless energy and vigour. She was like a woman possessed, in her need to eradicate all signs of the Evil Eva and get the place, *"Homely"* again. Homely meant transforming the building back into a 1960's or 1970's office building: with all the excitement and innovation that embodied.

Karen then proceeded to prod the exhausted Harry, sharply in the shoulder, and made her get to her weary feet. Harry and Bub were hot, sweaty, and covered in dust, debris, and old lumpy, blue tack. They had been working with Karen for over two weeks now and had just finished putting the main office space back together. They did it cubicle by cubicle, suspicious stain by suspicious stain and ragged safety notice by ragged safety notice. It was painstaking, tedious and backbreaking work. They were just glad that they didn't have to recreate the nicotine *"brown blush"*, that Karen was convinced was integral to the whole scheme. That particular task was given to the residents, and the continuous background hacking coughs of the reluctant chain-smokers were an added bonus, according to a jubilantly upright Karen.

Devil Keith had been in the working group but had whinged so much, so that on day three, it was a relief to send him off to work on his own room. They had tried to explain to him that Karen/Eva, or was it Eva/Karen? Hadn't actually touched his room during Hell 2.0, but he was adamant that it too needed some essential work. Devil Keith had actually said *"lifesaving treatment"*, but they decided to ignore that particular lump of drama and nonsense. They hadn't seen him since then, but they weren't too worried as they could hear him bumbling around in his room and talking to himself. However, the recent episodes of barking, growling, and yelping were out of character. The incessant banging, scrapping and intermittent electrical blackouts were also a bit bothersome.

"Hell 3.0, I think. There were many, many celebratory Falkirk Sewer's drank that night, I'll tell you. Can we have a wee break? Please. I don't think I have any more fluid left in me to lose. I've soaked right through to my knickers.... twice. It's like a sweaty swamp down there. I need a drink and a delicious Tunnock's caramel wafer to tide me over." Harry hadn't quite worked out that over sharing so early in a relationship wasn't all that romantic. In fact, referring to your private lady bits as a swamp wasn't great at any point in a relationship, or conversation, or generally at any time. She was rubbing her back and thought it hadn't been that sore since she dumped that stupid chuffing, hammock.

She had recently bought a super-king-sized divan bed with soft cotton sheets and a duvet that she was convinced was part cloud and part distilled love. She thought about her serene sanctuary and started shuffling towards her office. She made it a full five slovenly steps when Karen stopped her.

*"Glad you made the suggestion young Harry. A short tea break, then the executive dining room needs looking at. In fact, I think it might need a full re-model. Let's go. I didn't think we'd get this far today. It's delightful, just delightful!"* The ever-efficient Karen was consulting her black clipboard and making considerable notes. She had taken to dotting her *"i"*s with small sets of horns, and was in ecstasy when she could slip the word Mississippi into a memo.

Bub and Harry were quietly muttering about their potential mutiny (there's brave and there's taking on Karen brave) and reluctantly followed the ecstatic Karen.

The executive dining room…

*"Bub, are you sure that you've checked everywhere? Where are they? They can't just up and go. I don't understand, where are they? Who could have done that? I bet they've been shipped to Mississippi by mistake. Well, probably not, but I must write a memo. NOW! Stat."* Karen had been asking them this for nearly ten minutes. She had also shouted this through the tannoy system and had grabbed every unsuspecting resident, by the throat, to shriek in their face. Gone was the highly effective, cool manager and in her place was a frightening lunatic who was very likely to start severely maiming folks. Soon. Very soon. Very, very soon Harry predicted, as she edged her way from Karen, the berserker.

*"Erm, Karen. Is there anything else missing apart from all the vending machines?"* Harry was beginning to work out what might have happened, but she was really hoping that she was wrong.

Karen consulted her copious notes. *"It's all still such a mess, but I can't find the Moonshine Stills from the gym either. However,*

*I think they went into storage. I'll double check that later. All the old brown curtains are missing and Harry, most puzzling of all, your haggis has disappeared. Who in their right mind would go off with that stinky gunk?"*

Harry chose to ignore the haggis comment. She knew that only a highly sophisticated palette could appreciate the little fellows, and she actually felt sorry for people who weren't as lucky as she was.

*"We should go see Devil Keith."* Bub was on the same wavelength as Harry, and beginning to become seriously concerned over what they might find.

# CHAPTER TWO

In the corridor just outside of Devil Keith's door...

*"Devil Keith, open the fudging door! Open this door immediately. If you don't, I'll send in Karen... and Harry. But mainly Karen. You do not. I repeat, you do not want me to do that. Come on big bro. Open the door. If you open the door no one will be angry with you. We'll understand. I promise."* Bub pleaded with the big galoot.

*"I will. I'll be angry, Bub. Hell 3.0 properties are missing and presumed dead."* Karen crisply stated.

*"Please Karen, we might get lucky this time,"* begged a very anxious Harry. She was pacing in front of the door and trying to work out if a carefully placed kick would smash the door in. Bub thought that sometimes she could be so adorably naive.

Devil Keith eventually opened the door a fraction, then shut it quickly. Bub grabbed Harry and pushed her up against the wall. *"I want you now. Now. Come, come, come on. Don't be shy. Now my ferocious kitten. Oh, your gorgeous fudging boobs. Get your pink nips out. Get your fudging plump ass here. Just where I want it. Mine, all mine. Bite me. Hard. Draw blood. I want you to leave a mark. I need you now. NOW."*

Bub was kissing Harry and frantically ripping off her shirt. Buttons flying through the air and fabric tearing. Harry was equally frantically trying to push him away: struggling, slapping, and viciously kicking out at him. Karen was hitting him over the head with her clipboard, but there was no dislodging him. Karen then jumped on his back and started desperately choking him with her sturdy lanyard. Finally, she was able to drag him off the flushed, rumpled, and frightened Harry. A panting and sweaty Karen placed herself between the horny predator and his anxious prey.

*"Yep, just as I feared. It's bad. Really bad. That was barely a second of exposure and look at me,"* Harry gasped, whilst pulling the edges of her shredded shirt together and searching for her displaced buttons. Bub handed her his sweaty tee-shirt and shirt to put on.

*"We'll need some help. A lot of help."* Bub was looking shamed faced and asked Harry for a hug. *"I'm so sorry. It was just so overpowering. I just couldn't stop myself. I'm so, so sorry. You know I would never be rough with you or hurt you. Never."* He patted her back and gently smoothed down her ruffled hair.

# CHAPTER THREE

Harry's room an hour later...

Harry, Bub, and Karen had exhausted all their more reasonable options, and were now reduced to just throwing random words at each other in the hope that something would stick. However, Bub remained adamant that Harry was **not** allowed to brick Devil Keith in his room until he'd learned his lesson. No matter how much Harry tried to coax him into doing it.

*"But Bub, he ruined my favourite shirt. Well, he made you ruin my favourite shirt. He's always hated it. I bet he did all of this on purpose just so he could re-style me. He keeps measuring me and tutting. Plus, I've had to hide my favourite flamethrower, and I thought it looked really good in here. Very decorative. Tres's chic."* Harry held up a pile of rags that use to be her shirt.

*"Harry, I'm positive he wouldn't just do it so that he could get his hands on your clothing."* Argued Bub. He was just beginning to understand what a strange relationship his brother had with Harry, and Harry had with his brother. Why are they friends? Are they friends? How are they both still alive? And lastly, hadn't Harry's shirt always looked like that?

*"Proof. Oh, you need proof, now do you? Huh?"* Harry rummaged in her cosmetics drawer and handed Bub a diary. It was open on a page that read:

*"'1. Do something truly Devilish to get into Harry's wardrobe and bomb the abomination.*

*2. Question Harry about how much she knows about my grooming regime.... especially my glorious hair. She's a suspicious little harpy.*

*3. Remember to snip off some of Bub's hair.... supplies are running a bit low.'*

*Now do you believe me? Hah?"* Harry crowed and did an unpleasant bottom wiggle thingy around the couch.

Bub wasn't sure what to react to first. Harry has a cosmetic's drawer? Devil Keith has the discipline to keep a diary? Harry's right about that fudging oaf, and his hatred of her clothing? Bub was also mighty relieved as he had noticed quite a lot of hair loss and a bald patch recently, so at least that puzzle had been solved. Well, nearly solved. What was Devil Keith doing with all his hair?

*"Hurmmp, he thinks that because I never use make-up he can keep his fudging, diary here. Where it's safe, from the possibly unionising mannequins. The twit. Ha, ha, ha!"* Harry was clearly smug and had no qualms about reading Devil Keith's private journal. And sharing the contents with others.

Thirty minutes later and they were still no further forward: Harry reluctantly placed a call to her half-sister Dippit, the Horsewoman of Disease. She hoped that Dippit wouldn't get too mushy, slushy, and gooey all over her.

*"Hi Harry, how's the love life going? Wedding bells? Do I hear wedding bells a pealing? Doves a flying? Floral arrangements a smelling? White, cream, or pink dresses a calling? What creation is Devil Keith dreaming into existence? Whatever it is, I bet it's lush. Mmmm, and the delicious Bub? Dish the dirt, girly. Does he look as good without clothes as he does with? Come on girly; tell your wee sister all the good stuff. The X-rated gossip."* Dippit cooed, and there may have been a slurping sound in the background.

Dippit may have been a renowned expert in disease aetiology and chemical weapons, but she did have a pair of eyes, plus the McTavish curiosity. Oh, and a lust for life... or maybe just lust?

Cue Dippit's back story...

Dippit and Harry shared the same father: one Mr Roger McTavish. He came from a long line of *"escorts"*, and he felt it was his God given duty to decorate the world... with his beautiful offspring. Harry was the eldest and born to the stunning and enigmatic Morag. Morag was an unusual creature; in that she was the only female druid of her generation. A strong and mystical woman who loved sumptuous puddings and her daughter, unreservedly. Though thankfully, not always in that order.

Dippit was Roger's second born. Dippit's mother, the stunning Helena, was a studious woman who scrutinised the work of Hippocrates and Aristotle. She provided healing balms, basic surgery and poultices to her fellow Greek villagers. Helena was curious, kind and thoroughly enjoyed solving complex problems. Dippit learned her trade at her mother's knee, and she would have been a very serious child indeed. However, the riotous McTavish genes added much needed spice to the little girl's nature.

Dippit, although clever, philosophical, and practical, was also a die-hard romantic. She dreamt of being saved by a mysterious, sexy and clever stranger. A stranger who also washed his hands after having a pee, as that didn't happen all that often in her time period. She would plan for that wonderful day of romance, whilst lancing rancid boils, yanking out thorny splinters and amputating gangrenous legs.

Joining Harry as a Horsewoman of the Apocalypse was a dream come true, so Dippit merrily became the Horsewoman of Disease.

Back to Harry's room and the present...

*"Hi Dippit, yes I do. Just as good either way. If you much know. Thanks for asking."* Bub was broadly grinning and shaking his head at her predictable antics.

*"Don't believe you Bub; send me a photo or better yet a video...*

*prrrrr. Meow, tiger! Down boy!"* purred the playful Dippit.

*"Dippit. He so would send you a photo, so please stop asking him every time we speak! Dippit concentrate, you silly cookie-bun, we need your help."* Harry laughed and playfully ruffled Bub's hair.

Bub and Harry explained that they thought Devil Keith had acquired the Greed and Fornication Moonshine Stills from the gym, so he was probably heavily dosed up with their juices. They also thought he had pinched all the vending machines, so he was stockpiling food. Although the pairs of missing curtains and haggis were puzzling. In the extreme.

*"So, approximately how much of the juice has he got in there?"* Dippit pulled a pen from behind her ear. She enjoyed taking copious notes and solving equations.

*"We're not sure exactly, but he opened the door the tiniest of slivers, for less than a second, and that was enough to put Bub over the edge. And I mean right over that edge, and into a bubbling a river of lust. My favourite shirt didn't make it."* Harry confirmed.

*"Harry, I'm sorry..."* Bub said and hugged Harry again.

*"It's ok, really. Bub, it wasn't your fault. Not at all. No one could have predicted just how potent the juices were. So Dippit, what can we do? We really need your expertise on this one."* Harry cupped Bub's cheek and gave him a kiss.

Dippit explained that she had her hands full at the moment, or she would have been happy to come Down and help. However, she did give them a list of essential provisions, and warned them that they would need more hands-on deck as this was gonna be a *"doozey"*. A hellava doozey.

*"You really need a highly skilled chemist, and possibly an engineer. If you had a medic that would be good to. However, if you can deal with the worst of it just now, I'll be Down as soon as possible. Oh, if Angel Gab is still around, I'd ask him too. He knows the score, and he can flash you away to safety if things get bad. And I think it might just get that bad.*

*I wish I could be with you just now, but there's a few things that need my urgent attention. Bye for now and good luck, big sis. Bub, just email me the photos and the video. A striptease video would be greatly, and very regularly, appreciated. Grrrrr!"* Dippit hurried off to mix up a gurgling potion, and stick a needle where a needle had no business being stuck.

*"She's relentless. I just might send you up to see her. That'll teach her."* Harry was only joking but Bub looked, ever so slightly, panicked by the threat. The varicose veins incident was still too fresh in his mind, and his nightmares.

Harry hugged Bub as the ever-efficient Karen went to dig through Hitler's old bunker for spare gas masks, just in case they didn't have enough hazmat suits.

# CHAPTER FOUR

O utside Keith's room…

All suited up and carrying bulging backpacks: Bub, Harry, Karen, Dr Riel and Gab tentatively pushed their way into Devil Keith's room. They tried to be as quiet as possible, and they were grateful that Devil Keith's muttering, gurgling, barking, and slurping helped to muffle their slight noise. The room was only partially illuminated due to the shredded overhead lights, but there was just enough light to distinguish the shapes and catastrophe that was Devil Keith's room.

All of the stolen vending machines were against the left wall: some were smashed into tiny pieces by mammoth fists. Whilst others had been roughly topped like dominoes and the rest were ripped apart: their sparking guts hanging out and messily coiled onto the floor. There was partially eaten, decaying food scattered across the room, with small piles that had the appearance of being hastily constructed nests.

The room was smelling of rubbish bins left out on a blisteringly hot July day. Cloying and unrepentantly putrid. Despite the evident putrefaction even a swarm of curious bluebottles wouldn't touch Devil Keith's room. Harry was pleased as the pale, creamy, wriggling maggots would have been too much to deal with.

The disturbing noises were coming from the back of the cluttered, ramshackle room. Through the gloom they could just make out a fort constructed out of the large dress-making table and roughly a dozen mannequins. The fort was partially covered with the missing brown, striped curtains.

"*He's made an A frame fort using the mannequins? Poor Devil Keith. He must be bad. He's really scared of the mannequins and their sly way. Them, and spiders. Ah, that's why the brown curtains were taken. To cover the frames.*" Harry whispered to Bub.

The front of the fort exploded. "*Oh I smell you little girl. Mmmm peach lip balm, my favourite. How did you ever know? Oh, and little boys who want to be the all-conquering heroes. Trying to cover up the smell of fear and dripping sweat, with bravado and puffed out chests.*

*Oh, you smell so sweet little girly. I'm going to enjoy playing with you, little girly. You smell so deliciously sinful. I'm gonna gobble you all up, you little morsel of fun. We are going to play such fun games, my little one. Such entertainment. You'll never be the same again.... I promise. Oh, how I promise,*" spewed a malformed Devil Keith as he rubbed the saliva dribbling down his chin.

The repulsive thing that was, or had been Devil Keith, stood nearly nine foot tall. His gaping mouth was stretched over broken, needle like yellow and blackened teeth. His red-ringed eyes had grotesquely elongated across his skull and into his sparse, frizzy tufts of hair. In the centre of his face was blackened snout that was gleefully sniffing the air. His right hand was a pulpy mass of muscles, arteries, stringy ligaments, and trailing tendons. The blood clots were sludging off and piling onto the floor. His other hand was grasping what was left of a beaten mannequin. Her features having been frantically scrubbed off: the remaining lump of plastic was covered in blood, rotten tissue, deep scratches, and grooves.

Devil Keith dropped the badly used mannequin and picked up an old bottle of milk. He looked at the curdled mess, grinned then greedily gulped it down: the greyish lumps coating his lips and dripping down his chest towards his mangled abdomen, groin, and thighs. He slowly extended his fungi encrusted long tongue and licked his left eyeball: smearing it with semi-digested food, small mushrooms, and thick, gloopy, yellow mucus. He did a second slow, sweep then uncoiled his tongue further in order to rhythmically stroke the crusty, green horn growing from his buckled forehead. His feet were long gone and in their place were colossal, black hooves. Hooves that were rhythmically padding on the mauled floor.

Harry was sweating inside the suit as her gaze caught Devil Keith's feet, then she started to hyperventilate. She bent over and hugged her stomach. She was trying not to vomit. "*Hooves, he has fudging hooves. I don't think I can do this.*" Bub stroked her arm and pulled her back from the barely contained panic attack.

"*Harry, sweetheart. You can do this. You can. I believe in you. We have your back. You're safe. I'd never let you get hurt. Remember, we have a plan. We got this.*" Bub whispered, although now that he had witnessed the full extent of Devil Keith's "*make over*" he was less sure of their plan. They needed more help. More fire power. More everything.

The creature, that was Devil Keith, could smell their fear saturating the air. He dipped his mutated head and peered through his sparse, spiky eyelashes. He then cracked his neck. Left, then right then he dipped his head forward. He stopped...motionless for a second. He smiled and gave a slow wink. He went from standing upright to a full-on crouched charge. He was furious: rapidly decimating mannequins, and his domain, in his need to reach Harry and Karen.

Bub, Karen, and Harry had been warned by Dippit, but even they couldn't comprehend what they were seeing. The speed and sheer destruction was utterly catastrophic. An industrial sewing machine flew into the air and narrowly missed splattering a stunned Dr Riel across the back wall of the room. A knitting basket flew at an impossible speed and a needle skewered Karen's fleshy palm to the nearest mannequin. A box of dress making scissors doubled as small spears and ripped through fabric then gouged out flesh, muscle, and bone: Gab stared at the 10 inches of scissors piercing his left thigh then screamed out in agony. Bub dived in front of Harry and took a pair of scissors through his right lung. His lung deflated and his blood pooled in his chest cavity. The shears would have torn clean through her scalp, pierced her skull and obliterated her soft, vulnerable brain tissues. The barrage of scissors were quickly followed by a full dressing table mirror. The lethal looking glass sliced through the air and narrowly missed decapitating Harry and Bub. Harry fell over a dressing table stool and smashed her shin off a wooden box. The volley of destruction ensured that the hazmat suits were quickly losing their integrity, and everyone was in soul destroying danger.

Their first instinct was to flee: get away from the monstrous nightmare that was barrelling towards them. They managed to stand their ground as they scrambled, ducked, and crouched: barely avoiding the worst of the missiles. Bub grabbed his rucksack. He pulled, struggled, and fumbled but he managed to stretch out the heavy iron netting that lay inside the bag. It was their only means of saving themselves, and possibly saving Devil Keith. This was the tricky part as their line of sight was hampered by the gas masks and suits, so they had to hope that this would work. They had one shot. Just one. After that Devil Keith would be too strong: even if they tried using a battalion of armed soldiers to bring him down.

They all held the net in front of their bodies: trying to maintain tension despite their shaking limbs and palpable fear. Devil Keith, in his all-consuming fury, ran straight into the net in his pursuit of Harry and Karen. The sheer force of the charge pushed them all backwards. Despite this, the team held on tightly and with muscle tearing effort they pushed a vengeful Devil Keith back. They were desperately trying to hook his ankles with dulled scythes and flip him onto his back. He was screaming and spitting whilst ripping at the very air they were breathing. The viscous saliva was flying from his broken teeth, as he tried to bite and claw his way out of the iron net. Eventually the team had him down on the cluttered floor but not out.

How were they gonna keep him there? Panicked and adrenaline fuelled, they knew they would quickly become exhausted and start making mistakes. This was it.

Bub stumbled, just realising that his lung had completely collapsed, and he was drowning in his own blood, when Gab produced a sledgehammer and pegs from one of the other backpacks. Grasping his ruptured thigh, he began pinning the net to the floor whilst trying to avoid the worst of the punches, gouges and scratches. Karen tore her mushy hand from the mangled mannequin then she rushed to the damaged air conditioning controls. Despite the multiple electric shocks, she slowly started venting the juices and gases out of the infected room. They knew that it wouldn't entirely solve the problem, but they couldn't let Devil Keith inhale anymore of the cloying air. They were also beginning to feel the effects of the gases, so getting the air as clean as humanly possible was nearly as important as holding the beast down.

*"I know Dippit said we needed to get a gas mask on Devil Keith, but I don't think we can. He's too fudging strong. Too violent. I don't think anyone should go near those horrific teeth. He could be contagious,"* panted Harry as she threw herself across Devil Keith's abdomen and thankfully missed the worst of the oozing, green spittle.

*"Oh, now you want to play, Harlot. Oh, Harlot. Cooee. Come here my pretty little one. My little, little girly. Let me..."* Bub didn't let Devil Keith finish. He began viciously hitting Devil Keith in the chest with a baseball bat. However, the vomit-inducing Devil Keith continued to thread his bilious tongue through the net towards a disgusted and frightened Harry.

They couldn't hold him much longer. His strength showed no sign of abating, and they were all flagging. Dr Riel grabbed Harry's shoulder and frantically pointed. The highly complex sets of Moonshine Stills were in the corner. The machines whirred and spun with a dazzling array of tubes, buttons, knobs, and gears. The collection bottles were cracked and leaking juices and gasses into the air.

Harry wearily rose from the floor, and Dr Riel took her place holding a bucking Devil Keith in place. She limped over to the Moonshine Stills. Harry tried to make sense of the machine, but it was beyond her skills. The array of switches and wiring was mesmerising in its dastardly complexity. The ever practical, Karen joined her. She grabbed some wax and a lighter from the backpack and began sealing the fractured edges of the containers. Karen knew this was, at best, a temporary measure until they could find Stan and get him to isolate the highly convoluted valves and make the units safe.

*"Go Gab. Go, now. We don't have much time,"* screeched Karen. Gab, still holding his bleeding thigh, sharply saluted then disappeared to search for Stan.

Moments later a blood splattered Gab appeared with a surprisingly unruffled and gorgeous Stan. Stan was decked out in jeans, scuffed work boots, a sexily torn tee-shirt, and a thin DIY paper mask. He had a tool belt round his narrow hips. Harry was still gobsmacked every time she saw the adorable Stan. Well, that's until he opened his mouth.

*"Hiya Devil Keith, ma old pal. Ma pal. I say, ma pal. You're in a right old state. I say a right old state. Oh, this is a right old mess. I say, a right old mess. I think I can help you there though. Yes, I think I can."* Stan casually walked over to the Moonshine Stills. He traced the pipe work with his index finger, and stopped. He tutted then shook his mane of black hair. He then turned two small knobs and nodded.

*"There's a couple of washers missing, and the pipework's been hijacked. Been hijacked, I say. But that'll do it for now. Yes, that I'll do it nicely. Nicely, I say."* The Moonshine Stills immediately stopped spewing gases and loudly burped. Stan then sauntered over to the shredded air conditioner unit. He fiddled with a couple of the wires and managed to turn it up until the toxic gas

and juices were torn from the air.

"*Yep, that's it all sorted. I say, that's it sorted, yep. One last thing, I say one last thing. Yep, you'll be needing that, yep that's the ticket, I say the very ticket.*" Stan slowly ambled over to a mannequin hidden in the corner. He bent down and proceeded to tickle her feet. A pale blue, viscous substance appeared on the soles of her feet. Stan used his trusty screwdriver to scrape it into a small pot and mixed with the debris lurking at the bottom of his tool belt. He brought it over to Devil Keith.

"*This I'll fix ye up lad, I say fix ye right up. Good and proper. I say good and proper. Hope to see ye next week to sort out the ear wax patent, yeh the ear wax. Next week, right. I say right, next week.*" In less than five minutes Stan had saved the day. Harry thought that he was an extraordinary individual. Not as wonderful as her Bub, but certainly worthy of a second glance.

A few minutes later...

"*Is that Selena? In the corner over there? We thought she'd fossilised, or disappeared or... well we weren't sure what had happened to her. Stan how did you know she was here? How did you know that the Deadly Sin of Sloth would vanquish the Deadly Sins of Greed and Fornication? As far as I know, no one knew that. I didn't even consider it as an option, and Dippit never mentioned it.*" Queried a very puzzled but relieved Karen. She was wishing that she had a clip board to hand in order to record this unbelievably, lucky find.

"*Just did, I say I just did. Now I have to get back to my soft fried eggs, baked beans, and chips, I say I must get back. There's rhubarb crumble for afters. I say, crumble for afters. With pink custard too. Pink, I say. Nora makes a great Saturday night dinner. Mmmm. I say, mmm.*" Stan rubbed his hands together and smiled sweetly as he, and the injured Gab, disappeared again.

Cue Selena's back story...

Selena was always a very lively young girl and a veritable

chatterbox. Whilst her mother was giving birth Selena was able to tell the gnarled old midwife how everything was going. From, *"it's getting a bit tight in here"* to *"that's me baked and ready, here I come.... wheeeeee."* The slap from the midwife, then her mother, the village elder and Jack, her older brother, didn't stop the new-born from her constant narration: *"cut the cord. Oh, nice and tight. I don't want a sticky out bellybutton now. Yes, that's good. Now for a drink. Get them out. Here I come, ready or not."*

She spoke or sang incessantly: providing a running commentary on everything she saw, felt and was currently doing. Each morning she'd have the same conversation with herself. *"Time to get out of this lovely, warm furry bed. Oh, it's so, so cosy. Just so warm and snugly. I wonder how the bear died. Not of old age, I would think. Probably a hammer to the head or even a spear, but surely that would leave a hole? It might have been a big old, bear trap or maybe he ate poisoned berries? Maybe all four things did him in. Bit of an overkill. Ha, ha, ha,... a pun. That's marvellous. Now time to put on my bat skin shoes. Big toe, smaller toe, middle toe, fourth toe and finally the pinkie toe. Is it called a pinkie toe? Why a pinkie? The colour? The lovely cuteness of it? What is the fourth toe called? I'll just ask ma mam. Oh these shoes, they're getting ever so tight on me. I must have grown overnight. That's just wonderful. Oh, I wonder how much I've grown. I'll ask Jack. He'll know. Just have to find him now. He's always hiding and starting racing games with me. Sometimes I don't even know that I'm playing a game..."*

The only time Selena would stop talking was when her mother was decorating their cave with colourful drawings of the latest water buffalo hunt, or pictures of the most recent *"spacemen"* visits. Even then Selena would dance around and have to cover her mouth with both her hands to stop her from exploding with questions. She would stare at her mother: willing her on so that Selena could propose possible reasons why the *"spacemen"*, visited Bonnybridge, Scotland. Well, technically it wasn't called Scotland at that time, but you get our drift.

Then one day Selena yawned and... just stopped. The yawn was huge: if there had been an observer, they most definitely would have been able to count all her teeth (twice), and they would have been able to flick her tonsils. Not sure why anyone would want to flick her tonsils, but they could have, like if they wanted to, that is. She didn't just stop talking she stopped everything. At the tender age of twenty-one Selena had used up all her words and all her questions and all her theories and all her possible movements. Her family initially thought she was just resting and were delighted with the silence. Her mother painted away in peace, her father built a racing canoe, and her brother organised his prized collection of haggis skulls without her "*help*". Then, they quietly realised that whilst Selena spoke no one else had the opportunity to argue, quarrel or disagree. Without her constant chatter their lives slowly deteriorated into petty squabbles, fisticuffs, and in-fighting. Meanwhile, Selena was blissfully unaware and was enjoying some much-needed hibernation.

Several centuries later the sleeping Selena was disturbed by a grave robber, whom she greeted very warmly. Very warmly indeed. She wasn't sure who got the bigger scare, but as he immediately died of fright, she surmised that it probably was him, after all. Another few centuries went by until she was unearthed again. This time she kept quiet and was transferred to a cold room. She read the note attached to her left thumb. It said, "*An example of an excellently preserved Scottish Mummy.*" She thought that can't be right: I've never had children of my own. So, after some slow wiggling Selena managed to get out of the room and onto the street. She began gleefully chattering again, and dancing wildly.

"*Oh, big white birds, they fly really high. Where are all the caves? What is that shape? Oh, I heard there were things called wheels, but I've never seen one before. It goes round and round. Is that music? Oh, there are drums...*" then she started to slow down and yawned. She fell back off to sleep with a puzzled smile on her face.

Selena woke a few years later. She lay still and reflected on her life. She may have talked a great deal, but she retained her conversations and most of the information around her. She realised that if she did too much or too quickly then she would suddenly go back into stasis. Her only solution was to do as little as possible, whilst still being able to do a little bit of chattering. She realised that she had to pace herself. Take it easy. There in was birthed Selena the Deadly Sin of Sloth.

Oh, and for the record. Selena ended up in Devil Keith's room because she couldn't resist the allure of salsa dancing, despite the slowdown it would ultimately cause. As she froze into her hip shimmering pose, she was mistaken for a rather pretty mannequin. Devil Keith went through a lot of mannequins, so he was always on the lookout for a bargain. He picked up a job-lot of cheap mannequins and Selena was scooped up in the sale. She was the one responsible for starting the mannequin union, but don't tell Devil Keith.

Selena provided her whole back story at just less than the speed of sound, so she probably won't re-surface again until humans colonise then destroy Mars.

Back to Devil Keith's wee problem…

Dr Riel had the unenviable task of trying to avoid Devil Keith's sharp, sticky and frankly gross bits so that he could apply the waxy poultice. He quickly dabbed Devil Keith, then jumped back. Then there was another quick dab then another jump back. Finally giving up and yanking the arm off an unsuspecting mannequin, so that he could take care of the dangerous dabbing from a safe-ish distance. Dr Riel would have liked the distance to have included his consulting room, then a long corridor, several ex-SAS security guards and finally a steel enforced door but he did so want to impress Karen, so he agreed to the closer proximity.

With the liberal application of the wax, Devil Keith finally transformed back to normal. He yawned then calmly looked around the room. *"Oh, you've formed a band, goodie. Can I join? Why am I asking? Of course, I can. Bags lead vocals,"* and with that Devil Keith put his thumb in his mouth, turned over and went for a rather restful, sloth induced, nap.

# CHAPTER FIVE

**H**arry's room and one cosy nap late…

*"Harry, Harry. You horror. What have you done to my room? You've wrecked my room. Where's Bub? Answer me. Answer me woman. Where is fudging Bub? I know he's here."* Devil Keith was screeching this into Harry's left ear whilst bouncing her around the bed and peeking under the quilt.

Despite his apparent distress over the condition of his room, he had taken the time to don a sarong decorated with flamenco dancing parrots, a glittering purple tube top, goat skin flip flops and azure blue, fingerless gloves. He wasn't sure about the gloves and decided he might change them for one of his many pairs of lace edged gauntlets.

Harry slowly opened an eye then quickly closed it again, *"mmmmm spleeleepinklis…"*

*"What? What, are you saying, you slattern? Answer me. Answer me this instant. What have you done? You ginger, vixen! Where is Bub? Where have you hidden him?"* Devil Keith hollered.

*"Speelsspeig……"* Harry mumbled into her lovely duvet.

Devil Keith pulled up Harry's eyelids, and slowly but loudly shouted into her eye sockets. *"What have you done to my room? You slattern."*

Bub slumped into Harry's room. *"She didn't do a thing: you did that all on your ownsome. Come on Devil Keith, get back to bed. We're all completely exhausted. We've been dealing with our cuts and bruises all night. Let her sleep. Come on out of here. I'm off to my bed. We can talk about it tomorrow,"* Bub's hair was standing on end, and he was sporting a rather nasty black eye. His ribs were probably cracked, he thought. He generally ached all over and was coughing up lumps of old blood clots. He knew Harry hadn't faired any better and had her shin in a splint.

*"No. I refuse to go until I get an explanation, and it better be a good one. An epic one, in fact. I'll never recover from this, this...betrayal. By the way, have you never heard of concealer and a hairbrush?"* Devil Keith spluttered, and rose to his full height. Devil Keith then realised that his legs had regained the ten inches that he had previously lost during the Snow White debacle. He still maintained that God was just being vindictive and needed to get a sense of humour. He thought it, but for some reason never quite got round to saying it to her.

Bub had seen that petulant look and heard that particular tone before, so he knew that he wouldn't get any peace until he gave Devil Keith a summary of the last few days and weeks.

One summary later...

*"Great. Well, at least that got rid of one of Harry's awful shirts, bit extreme but worth it. Any chance we could have another go? Get shot of more of her clothing?"* smiled Devil Keith whilst dotting foundation on Bub's flaming red cheeks.

*"Quit doing that, and step away from the eyeshadow palette. That's what you've taken from all this? Not the near deathly fight? The horrific destruction of people and property? The theft of part of my room? You do know that you stole a chunk of my room when you pushed your walls out? I still can't work out how you got those rollers up the stairs without anyone noticing. The probable PTSD?"* Bub blustered. He was exasperated by Devil Keith's thoughtlessness.

*"You're right. Not your colour. Not your colour at all. Well, my room is rather messy but that can all be fixed. Obviously by the culprits, hint, hint."* Devil Keith was looking around, trying to work out how much of Harry's room he could appropriate. He'd pop in later with his measuring tape and a nail gun. A bigger room and an opportunity to get rid of the monstrous wardrobe.

Winner, winner...chicken dinner.

*"I'm just gonna ignore you. So, we've hidden the Moonshine Stills, for now. Stan is heading Down later and he's going to make sure they're closed down tight. Apart from that, no one and I mean no one, is getting their hands on them. They're just too dangerous. You could have killed everyone, Devil Keith. I mean really killed us all."* Bub was staring at Devil Keith and wiling him to listen to reason.

*"I want them back. They're mine. I want them back Bub. I want them now. Finders Keepers. Yes, I'm gonna have to use the ancient and unbreakable, Finders Keepers law. You're making me do this. I'm drawing a line in the sand over this,"* Devil Keith was stamping his feet and Bub feared that he risked waking up Harry.

*"Devil Keith, seriously mate, you have to think about what I've told you. It's too risky. If they fall into the wrong hands, well, we're all done for. I can't stress this enough,"* Bub was trying to be patient, but this exploit had tested all of their fortitude and he was just too tired to discuss it any further.

*"But they look really good in my room, and I so wanted to make my own gin. Save a few coins and all that,"* whinged the unrepentant Devil Keith whilst admiring his elbow length, embroidered evening gloves.

Yes, Devil Keith had managed to change his gloves during this important exchange. You could ask Devil Keith for a lifesaving bandage to staunch the blood from your severed limb and he wouldn't have one. Ask him for a fluffy, wuffy accessory and he would have many, many of them secreted about his person. You still wouldn't get one, but they would be there for his use.

*"Ok... we'll compromise. I'll ask Stan to make you a gin Still, if and only if, you let this go. Deal?"* Bub sighed.

*"Ok, ok. I agree but I'm the big brother, so I need to know where they are. Another line in the sand, and all that jazz, Bub."* Devil Keith whined. Again.

"Not happening," mumbled Harry. "Get out the pair of you. I have work in the morning."

# CHAPTER SIX

Harry's room a few days later...

*"So, what have my two favourite scallywags been up to today?"* Harry enquired. She was in such a good mood as she had just visited Neville, Carmen, and their rambunctious, four-week-old pups. She so wanted to foster or possibly adopt one of the puppies but didn't really want to take one of Neville's babies away from him. He was very protective of them. However, he and Carmen were truly exhausted.

If Harry took on this responsibility, she felt that it would help their small family to cope. She wanted to discuss it with Carmen and Neville so that they could express their feelings and receive the reassurances they would so desperately need. It was a delicate and sensitive topic. Harry was considering drinking her own urine so that she could speak with Neville and garner his opinion, but she thought that she had a urinary tract infection so thought she didn't want to risk it at the moment. Well, that was what she told herself anyway.

*"You're in a good mood. Just seen the puppies? How are the little goofballs? Did you speak with Neville and Carmen? Oh, going by the look on your face you haven't yet. If you're not ready Harry: I'll go speak with Neville. I'll happily take a urine tea if that would help."* Bub had offered to do that on a number of occasions, as he could see that Harry was so torn over this. He wanted to make it as easy as possible for her. He really is a bit of a sweetheart underneath all the snarling and tailored suits.

*"Bub, honey. I am tempted, I really am, but I think I should*

*speak with them first. I trust you to put forward my reasons, but it's my responsibility and I just need to put my big girl pants on. Then get on with it. To be honest it's not the urine drinking that's putting me off: it's more the thought of hurting Carmen and Neville. They might think that I don't trust them as new parents. Or even worse they might think I want to take all their babies, so I'm trying to undermine them. I'm a bit conflicted and I think it would be easier and demonstrate more integrity if I did this myself. Thanks for the offer though, ma big lug."* Harry ruffled Bub's hair then sat on the arm of his chair. Bub went to get up to offer Harry the chair, but she pushed him down. *"I'm quite happy where I am, babes."* Harry hadn't decided what cutesy name to give Bub, so she was trying them all on for size. The next ones on the list were *"My Moonlight"* and *"My Wee Chicken Nugget"*, but she wasn't entirely convinced she could get them past her gag reaction.

Bub and Harry had been taking it slowly. Harry was still trying to equate this kind, funny and affectionate Bub with the guy who had ignored her for such a long time. Whilst Bub was still getting over being Karen/Eva's unwilling plaything. He was still struggling with being in the same room as Karen and so far, had avoided discussing it with her. However, he could see that she had questions and was looking for some straight answers. He really couldn't blame her, but he also knew that he needed some time before he could discuss it and finally put it to rest.

*"Harry, Harry here's an idea. I'll distract Neville with an ever so witty original poem, and you take the one you want. Hint, hint. The tiny one gets my vote. Hugo is such a cutie pie. Ohhhh yeah."* Devil Keith was shivering with delight then quickly added, *"Neville's not the brightest, and with all the sleep deprivation he's totally daft just now. He'll be fine about it. One less mouth to feed, and all that. We're only doing him a favour after all."* Devil Keith tried to look buff and manly as he made the outrageous suggestion.

Harry was about to go ballistic when she looked at Devil

Keith and realised that he also wanted a puppy. Needed a puppy. There was a tiny pit of desperation beneath his attempt at being an alpha male. She thought that he probably wanted a puppy even more than she did. Devil Keith was having a little trouble adjusting to Bub and Harry's new relationship. And Harry wondered if Devil Keith was missing his Nora and the challenges she unwittingly provided.

*"That's a hard no, but I will speak with them...."* Harry firmly stated.

*"Look Harry, I'm trying to be more responsible. I've loaded nearly all my 'loud clothes,' to the back of my room so as to not upset the puppy. Although I'm not entirely convinced that dogs are allergic to sequins, bustles and the colour chartreuse, but I trust you. You wouldn't steer me wrong. Plus, I now have.... gulp, jeans. Only the one pair, mind you. So I can go to the playpark and fetch a stick for the little puppy. I'm not sure about me having to poo in a bag then hanging the bag on a bush but I'm game. But I'm totally behind all that dog butt sniffing. I want to know if the dogs, my puppy is associating with, have a chewing tobacco issue. Yep, I'll sniff that right out."* Devil Keith was getting paler by the second: not due to the olfactory overload but due to the jeans. They were not his thing. Not at all, but it was clear that he was trying to commit to change and being a good puppy daddy.

Harry decided to chance her arm a bit. It would be decidedly odd if she didn't. *"Well Devil Keith. That's certainly a step in the right direction but I think it would help if you stopped wearing those tee-shirts. They're a bit.... much, don't you think? A bit crass?"*

Karen had been fizzing mad when she got out the filing cabinet, for the second time. (The end of *"The Devil's a courting"*). Luckily, she hadn't realised that she had been found an hour earlier by the much-harangued Angel Gab. Devil Keith then did the honours and Karen, although understandably in quite a temper, quickly pronounced that Devil Keith was the hero of the hour. Her saviour.

Since then Devil Keith had taken to wearing tee-shirts with terrible slogans, suggested by his mate Alan. The slogans included classics such as: *"I am the hero of the hour,"* or *"who has 2 thumbs and found Karen? This guy"* or *"I don't wear my pants over my tights, but I'm still a great big hero."*

Karen had raided the budget and bought Devil Keith three dozen of each design, so Harry knew that they were gonna be around for a while. Harry wondered, not for the first time, why there were no public relations, marketing, or advertising executives in their Hell. She reasoned that there must be a bunch of them somewhere: after all some of their pre-death campaigns had been out and out sins.

Back to the present and the puppy problem…

*"But Harry, if I stop wearing my tee-shirts how will people know what a brave and devilishly handsome chap I am? How will my Nora know? I know everyone can see how gorgeous I am, but my colossal bravery is hidden within my many layers of humility. I think I owe it to my adoring fans to keep wearing them. Afterall, they keep throwing their panties at me when I walk by. Who would they all look up to then? Mmm, who would they admire and want to emulate? Where would those poor, lost tiny panties go?"* Devil Keith smiled and pouted in the mirror.

*"Devil Keith, I'm not entirely convinced that the 'panties' are all that clean or that small. However, I am sure that they're mainly well-worn, baggy, greying, y-fronts. So, no real loss there."* Harry pushed him away from the mirror so she could check her teeth for basil leaves.

*"Ok Harry, the tee-shirts can go when that wee cutie arrives and is cuddled up in my manly arms. But I want a humongous shiny medal, Harry and a mile long ticker tape parade, Bub. Deal? Pinkie promise or no deal, ok? You have to promise first. I know how deals work. Afterall, I am the Devil, supreme being and maker of non-stick frying pans. Harry, you have something in your teeth."* Devil Keith

stuck his hand in and pulled a whole lettuce leaf from between Harry's front teeth.

Harry and Bub quickly agreed. Anything to rest their eyes from all the sequined tops and stop the random, unpleasant smells seeping from Devil Keith's panty (y-front) strewn room.

# CHAPTER SEVEN

Harry's room and a breakfast raid...

*"Yo, yo, yo. Harry what you doing?"* Devil Keith swaggered into her room to conduct a smallish heist.

*"You know very well what I'm doing and while we're on the subject of doing. You two fudging chancers can't just walk into my office, especially when you're not even coming to see me. You're just here to steal some breakfast. My breakfast. Every fudging day, this week."* Harry pretended to be angry, but she loved seeing Bub every morning and she accepted that Devil Keith would hang around too.

*"Now, now. Well Harry, you're such a good cook and it's such a delight to see you in the morning."* Bub was trying to distract Harry with a sexy fumble whilst Devil Keith sneaked the crispy French toast from her plate.

*"Hands off you mongrel."* Harry whacked Devil Keith's hands with her spatula and scowled at them both. *"You need to finish putting Devil Keith's room in order. Then we could rotate the breakfast duties. I could steal your French toast for a change."*

Bub had been filling Harry's kitchen cupboards with little treats and leaving her silly, naughty love notes so they both knew that she loved their breakfast squabbles. Harry retaliated by leaving Bub chocolates, shaped as boobs, on his pillows. He still had part of one of the melted chocolates stuck in his delectable hair.

Bub and Devil Keith had managed to move the broken vending machines, dismantle the disgusting curtain fort and dislodge the sewing machine from the wall. They had found the missing haggis lining the walls of Devil Keith's many food nests. The haggis disposal duties had needed a double set of hazmat suits all on their own...yuck. Most of the mannequins couldn't be saved, but Selena was given her own silk lined cupboard with a sign telling everyone to leave well alone. Unfortunately, Devil Keith still couldn't decide on how he wanted to categorise the remaining mannequins during this year's "*sort*". He thought he could try sorting them by the weight of lace on a garment, or by the square footage of embroidery, or evening wear versus day wear. All three possibilities had their merits and their own unique limitations, so he was still spit-balling at the moment.

"*We would finish it, but Devil Keith stole part of my room and still hasn't moved the wall back. So I only really have half a room just now.*" Bub grouched. This was a slight exaggeration. However, Devil Keith had used Eva's Hell rollers and surreptitiously moved the walls a few inches... Every day and was still doing so. On second thoughts: maybe not such an exaggeration after all?

"*You say 'Devil Keith,' like it's my fault when we all know it was Greed's juices that took the teeniest part of your room.*" Devil Keith was rolling his eyes, but he was making no plans to move the wall back. He had his own secret, covert operation in place for that extra space. Less covert and more shoes based closet, to be honest.

"*It may have been* **'the influence of Greed'** *that took the extra space from my room, but it's definitely* **'Devil Keith'** *who won't give it back.*" Bub and Devil Keith had engaged in the same squabble many, many times over the last few days. Harry was hoping that it might escalate into them wrestling, naked-ish, in melted chocolate pudding with tiny marshmallows bobbing on top. Well Bub would be naked in the pudding, and Devil Keith would be fully dressed and on a distant continent.

"*Picky, picky,*" and with that Devil Keith, unashamedly, stole Harry's substantial lunch box and emptied it: directly into his cavernous mouth.

*"I'll leave you two to sort it out. I'm off to work Please, please do the dishes or this time I really will get the locks changed."* Harry gave Bub a kiss and a cuddle, then had to give Devil Keith a bigger cuddle. Big baby.

Bub tidied up then realised that he was free for the rest of the day. It didn't happen very often as he was usually working on a commission, so he was at a bit of a loose end. He reasoned that if he went to see Devil Keith, he would be talked into being his decider or designer or lowly assistant. Basically, something Bub didn't want to do. If he went to see Karen, then he risked being asked about the whole Eva debacle. Something he really, really didn't want to do either. So, he decided to go and see The Oracles, after all he hadn't been to see them for quite some time. Also, they made the most smashing cakes, biscuits, and cream scones. The ridged plastic coverings on the sofas were challenging, but the treats were yummy enough for you not to mind the slippery, sweating and farting sofas.

# CHAPTER EIGHT

The Oracles...

Marjorie and Gilbert had passed the multiple-choice theory part of the Security and Data Protection training. However, they were struggling with the practical section of the course. They knew that they had to get organised if they were going to store their riskier artefacts, *"effectively, securely and safely"*.

During their Security Course coaching session, they were advised to look at the *"positive"* and *"less positive"* aspects of their life. And where possible they were to sandwich the positive and less positive so that they could learn lessons and celebrate successes. So, ...

On a *"positive note"*, they had safely secured the crust of the evil French Loaf in a filing cabinet that at some point had a functioning lock. They felt that they had dodged a bullet over that particular escapade. They felt exceedingly smug that they hadn't been fooled by Eva's disguise and still recognised her when she pretended to be Karen. Well, they didn't realise that she was pretending to be Karen, but they did see Eva rather than Karen. No one else was able to do that, so they counted that as a win.

On a *"less positive note"*, they had maybe, just maybe, told Eva too much and may have been the catalyst to the whole event. They felt that wasn't entirely conclusive, so they still felt the previous positive was still worthy of note.

On a *"positive note"*, they hadn't been trusted with the

Moonshine Stills. Stills which Devil Keith had misappropriated, then had a very bad reaction to. They were intrigued by that event as they had never heard of such a strong reaction to the Sins. They thought that Eva or Stan may have stumbled on a dangerous chemical weapon, and that warranted more investigation. However, the Moonshine Stills were in hiding or being hidden at moment. The Oracles hadn't listened after they found out that it wasn't going to be their responsibility to look after them. They just breathed out a sigh of relief and decided the investigation could wait. Indefinitely.

On a *"less positive note"*, again. The Oracles still couldn't find the Big Bang Runes. That was a big, big, big *"less positive"*, and they were deeply concerned about it. That is despite not being entirely clear on how or even when that had actually happened. They didn't live in one cohesive timeline and the lack of the ancient Runes was making tracking time that much more difficult. The Runes acted as a beat to their internal clocks.

On a *"positive note,"* again. The grease stained pizza box was still producing prophesies, but the predictions were a bit sketchy at times.

The last sentence should technically have been two items with The Oracles finishing on a *"less positive note"*. However, the authors are a wee bitty scared of doing that to them. They are **The Oracles** after all.

Day one of The Oracles getting organised…

*"Let's get started, shall we Marjorie, darling?"* Then they both looked around their cramped sitting room and realised that they couldn't even remember what or if their carpet had a pattern on it. They did hoover, but it was a rarity. And they basically just used the hoover to push their Nile packages around…a bit…sometimes. They did even less housework now as Clive aka Carmen wasn't living with them any longer. Gilbert and Marjorie decided to eat some toasted crumpets and see if the room looked

better on a full stomach.

Still on day one of The Oracles getting sorted...

*"Oh, well g'day young Bub and what brings you here?"* Cooed Gilbert. *"We haven't had the pleasure of your company for quite some time. We think. We're ever so popular since we solved the Eva problem, mate. Devil Keith, Karen and now you. Lovely, jubbly, mate."* Marjorie was busy planning a celebratory cream team and ironing the penguin tea cosy, whilst Gilbert got down to some serious hosting.

*"Hi, just thought I'd check that you were all right. I know Karen told you about the Moonshine Stills and you not having to be responsible for them. I just thought I'd make sure you were fine with that. Not too gutted by the Hell team taking over."* Bub said this whilst farting, wriggling, and finally sliding right off the offending plastic coated sofa.

*"Disappointed but we totally understand, mate,"* lied Marjorie. She was trying her best to look upset and guilt Bub into visiting them more often.

*"Oh, we heard about you and the lovely-ish Harry. About time that prophesy came true, mate. We thought that would have happened before this time. Eh, what time is it anyway? Oh, did you ever hear the rest of the prophesy, mate?"* Gilbert added.

*"There's more?"* Bub queried.

*"Yes, lots. So when..."* Gilbert was interrupted by quite a sight.

The sight...

Devil Keith walked in wearing extremely tight black bike shorts (as an aside: it was all too clear that he hadn't been circumcised), a green polka dot halter neck top, beribboned Doc Martens boots and carrying a large violet, leather handbag.

*"Oh Bub, didn't know you were visiting. I was coming to help tidy up a bit in here."* Bub was surprised at Devil Keith's offer. The Oracles were hoarders, and the tonnage of lace doilies

were bringing him out in hives so he couldn't fathom how the fashion-conscious Devil Keith would cope.

*"In here? Devil Keith, you're helping here? You sure about that? There's a crocheted, crinoline lady toilet roll cover: you do know that don't you? And you've still not finished with your room,"* puzzled Bub. *"Harry is gonna lock down the fridge. Tight. And she'll glue the sweetie drawer shut if we, and by 'we,' I mean you, don't pull your finger out and get it sorted. As it is, she's using your latest wedding dress prototype to fill her sofa cushions."*

*"What? What? What? The heathen! The Harlot. The philistine. That's it. I'm not lifting a finger to tidy my room. Well not today anyway. Well not this morning. At least not for another hour. I'm in no way scared of her and her glue,"* blustered Devil Keith, shaking his fist and marching around the room. Well, sort of marching and awkwardly climbing over boxes, around the room.

Still at The Oracles on sort day…

Devil Keith and Bub thought that since they were there, they may as well make themselves useful and got stuck in to tidying away some of the boxes and parcels. They also couldn't help having a good nosey around, as you could never predict what you might find casually lying around. An evil apple pie, anyone?

*"Bub, Bub. Over here. What do you make of this?"* Devil Keith excitedly declared. That made his fourth excited declaration in less than ten minutes. The other three were all hat related.

Bub reluctantly walked over to the corner and picked up a box containing a battered blue and silver power Drill. *"It's a power Drill, duh."*

*"No, no. Look at the symbols on the Drill. On the handle too."* Whispered an excited Devil Keith.

Bub peered at the letter and numbers. *"Sorry Devil Keith, I think this is written in Devilian. I'm not that great at reading or speaking Devilian. You were always better at that than me. What does it say?"*

"Well, I think that bit says something about dimensions. Units of size? Units of currency maybe? Not too sure about the rest of it." Devil Keith turned the Drill around and ran his finger along another set of writing. "Bub, Bub. I think we can use this to visit the other places. Specifically, other Hell dimensions. The ones G.O.D. mentioned recently." Devil Keith excitingly whispered, again. And he turned a small knob on the Drill.

The Drill, with a capital D, disappeared then re-appeared a few seconds later, "Wow Devil Keith, that disappeared quicker than your wallet when it's your round in the pub."

"Funny, you're just so funny…not." Devil Keith huffed.

"Wow. It's interesting though. Very interesting. Wonder when it was last used. It looks a bit beaten up. Do you think The Oracles would know more about it? Do you think they'd let us borrow it for a bit? More importantly, do you think it's even safe to use? The buttons seem a bit sensitive." Bub tentatively turned the Drill over in his hands and he was careful to avoid the buttons and knobs.

"Lots of questions there. Don't know, Bub. We should so try it out. It'll be a scream. A guy's adventure, and all that. Best not tell The Oracles or Harry though. They're still a bit on edge after the whole evil French Loaf episode," giggled a naughty Devil Keith and with that he slipped the Drill into his spacious handbag.

# CHAPTER NINE

**H**arry's room and the promise of cocktails…

Harry had just returned from her work placement and a wee after work glass of red wine with her friend Amanda. Despite Devil Keith and Bub trying to ruin her interview she had gotten the middle-management job. However, she wasn't entirely convinced that this was her passion. Her true calling in life. She loved talking about leadership, and she could see the reasoning behind project management, and she absolutely adored the stationery, but she wasn't sure if she wanted to manage people. All those budgets, meetings and other things. She felt that she had spent, and was spending, such a lot of her time coaxing, cajoling and, quite frankly, threatening Devil Keith, that she wasn't too keen on doing that as a fulltime job too. So, she decided to give it another few weeks then she'd re-evaluate her options…. oh, but she did so like the jargon.

Talking of threatening people. Harry had opened her briefcase earlier that day to find a note from Devil Keith. It said, *"Enjoy your de-constructed ham salad sandwich. Love and kisses, from your favourite man in the whole, wide world."* With some trepidation she checked her lunch box and found a small piglet eating bread, scoffing her salad, and licking butter from his snout. So, no lunch today. Plus, the added joy of having to explain to work colleagues why she had the foundation of her own small petting zoo in her bag, took up most of her lunch break and all of her patience.

Outside her room and the first thing Harry noticed was the

sweet, sweet smell. Mmm coconuts. Delicious. *"Mmm, possibly a pina colada? No, I bet it's pina coladas, plural,"* thought the delighted Harry. Oh, they're both so thoughtful. A long, deeply relaxing foot rub, a jug or five of cocktails and a meaty, sauce dripping BBQ, what could be better? Sumptuous.

She was wrong, so wrong...

Devil Keith and Bub were standing, in a couple of large buckets of water, as they clearly couldn't sit down. They were both bright, fire-engine red and painfully wincing as they tried and failed to cover their scorched bodies in gallons of after-sun lotion.

*"Ouch, it stings. Oh, oh, oh it's so sore. Nippy, nippy. So nippy,"* cried Devil Keith, jerking away from Bub and falling out of the bucket onto the floor. *"Aaahhh, this is worse. My bum. Oh, my lovely, pert bum is burnt too. I have a boo-boo... Oh, but no white bits so that's a bonus."* Devil Keith had a certain way of finding the positive aspects in situations. He listed this as his hobby in his extensive CV.

*"Hold still. Come on...hold still. Quick, come on, we have to get this on then some foundation to cover the redness before Harry gets home. She's gonna kills us. Quick, stop messing around and pass me the frosted beige concealer and I'll do your back,"* Bub was trying to move the process on whilst furtively watching the door.

*"Going to kill you, am I? Ermm, something to tell me my favourite guys? Something you want to get off your chest? Well apart from the raging sun burn, blisters, and ground in sand. Something else? Eh guys? Sharing is caring after all,"* what on earth have they been doing thought Harry. This cannot be good!

*"Well Harry. I'm not sure we need to answer to you. Do we, Bub? We are the masters here. Well, I'm the older brother so I'm the bigger master. We don't and won't tell you...you nearly woman thingy. You."* Devil Keith brazened it out.

*"Devil Keith, please shut the fudge up. You're making it worse. So much worse. Let's just get it over with. The sooner the better*

*and all that...*" Bub explained that earlier that day, after they had had a leisurely breakfast. And Bub cleaned up the dishes, whilst Devil Keith swanned off to wash his smalls. They, totally independently, had the bright idea of visiting The Oracles. Separately and not at all pre-arranged.

"*No, no not the fudging Oracles. Nothing good comes of Devil Keith visiting The Oracles, and I'm not all that keen on you going either,*" Harry could feel a monumental headache appearing. Encephalitis or meningitis she feared. She was currently reading about medical conditions that had "*itis*" in them. She was still struggling with the difference between endorphins and pheromones, but the "*itis*" seemed to be making sense.

"*That's probably not the bit of the story that you should be worried about, Harry,*" replied an anxious Bub.

Back to what happened earlier that day...

"*We visited The Oracles and Devil Keith noticed the most amazing contraption. Well, we had to try it...*" Bub started to explain.

"*But did you? Did you really have to try it?*" Harry plonked herself onto the sofa, and could see her lovely foot rub and cocktail night drifting out the window.

"*Hmm...yes. Devil Keith's been feeling a bit down, haven't you mate?*" Bub looked for some back-up.

"*As it happens, yes. Terribly down, not even my fuchsia embroidered evening gloves can cheer me up. And you still haven't sorted out my room. And Harry you promised you'd do it today.*" Devil Keith lied.

"*No, no I didn't promise. I absolutely didn't so don't even bother trying the old pigeon recordings trick with me. That ship has sailed. No way buddy. Just no way.*" Harry was throwing a bottle of water from hand to hand.

"*But Harry....*" Devil Keith whinged.

Back, back to earlier that day...

"Anyway, back to the story. The contraption looked like any other ordinary Drill, and I suppose technically it is a Drill...... but get this, it creates a hole so that you can see and visit other dimensions. Other Hells. Just imagine it. Other Hells? We could spy, or vacation, or even spy on them. It's amazing. So Devil Keith pinched it. Okay Devil Keith, you borrowed it for eternity. Better?" Bub was beside himself with joy, but his mood quickly sobered as he realised what he had said and what they had actually experienced.

"Oh please, no. Not another adventure." Harry was now convinced that she must have many, many medical conditions with "itis" in the name.

"Oh, Harry apart from the searing heat, bites, burns and hallucinations due to heat stroke it was a marvellous day. Eh, Bub? We had a blast?" Devil Keith nodded encouragingly at his brother.

"I'll need a Falkirk Sewer if I'm gonna listen to the rest of this," mumbled Harry, rising to fill her handy and much used sippy cup.

"So, we decided to do a little fact-finding mission to the other Hells. That pretty much covers it, Harry." Bub added and tried to leave whilst Harry was grilling the haggis bits for her cocktail.

"Please continue Bub. I can sense, and definitely smell that there's more. Much, much more to this tale." Harry tipped the steaming haggis into her cup.

"You're so nosey and bossy. But I know you'll keep snooping until we tell you. We went to Hell number three.. so there. The Beach Comber's Hell... so there. We had such a blast and we brought you back a present. Not that you deserve it. You'll be so excited, but you have to wait until we're ready to present it to you," shrilled Devil Keith. He started clapping his hands and instantly regretted it.

"Ermm, Devil Keith it really wasn't a blast. Not at all. Unless you're talking about being sandblasted and having most of the skin stripped from our backs." Bub was shaking his head and looking at his brother incredulously.

"*Ohhh, Bub. Well, I suppose there was that. Spoil sport,*" huffed Devil Keith. He did so enjoy a good exfoliating. Alright, it was a bit rougher than usual, but Devil Keith thought that his de-skinned back muscles were really rather attractive. And usually no-one was ever lucky enough to see them. Except that one wonderful time.

"*You're obviously upset and hurting. You're hiding things from me to spare my feelings. But I can take it. What else happened Bub?*" Harry coaxed Bub onto the sofa and began liberally coating him with after-sun lotion.

"*That's so good, thank you.*" Bub sighed in relief.

"*Me, me. Me first. I'm the oldest and most fabulous. Me first.*" After a few minutes Harry moved to sit behind Devil Keith and massaged his shoulders. Luckily, Devil Keith's shoulders weren't quite so raw. Harry thought she couldn't have coped if Devil Keith was in as much pain as Bub. Devil Keith would have been an unbearable baby about it.

Bub began describing their, and the unfortunate residents, harrowing experiences…

"*We messed around a bit then finally got the Drill to work. Devil Keith set it to Hell number three and pressed it against the wall over there. A portal instantaneously appeared. It was like looking into an immense eye. The outside circle was bright blue fading into grey and there was a dense black circle in the middle. Colours started to appear in the black pupil of the eye. It was amazing. Harry, you would have loved that part of it. We started to see shapes: it was an idyllic beach scene. Miles of sand, crystal clear water and sand dunes. There were beach huts, a kiosk, and trees. It looked like paradise, so we thought let's do it. Let's explore. It was so inviting and as it was Hell number three, we thought it wouldn't be too bad. Give us a baseline so that we could work out where our Hell sat in the grand scheme of things.*" Bub explained.

"*You're both still bothered by this being Hell number one? Aren't you?*" Harry offered him a sip of her drink.

*"A bit. It came as a bit of a surprise when we were told that we were basically an open prison."* Bub was obviously more than a little bit bothered. Harry was still building a relationship with Bub and learning more about him every day. She was surprised that he was concerned about this as he usually appeared so comfortable in his own skin. He rarely seemed upset unless it mattered to people that he cared about. He was content with his lot in his non-life. Especially now as he was sort of with his feisty Harry, well that's what Devil Keith told her. Bub was such a pleasure to be around, and Harry loved his dry sense of humour. His ability to spin a yarn had her in stitches.

*"Anyway, we stepped through the portal and onto the beach. Wow, it was hot. Really hot. So, we thought we'll stay for the day and gather some info."* Bub added.

*"Bub, you look like you stayed much longer than one day."* Harry swallowed and looked at their crispy skin.

*"Eh, no. We didn't stay long at all. Harry it was horrific. We couldn't believe that it is only two increments away from our Hell,"* Bub gulped and reached for Harry's Falkirk Sewer.

*"We were greeted by a dozen, dancing red squirrels. They were wearing grass skirts, playing teeny, tiny guitars and limbo dancing. They were fantastic little movers. It was so cute. Their tails were decorated with brightly coloured, scented flowers and trailing ivy. It was really funny. Erm, little did we know but they were distracting us while some of their less cute mates robbed us blind. Devil Keith and I had brought some supplies; bottles of water, a Swiss army knife each and some basic food rations. All gone in a blink of an eye, and they even managed to steal our shoes. Our shoes Harry!"* Bub looked at his crispy, smouldering feet.

*"We then looked around and that's when we realised that we might have been a bit overconfident with our spying and vacation plans. Some of the residents were walking skeletons. Literally skeletons just held together with ligaments, thin threads of muscles and the odd artery. We couldn't understand why, as there were coconuts and dates just lying around for the taking. Initially we*

thought that the residents had been there for so long that, maybe, they had just given up and couldn't take the heat any longer. We were wrong: they were starving. The enormous seagulls were employing bully boy tactics in order to extort all the available food. The seagulls were also randomly stealing the residents' bones and gobbling their plump eyeballs from their sockets. The skeletons didn't stand a chance. Once the skeletons were pitifully crawling on the ground, they began to lay down sticky muscles, lengths of tendons, veins and finally skin. Fully restored and functioning bodies emerged from the glutinous, sticky mess.

The starving then started again. It was a relentless cycle of starvation, ridicule, death, and re-animation. It was sickening." Bub gagged.

"Bub, you don't have to tell me anymore. It's obviously really upsetting you." Harry stroked his hair. It was probably the only piece of Bub that didn't hurt.

"No, I think maybe talking it through will help. There were 12 feet tall, giant Crabs carrying Kalashnikovs and smoking cigars. They moved at a hellava speed and indiscriminately shot off resident's limbs. Some of the skeletons looked and sounded like maracas due to the number of bullets lodged in their rib cages." Bub mimed the Crab's significant height and actions.

"Bub, Bub. Tell Harry about the gerbils." Devil Keith was obviously entranced by the gerbils and their antics.

"I'm getting there. Give me a minute. The sun was blisteringly hot, so we ran for some shade under a pine tree. We couldn't believe what happened next. The tree promptly pulled up its roots and draped them over its lower branches, like Victorian lace petticoats, and then the tree legged it up the beach. Seriously it ran away: taking our much-needed shade with it. We saw other pine trees pulling the same trick." Bub shook his head in amazement.

"No Bub, tell Harry about the fudging, gerbils." Devil Keith shook both his fists in frustration. Then gave a whimper when he remembered how sore his hands were.

"I'm getting to that, sheesh. Devil Keith and I ran for another tree. A palm tree this time. It stayed still so we thought we were in the *clear. But no, it started straining, gasping, and groaning so we looked up. Oh Harry, it was giving birth to coconuts, areca nuts, sacks of dates and things that kinda resembled gerbils. Actual birth to them: dilation, blood, sticky bits, and all,"* Bub finished the Falkirk Sewer and was looking around for more.

*"Finally, Bub you take too long to get to the good bits."* Devil Keith grinned manically.

*"Devil Keith, please let me finish. The tree began lobbing the coconuts, nuts, and dates at us. Wow, they are heavy fudgers. That was sore. Really sore. I think the bones in my forearm are crushed. A mega coconut nearly took my head clean off, but the tree's aim was knocked off due to a great white shark."* Bub shook his head and blew on Keith's red hands.

*"What, a shark? How did that happen?"* gasped Harry.

*"Harry, ma darling, I'll get back to those creatures in a minute. Then the sort of gerbils started to drop. They didn't have any fur. Oh, they were ugly, scaly creatures and they were pure, concentrated evil. They sunk their teeth and nails into us. Reaching through shredded tissue to scrap at our bones. Oh, that noise will haunt my nightmares. We threw them off, but they just kept coming. We were covered in a wriggling mass of their claws and teeth."* Bub was shaking but Devil Keith was surprisingly calm.

*"Devil Keith you're taking this well. Too well."* Harry was puzzled. She'd seen how much Devil Keith hated tiny spiders.

*"Superior being and all that, Harry,"* and with that nugget of wisdom, Devil Keith began applying a layer of rainbow nail polish to his manicured hands.

*"We managed to get away by rolling in the sand. That was a double-edged sword as there were rivers of molten glass just below the surface of the sand. Our burns aren't just from the sun. The molten glass did a fair bit of damage too. My feet are just starting to re-grow skin now."* Bub checked the progress. They would still need some more time before he could put on any footwear.

*"We hopped and jumped our way towards the churning sea. Devil Keith's currently fascinated by gloves, so he was able to do*

*handstands and take some pressure off his feet. Now that I think about it, what kinda gloves were they?"* Bub re-checked their hands.

*"Good ones, duh,"* Devil Keith had started applying the nail varnish topcoat then blowing it dry.

*"The sea was just as bad, if not worse. There were hulking great big mermaids trying to entice us into the water: using come hither looks and obscene suggestions. I managed to hold Devil Keith back a few times, but it was touch and go. He was fascinated by their anchor tattoos and rippling, bulging muscles. Contrary to belief, Harry: the mermaids aren't the most attractive women. They looked like they spent their down time wrestling great white sharks. And Harry, they were. They were fighting with sixty-foot-long great white sharks then throwing the beasts onto the beach.*

*The savage sharks landed on the beach, in the sand dunes or in the trees. That's how I managed not to get pulverised as one knocked the palm tree off course. The marooned sharks then puckered up their lips and spat their teeth at the residents. They too, were like machine guns but they didn't need to re-load. They just kept spitting until the sharks agonisingly, suffocated. There were shark carcasses hanging in amongst the treetops. The smell was nearly as bad and debilitating as the bullet teeth.*

*We also saw a couple of decomposing sharks that had people imbedded in them. We weren't sure if the residents had braved the sea and had then been eaten or if they had been eaten on land. Nowhere was safe.*

*By then the mermaids were flossing their teeth with vicious fishhooks and then they started on the hammer head sharks. They were arm and fin wrestling the hammer heads then; they too, were thrown onto the beach. The sharks grew muscular legs and began chasing us. They had hammers on their heads. Actual hammers. Massive, shiny steel hammers. When they caught a resident, they smashed them to smithereens. It was so grim. Just so grim."* Bub shuddered.

*"You're making it sound bad. It wasn't all bad. The sharks*

*looked hilarious. Chase, chase, chase...whack, whack, whack. If they wanted to be taken seriously, they really should have shaved their legs first."* Devil Keith was happily coating his hands with peach moisturising lotion and putting on his cotton night gloves.

*"Devil Keith, it was bad. Real bad. We both saw it. We then saw what we thought were balls of clothing and thought we could make some sort of shelter. But it turns out that they are another part of the residents' 'Life Cycle.' We think it goes normal person, ball of clothing person, start of the starvation process, ridicule, skeleton, death and then they all start it again.*

*Whenever a resident starts to remove their clothing, in order to cool down, they're given another duffle coat as punishment. So, they're slowly being casseroled until they start the process of becoming an emaciated, walking skeleton again. I think that the residents retain the memory of the previous Life Cycle, but they can't seem to stop the sequence of their actions. Sorry, I'm not making much sense but it's taking me some time to get my thoughts into order."* Bub blushed. He couldn't believe how much this had impacted on him and it was only two levels away from their Hell.

*"That's ok. Take your time. No rush. I'll get you another drink. You look like you need one."* Harry carefully patted Bub's arm then kissed the very tip of his burnt nose.

*"Make mine a double and would it hurt to have some nibbles, Harry? Some hostessing skills maybe? Bub, you need to get her trained, really!"* Huffed Devil Keith.

Harry added that comment to her, *"why Devil Keith regularly needs a good kicking"* list. Again, where are the public relation, marketing, and advertising execs when you need a good slogan or an inventive title for a *"Devil Keith list"*?

*"We then picked up a sunbed to hide under, but it appears that their only purpose is to brand the residents. I left most of the skin from my right hand there. It smelled like crispy grilled bacon. Harry, please don't cook that for a while, or I'll probably throw up on you.*

*We distracted a couple of the seagulls...turns out they're not so keen on Devil Keith's singing."* Bub sorta laughed.

"*Barbarians! The lot of them.*" Devil Keith huffed.

"*And picked up a couple of coconut shells. We desperately needed water, or basically any fluid. Even the sea was looking pretty tempting by then. Harry, the gerbils slurp the bone marrow from the residents' femurs and use the empty bones as straws. As soon as we picked up the coconuts, and just as quickly dropped them, we had the most horrendous hangover. Sick, dizzy, dehydrated and pounding headaches: a four-day weekend hangover. You know the kind....it makes you promise never to drink again. I only had that Falkirk Sewer due to extreme mental health needs.*

*So, there we stood, well sort of stood. Ripped, torn, burnt and thoroughly miserable. When we clocked the smell. I think they have a local sewage plant that dumps raw sewage into the sea. So, between that and the mounds of rotten flesh and bones the smell had us both retching.*" Bub swapped Harry's drink for a glug of water.

"*Oh, Bub I'm so sorry, what a terrible day you've both had.*" Harry gently rubbed Bub's arm, avoiding the worst of the injuries.

"*Harry, we weren't there very long. Less than an hour. It's so bad. We managed to get out just as we heard a funfair start up. The residents were clearly terrified and started wailing when they heard the first notes of the Waltzers. We knew we had to get out. I don't even want to imagine what that could have meant.*" Bub shuddered again. Harry thought he might have heatstroke.

"*And I so wanted to go on the Dodgems or the giant spinning teacups, but Bub just wouldn't let me. He was shouting... 'run for your life.' Huh, I think it might have been fun to have some hot dogs with mustard,*" added Devil Keith whilst blowing on his nails.

"*I'm not even going to grace that nonsense with a response but if I were to respond I'd say you were a fudging idiot. If they had hot dogs, they were probably still barking and trying to lick off the mustard dressing.*

*You nearly got us killed when you ran towards the sound of the funfair. Everyone, and I mean everyone, was running away from it. Some residents were even chancing the mermaids to avoid it. We also saw a few of the sharks trying to get back into the sea. There were a couple of people surfing but we couldn't make out what was happening to them. To be honest, by then, we couldn't think of anything but survival.*

*And to think, that Hell is only two places away from our Hell. It beggars belief. It was so lucky that we brought the Drill with us."* Bub was pleased to see that the skin has stopped sloughing off his feet.

Just then Chick the portly mouse jumped onto the table wearing a rather dashing new hat and jacket combo. He bowed to the startled Harry then just as quickly disappeared.

*"Oh Harry, I meant to say. We accidentally brought a feral gerbil back with us, but Chick and his assistants took care of that vermin. They are amazing little fencers. Who would have thought it? Their darning needles are sharp little fudgers and the gerbil didn't stand a chance against the six of them. Chick's wearing the prize of war just now."* Bub nodded at the stylish mouse.

*"Wish we had brought back more gerbils. I want a new coat. A scaly one would have been so chic."* Devil Keith flicked his petted lip and batted his eyelashes.

*"I don't think Chick could have fought off that many gerbils,"* Bub smiled and winked at Harry.

*"So, is this a never again scenario? A onetime adventure, never to be repeated guys thing?"* Harry sought some assurances from the frazzled pair.

*"Yes, yes, yes. No way am I doing that again. I will never, ever, ever use that Drill again. It's going back to The Oracles tomorrow… with a neon warning attached, in case some other foolhardy adventurer thinks about trying it out."* Bub was vacuuming up their flayed, brittle flesh and he handed a mop to Devil Keith so he could get rid of the glistening red viscera.

Returning the Drill was wishful thinking…

# CHAPTER TEN

A bacon breakfast morning...

*"Harry, did you see a brown rucksack?"* Despite the threats Bub and Devil Keith had broken into Harry's rooms to try to pilfer yet another breakfast. Although, going by the smell, Bub was fearful that it might be a fried breakfast morning.

*"Over there. On the empty table. Well, empty of all breakfast items. I hope you've eaten,"* threatened Harry whilst quickly scoffing down her pancakes and maple syrup then hiding the evidence in the sink. She had conveniently *"hidden"* a plate of cream cheese laden croissants in the microwave just in case the guys were hungry. However, she would hotly deny this to all who asked.

*"Coffee? A Coffee would be nice."* Devil Keith mooched whilst opening and closing the kitchen cabinet doors.

*"Devil Keith, you know where the vending machines are."* Harry skelped him with a Visit Falkirk tea-towel.

*"Ohhhh, you know they aren't quite working yet. They'll only issue pilchard tea, and I can't drink any more of that...well not until later in the day,"* Devil Keith mumbled this through the six Tunnock's caramel wafers he had just rammed into his mouth.

Bub retrieved his rucksack and handed Harry a book. *"Your gift ma lady,"* he bowed with a flourish and a pinch of her bum.

*"Oh, I do like me some presents,"* Harry twittered then added, *"Devil Keith, if you value your life step away from the petticoat tail shortbread. It's a new packet, and you know if I open it I won't be*

*able to stop eating them until it's finished."*

Devil Keith slipped the buttery biscuits into his pocket and grinned beguilingly. Well less beguilingly, and more like he needed to loosen his jet beaded choker an inch or two.

*"This book. It's written in Devilian, Bub. I can read some of it, but it will take me some time to make sense of it. I think Karen is fluid in Devilian. We could ask her."* Harry was delighted that it was a book. She wasn't too bothered about getting flowers, as they attracted too many pesky fruit-flies.

*"I could try,"* Devil Keith's offer was greeted by stunned silence.

*"Eh, all right. Go for it."* Bub shrugged as he handed over the manual to Devil Keith. Harry loved to read so was disappointed that she couldn't curl up with a coffee and delve into the guide.

The manual...

*"So, this is the instruction manual for Hell number three."* Devil Keith had a gold framed monocle wedged in his left eye. It had plain glass but that wasn't the point, he argued.

*"Devil Keith, isn't that an eight?"* Harry went to remove the book from his hands.

*"Ooops sorry Harry. Yes, Hell number eight. Ma bad."* Devil Keith pulled the book into his chest and swapped the monocle over to his right eye. He sighed.

*"Oh, that's such a relief. I thought that if we had gone to Hell number three and it looked like that, then I couldn't imagine what the other Hells had in store. Hell number eight makes so much more sense. That's seven Hells away from us."* Bub looked slightly less tense beneath his oozing blisters and rumpled, red skin.

*"Ah, here's a list of the other Hells and a brief description. Oh, they use horns as a guide to the severity of the environment, food, punishments and over all ambience. Now that's handy. Karen will love the horns. As an aside, do you know that she's trying to send memos to Mississippi again?"* Harry poked at the book.

*"Yep, we knew about the memos. They make her ever so happy.*

Horn rating? Handy? I suppose so, but as we're never going to any of them again, I'm not sure that it matters. Although I'm intrigued as to why they have a manual. I didn't think the Hells knew about each other," puzzled Bub.

"Maybe we'll find out later...." Harry added as Devil Keith gave a particularly loud tut.

"Quiet minions, I am talking here. Right...let's start.
'Hell number one
One Horn
The Office
This Hell will leave you cold and bored. The decor is dreary, the food combinations are the work of a buffoon, and the punishments are sloppy and lack imagination. The management are permanently out to lunch. It's blah, blah.' Oh, not good. Wonder what poor sucker runs that sad heap, ha, ha, ha." Devil Keith tittered and slyly stole the last cream egg. Harry just as slyly made him spit it right back out again

"Devil Keith, that sucker would be us. One horn? Just one horn? Out to lunch? Fudging cheek. Our Hell was designed so that the residents would have the time to reflect and be miserable. Its whole ethos is based on psychological pain and sorrow. It's meant to be dreary and lower the mood. That's our whole look. The additional punishments are only there as a deterrent or to add a little spice. They're only a small part of the package. They obviously didn't speak to anyone here when they were writing the guide," Bub was flabbergasted. "What about Hell number eight? It had no finesse? No underlying meaning. Huh? How did that monstrosity measure up?"

"Hell number eight
Four Horns
Hardy Beach Combers Delight
This Hell takes all joy out of a beach holiday. The sun is blistering and the sand more so. There is evidence of real imagination and innovation. The food is scarce, and the immediate

hangover is a touch of genius. Would recommend." Devil Keith nodded. He thought that was a fair review, although instead of horns he would use the more elegant vulture method.

"Would recommend? Would recommend? To whom? Who would want to go there?" Bub's dander was well and truly up. The book received a punishing poke in its spine.

"I may be wrong, but it sounds like this is a review and recommendations by demons to fellow demons. It's not for the residents at all. That's probably why it's written in Devilian. Maybe? Eh?" Harry tentatively offered her reasonable suggestion. "What about the other Hells? Keep going."

"Hell number two and three
Two Horns each
Meet the Brownies and Medieval Chivalry at its Best.

Hell numbers four, five and six
Three Horns each
The Health Inspectors Non-recommendations, The Nursing Home Mystery Tour and the Gambler goes Large.

Hell number seven and eight
Four Horns each
The Midnight Gardeners go a Cutting and the Hardy Beach Comber's Delight.

Hell number nine and ten
Five Horns each
The Cruise Ship/love boat and the Va-Va Voom Volcano not to be mistaken for the Va Voom Volcano. The additional lava makes all the difference to the volume of screams hence the extra Va.

Hell number eleven, twelve and thirteen.
Ten Horns each
For the connoisseur otherwise leave well alone. You have been warned." Devil Keith removed his monocle and gave it a wipe.

"Interesting," mused Bub, and scratched under his nose. The sunburn peeling was so itchy.

*"I'm getting bored with this."* Devil Keith moaned. He had obviously used up all of his supply of goodwill for that day.

*"Devil Keith, before you go, can you see if they explain why we didn't know about the other Hells? Why we don't have a list or a manual."* Harry enquired, and gave Bub's back a satisfying scratch.

Devil Keith flicked the manual pages back and forth. *"It says here that the insignificant Hells, or Hells with only one horn, have no requirement to know about the others due to their lack of influence and power. That seems about right to me, Bub. Why tell those one horn nobodies anything? They're pathetic."* And with that pronouncement Devil Keith put on his pink fake fur coat and headed home for a well-deserved nap. *"Bye, bye, have fun my cool cats."*

*"Well, that's that then. Can't say that I'm not disappointed. I have to admit that One Horn is a bit sore, but Devil Keith and I have left most things to Karen to deal with on her own. That's a big ask of her. We didn't even notice that Eva had taken her place so, on reflection, I think the review is justified."* Bub was slightly dejected.

*"Bub, the next sections are for the residents. It says, 'Rules and punishments.' That might give you some ideas to work through. And I think Karen would appreciate seeing your find. How about a cuppa, a few biscuits, and a chinwag with Karen?"* Harry gave him a hug then put the kettle on.

# CHAPTER ELEVEN

An hour later in Harry's office

Karen couldn't believe that Devil Keith and Bub had visited another Hell without asking her to go with them, or asking for her help with the planning and preparation. That was her forte, and she could have done with the exercise.

*"This has real potential. We might have known about Eva's plan much earlier if we had known there were other Hells out there. However, you and Devil Keith were poorly prepared, and it could have gone seriously wrong. Even Devil Keith did better than you did, Bub. At least he wore a pair of gloves.*

*Plus, and most importantly: a full head cannot be re-grown. You know the rule, Bub. We could have lost you yesterday. Both of you. Cause of death; the main ingredient in a Pina Colada cocktail. We just can't afford that level of risk. Harry, you must agree?"* A slightly miffed Kared nodded over at Harry.

*"Yeah, the experience sounded really awful, but Bub said that he would never use the Drill to do it again. So, I'm not so sure about considering that any of this has much potential,"* Harry was holding Bub's hand and rubbing his arm: as much for her comfort as it was for his. She was beginning to believe that he could be *"the one."* She was so happy with Bub, as it felt like a real and equal partnership.

*"So, what does it say...?"* Harry enquired. She opened a packet of prawn cocktail crisps to munch during the reveal.

Extract from the manual
*"The punishments. Guidance for unlucky residents.*

*The red coloured squirrels are in full sunburnt grey squirrels from Wales, UK. They will report you for:*

- *Mispronouncing a Welsh word or a place.*
- *Referring to them as red squirrels. Even if you whisper it in absolute delight.*
- *Referring to them as vermin or dirty, red thieves. Despite them deserving those names.*
- *Stealing their guitars, pompoms, or limbo equipment. They scratch their names into their possessions and do regular stock audits.*
- *Joining in when they sing their songs.*
- *Referring to them as cutie pies or adorable.*

*You have been warned."* Karen couldn't believe the utter cruelty, as everyone knows that red squirrels are soooo adorably cute.

*"Wait, wait, doesn't that give people who are originally from Wales an advantage, as they would know how to pronounce the words already?"* Bub was also astounded at the Hell's cunning ways.

*"It would Bub, but people from Wales are usually excellent singers, and would really struggle not to join in with the squirrel's choir. So it all evens itself out in the end."* clarified Karen with a sage nod.

*"Oh, there's a little bit more. 'You must attend the Funfair once per week where you will be:*

- *Traumatised by a socially inept clown (details to follow).*
- *Shot out of a cannon into the arms of a robust, sexually starved mermaid. Helmet not provided.*
- *Made to shave, pluck, wax and exfoliate one of the ferocious and biting, Bearded Ladies during their bi-weekly beatification regimes. Gauntlets will not be provided.*

*You have been warned.' That all sounds horrifying and very specific."* Karen finished with the manual and shook her head. The Devils running that Hell had thought of everything.

*"The clowns sound terrible, and I wouldn't fancy my chances with the hulking mermaids. That last one sounds a bit tame though. Quite relaxing even. I enjoy being pampered. In a manly way. I'm sure the Bearded Ladies would be grateful, rather than annoyed or bitey during their beauty sessions."* Bub laughed and stole a handful of crisps.

*"Harry, would you mind getting some wax and my tweezers so Bub can try the last one?"* Karen laughed too. A wicked laugh.

Thirty minutes later...

Bub now realised that the last punishment was, by far, the worst thing imaginable, and he'd seen a fair few peelings in his time. He now had random tufts of chest hair dotted about his scarlet torso and one badly waxed oxter (underarm to non-Scots). He had nearly chewed Harry's hand off during the waxing and plucking, so he could now picture how wild and savage the Bearded Ladies would be during their twice weekly beauty M.O.T. Plus, not providing safety gear to the Beach Combers residents was a stroke of evil genius.

*"Oh, sorry. There's another page here. 'Removal of clothing for comfort will result in:*
  - *The addition of one duffle coat per broken rule – slow basting optional but highly advised.*
*Residents ganging up on the seagulls will result in:*
  - *A salty bath with sharks as your very own rubber duckies. Please note: the shark's school report cards always stated that they do not play well with others and hate sharing their beaten seal carcasses.*
*Theft of Pincer James' or Pincer Stuart's cigars will result in:*
  - *A hula dance to the death. Hint: your opponent is likely to be a hammer head shark who is suffering from a pounding headache. Paracetamol not provided.*
*Peelings timetable, refer to appendix A.*
*You have been warned'* There's more, but it's roughly the same message. It was written a few years ago, so I'm not sure if the*

*manual's been updated recently. We might even have more horns. Unlikely, but maybe. Fingers crossed."* Karen tried for upbeat, but failed miserably.

Harry, Bub, and Karen decided that having their own Hell manual would be useful as their Decider was incredibly temperamental. And occasionally just mental, so having something more substantial would help them all. Harry was delighted with a future management project, and was planning her stationery needs accordingly.

# CHAPTER TWELVE

The smell of smoke, and Harry's disintegrating room…

It was the smell that warned Harry that something was wrong. Badly, badly wrong. She opened the door to her room and immediately began wheezing due to the overwhelming smell of hot sulphur and brimstone. She feared that she was suffocating and fell to the floor. She crawled to the air conditioning unit and tried to vent the smoke and steam. It was a pointless exercise, as the system was immediately overwhelmed by the stench and belching smoke.

Her eyes were streaming but she could just about make out what she presumed were the cause of the smell, gases, and smog. In the middle of the room there were two large lumps of white-hot rocks. Sizzling, spitting, and belching steam; they polluted the atmosphere. The sweltering heat was unbearable as it sucked all the oxygen from the room. Pints of hot, sticky sweat was puddling beneath Harry's prone body. She knew she had to act, and act quickly, as the rocks were burning through her floor and looked as if they were seconds away from burrowing through into the rooms below.

Harry slowly and painfully crawled into the corridor. Gasping, spitting, and choking she grabbed the fire hose. She opened the office door a fraction and aimed the hose at the centre of the room. The water was evaporating and turning to mist before it even reached the rocks. It was another pointless exercise as it was adding to the destruction of the fabric of the room.

*"God, oh God help. The whole place... is gonna go up in flames."* Harry was crying and bent double as she slid down the door onto the sodden floor.

*"Yes, dearie. How can I help?"* God appeared with her new hostess trolley, and a 1960's soda fountain clutched in her hand. She looked around and peered through the steam and smoke where she noticed the burning rocks.

**"Harry. HARRY, WHAT HAVE YOU DONE? WHERE DID YOU GET THE OCCULITES? HARRY, ANSWER ME. NOW! THIS IS AGAINST THE RULES! Gab."** God bellowed as a cyclone blew around her body, and fluttered her checked gingham apron. It was a terrifying sight, and Harry was frozen with fear. This was not the God she knew and loved.

Angel Gab appeared in a blind panic. He was cursing and swearing as he rushed to comfort a breezy God. Gab was usually very cold, and calculating, and reliable, and a bit dull. The fact that he was panicked and promising some mighty imaginative threats told Harry that this was serious. Very serious. He scowled over at Harry, and growled, *"Harry, how could you do this? This is a significant breach of protocol and procedures. Look at what you have done to her, and on her day off too. Selfish and stupid. No wonder you lot are always kept in the dark."*

*"Oh God, please... I don't know what's happened... Gab, I just got back from work... I swear... and they were there. I don't know where they came from or what they are... I don't know anything about the rules... or what's going on. Please...please can you help? God... please."* Harry was crawling on the floor in the corridor: coughing and hacking up her lungs. She had used the last of her breath to call for assistance. She was having to rest in between each pitiful plea for help and understanding.

*"Harry, I'm sorry. So sorry but I can't help you. I can't interfere in Hell related politics. This is something you'll have to face alone."* God held an embroidered hanky to her nose and mouth. She helped Harry to sit up and encouraged her to take slow, even

breaths.

*"God... I don't understand. Can't you cool those things down? Give me a chance... to stop this catastrophe. The fire hose... it isn't making any difference and people are gonna get hurt... seriously hurt."* Harry was covered in soot and her tears were running freely down her dirty face.

God reluctantly agreed to put out the worst of the fire. She threw several black storm clouds into the room and quickly closed the door. However she finished with, *"I'm helping just now because I can't stand to see you so upset. But Bub and Devil Keith have done a stupid, deadly thing that will have significant repercussions. You and many others will suffer due to their selfishness. I can't help with any of that. I can't answer any more of your pleas and requests, so please don't put me in that position again."* God started putting in her pink foam curlers and applying her night cream. Her help was over.

*"I know you just said that you can't help but .... where are Bub and Devil Keith? Are they safe? Are they hurt? What have they done?"* Harry rubbed wet soot over her forehead and through her hair.

*"Just keep cooling the rocks down and you'll have your answers. I can't stay any longer. I'm so angry, and I know that I'll do something truly terrible if I stay. Sorry. Take care little one."* God brushed away her tears and left with the furious Gab.

Harry shouted on Karen, and when she appeared she asked her to evacuate the floors below and bring more fire hoses. Karen was deeply worried by the calamity and quickly arranged the hoses. She added barrow loads of ice to the order, so as to speed up the cooling process. As they worked to control the heat and smoke Harry gave Karen a very brief update.

*"What do you think God meant?"* Harry hoped that God would appear, but she didn't.

*"I don't know but I have a feeling that Bub and Devil Keith may be in those rocks. I don't know any more than that, and I'm not even*

*sure if I'm right. Karen, I'm so scared. I think they may be really hurt. The heat was so intense... what if they don't survive?"* Harry was sobbing as she leant on Karen's shoulder, and they started their vigil.

# CHAPTER THIRTEEN

Karen and Harry on day two of their vigil…

Harry slept fitfully and awoke to the ominous sounds of cracking and the grinding of massive rocks. The mounds of lava were splintering open to reveal two large, crystal-clear diamonds and one very sorry looking Drill. The diamonds began slowly vibrating. The vibrating increased in its intensity until there was a blinding flash of red light. The light bulbs exploded, and the room was plunged into total darkness.

Harry and Karen scuttled backwards and hid under Harry's bed. Not sure what they would be dealing with. Harry was fearful that they could be facing another scenario like the mess Devil Keith had previously made. She immediately regretted her lack of planning and her subsequent lack of weapons.

There was a lung shredding cough and a whispered word, *"Harry…"*

Then silence. Harry wasn't sure what to do. The word was steeped in pain, but what if it was a trick? What if a demon rushed them?

*"Help us…"*

Harry was out from under the bed in an instant. *"It's Bub…Oh it's Bub."* Harry banged her shins on the edge of the decimated couch and slid across the wet floor, where she found a mound of stinging hot, wet flesh.

*"Pain, Harry, pain…….so much pain,"* gasped Bub into the dense darkness.

*"I'll get us some light…."* Karen skirted around the edge of the room and balanced on the exposed ceiling beams of the room

below.

Harry and Karen were quietly weeping as they looked at the pitiful, wailing creatures that were Bub and Devil Keith. *"Oh, you poor, poor wee souls. You're in so much pain and I can't do anything about it. I'm so sorry; this is beyond our meagre skills. We need Dr Riel. Oh Karen, I don't know if they'll survive the night. Just look at them. They're in bits."* Harry was now openly sobbing, and so frustrated with herself. She couldn't touch, or even offer comfort to either of them without risking sloughing off their remaining fragile skin and soft tissue.

Twenty minutes later...

*"Well, they're comfortable or as comfortable as I can make them. I've never seen anything like it, and I never want to, ever again. What did that to them? Bub and Devil Keith are designed to withstand virtually anything. Their healing is normally so quick, but this is something entirely different. They'll need some close monitoring. I'll take the first watch. You two get some sleep. Harry, no. Please don't argue with me. You were awake most of last night. You're no use to me or them in your current condition. Bed now. Off you go."* Dr Riel shooed the exhausted pair away off to bed.

Despite the screams of pain and torturous whimpers. Noises that froze the very blood in Harry's veins, Bub and Devil Keith survived the night. Their recovery still hung in the balance, but Dr Riel was quietly confident that they would live but he wasn't sure about the quality of that life.

# CHAPTER FOURTEEN

Harry's partially repaired room...

Harry was a total mess and knew she couldn't sleep any longer. The pacing, worry and lack of sleep was wearing her down. She needed someone to shout and scream at. She decided to call Dippit and leave a message. *"Dippit, it's Harry. When you get this message, please get back to me. I need you. Karen's here too. Please help me."*

Dippit dropped everything and came straight away. She knew that things were really bad if Harry asked for her help again. She enfolded Harry in a much-needed cuddle, and they settled on the patched-up sofa.

Karen had brought warm blankets, hot cocoa, and some calorie laden comfort food. *"Harry, it's alright for you to feel terrible and confused and angry and relieved. It's alright. You need to try to process this. Think about it. Your emotions have been all over the place. You've gone from heartily disliking Bub, to caring for him, to nearly losing him. All in such a short space of time. Plus, there's your strange relationship with Devil Keith and nearly losing him too. It's been frustrating and exhausting."* Dippit rubbed Harry's shoulders and tried to get some warmth into the stressed young woman.

*"I know you're right. But I can't think about losing him. Not now. Dippit, can you distract me? Please. Ask me nonsense or something."* Harry opened a bag of Maltesers. Although she wasn't really hungry or in the mood to binge on chocolate.

*"Ok...You asked for it. Harry, when did you know that Bub was who you should be with? The One?"* Dippit giggled. She had such

a strange profession and kept such odd hours that she feared she would never have a meaningful, romantic relationship. She was also very clever, so people were intimated by her and would nearly always give her a wide berth. However, that didn't stop her from loving all things mushy and romantic.

*"Oh, you minx. Interrogate me when I'm at my weakest? Okay then. Well, no one. But no one, was more surprised than me when Bub told me that he 'liked' me. To be honest I was always a bit afraid of him, well not exactly afraid but in awe of him. I did fancy him as well. Well who wouldn't? He's kind, thoughtful, talented and finger-lickin' gorgeous. Yummy!"* Harry popped a sweetie in her mouth and gave it a crunch.

*"He's a twin. So, do you fancy Devil Keith too?"* Dippit was clearly horrified by that thought. Karen looked like she was going to spew into a pile of carpet samples.

*"Oh no, no, no. Yuck. That's sick. Devil Keith's like the puppy you have to prevent from licking the electric sockets. No, what I mean is. Bub has the career, the common sense and he seemed to always know what to say and what to do. He's so polished and way out of my league. He's a bit of a golden boy."* Harry offered the bag of Malteser's to Karen.

*"Harry, I never ever thought that you lacked confidence in yourself. You're always so feisty and decisive. You're sometimes so focused that it's a bit scary. I have always wondered though, is that why you call your home an office or a room but never use the word 'home'? Because this is your home. It's a beautiful apartment. Tasteful and unique. Just like you."* Karen passed round a family sized bag of Revels.

*"I've never thought about that, but yes ...maybe? I'm not sure. I need to think about that. Bub decorated this office. I mean home, for me recently. I thought it was Devil Keith, but it's sensitive and so gently done. I should have realised. The lack of mirrors above my bed should have given it away.*

*Bub is pretty awe inspiring and a little intimidating. Anyway, before, when Bub was angry or dismissive towards me. Well, I thought I deserved it and then I took it as a challenge to get into even* worse scrapes. 'Cutting off my nose to spite my face'...as my mother would say." Harry scrapped the chocolate off a Malteser with her front teeth and contemplated the crispy filling.

"Well just get that outta your head, missy. You're so worth it. If he ever even implies that again, I'll steal your bra wires and he'll never be the same again." Karen harrumphed.

"Okay, tiger. Can't you use your own wires, Karen? Sorry. Not the time for jokes. No, no. I know better. I never even thought he was worried about me. He thought I was taking on too much when I was looking after Devil Keith. He was also jealous of the way Devil Keith would make me laugh. Imagine Bub jealous of anyone or anything?" Harry laughed and expected the others to join in.

"Takes some getting used to, but I think you're the exception. He's definitely jealous and a little bit insecure when it concerns you. Keep it up." Karen rubbed Harry's arm.

"Thanks Karen. You're making me blush. Since we had our 'talk,' we've seen each other's flaws and strengths. He wants to look after me but gives me space. I want to dirty him up a bit." Harry grinned and wiggled her eyebrows.

"Ohhhh. Do tell." Dippit cheekily crooked her finger at Harry.

"Dippit...I don't mean like that. I mean, push him to try new things and recognise that he doesn't have to be perfect all the time. I've found out that he has an absolutely brilliant sense of humour and he's so kind. I mean so, so kind and considerate. Although the other bit of dirtying up is pretty damn good too. I just can't believe he'd do this though. Put himself in that much danger. It's just inexcusable." Harry did a hiccup sob.

"Harry, you need to know what happened first. There might be a reason that Bub broke his promise. There could have been a mistake, or the Drill might have started on its own. Please try to give Bub the benefit of the doubt before you unleash the famous McTavish temper." Karen stated. Although she was pretty mad too.

Harry promised to try.

# CHAPTER FIFTEEN

Harry's fully restored room a good few days later...and a good few arguments later....

*"I'll sort it out, Harry. Hell number ten didn't even know we were there. It all happened so quickly. God might have been wrong. It might not be too bad after all."* Bub looked around and was disappointed by the lack of a wobbly hostess trolley and it's driver.

*"Oh, the great and mighty Bub. You'll sort it out, will you? You'll tell God she was wrong? Go on then. Go for it. You weren't even there when she arrived all pissed off and windy."* Harry threw her hands up in the air and blew her fringe out of her eyes.

*"I can assure you that I was there, and I have the multiple scars to prove it."* Bub raised an eyebrow and tightened his lips.

*"You're just being bloody facetious now. I know you were there, but you were in the rocks. I was the one getting a bollocking from God and trying to save your life. I was the one being told that God wouldn't help us anymore. I was the one dousing you in water and hoping that the floors and ceilings didn't cave in. Killing us all in the process. I was the one who sat up all night hearing your nightmares and collecting the skin and muscle you were shedding."* Harry was beyond livid. Too angry to cry. All the support and guidance from Dippit and Karen was well and truly out the window. Harry had opened the emotional floodgates, and nothing was going to turn that tide.

*"Harry, I know you were amazing and brave and wonderful, but I've said I'm sorry. I've tried to explain but you're doing your*

*usual and thinking the worst of me. You won't even let me tell you the full story. What happened."* Bub was trying to calm the argument, but it was quickly spiralling out of control.

*"The worst of you? The worst of you? You promised to put the Drill back where you found it, then you fudging well used it. You promised me. What more is there to say? You deliberately put yourself and everyone else in danger with your selfish actions. You're fudging pride. You and your one bloody horn. What does it even matter if this Hell has one horn? We all managed before we knew about the other Hells. We were happy in our ignorance."* Harry slammed a pot against the wall and watched the chilli slide down the wall.

*"I've already explained or tried to explain. We were just having a look at it when it went off in Devil Keith's hands. It was an accident. He was sucked into the dimension. What did you expect me to do? Leave him there on his own?"* Bub was exasperated and paced around the room.

*"No, I expected you not to look at it, or breath on it. And just PUT IT BACK WHERE IT BELONGS. AWAY FROM HERE! Back with those fudging Oracles. Let them be sucked off. Drawn into who knows where. Turned into tortoises for all I care."* Harry dipped a salty chip into the warm, sliding chilli.

*"Harry! You have to listen. Devil Keith and I have a duty to know what's going on in our domain. A duty to protect our people. The Drill has so many applications that we thought we were doing the right thing.... and I know you don't want to hear this. But I'd do the same thing again. I'd rescue Devil Keith again."* Bub was slow to anger but he was losing his patience and was about to blow his top. He could feel a tiny bump forming on his forehead.

*"The same again? Seriously? So, you'd step into Hell number ten and immediately be obliterated? Again? You'd welcome being crushed under a mountain of rock and put under so much pressure that you become a diamond. Again? You'd also want to go through that horrendous rehab. Again?"* Harry sarcastically stated.

*"Now look who's being facetious?"* Bub pushed the bump down and took a steadying breath.

"*I'm not being facetious. I'm talking to an imbecile who has no idea what's going on, and who doesn't seem to understand right from wrong or lunacy from rational thought. You're an idiot. A fucking idiot. And don't you dare even think that I'm sexy when I swear.*" Harry turned her back on Bub. He was silent for a few minutes but Harry could hear him trying to control his temper.

"*You know what's really wrong here, Harry? You fudging well treat me like a child. Like you treat Devil Keith. I've done plenty of sa...*" Bub hollered.

"*If you act like a bloody child, you'll get treated like a bloody child. You should know bloody better. Imbecile.*" Harry belted back. This was proving to be the worse argument yet.

"*It's not your place to tell me what to do.*" Bub shouted.

"*Not my place. Not my place. What do you mean by that? Is it because I'm a woman? Less than the mighty Bub?*" Harry was spitting mad and pulling unfounded arguments from the ether.

"*No, I don't mean that. And you know it. I've never felt like that. Every. You're twisting my words and I won't have it.*" Bub shouted again.

"*Oh, you won't have it? You won't have it?*" Harry taunted.

"*No, I won't you bloody...Harpy.*" Bub barked at Harry.

"*Now it all comes out. Harpy, I'll give you bloody Harpy. You're an arrogant imbecile who doesn't deserve me.*" Harry taunted again.

"*Yeh, I agree. I don't deserve a 'know it all Harpy' who spends all her time telling stories about her biiiiiggggg adventures, but really all you've done is tag along with other people and stole their glory.*" Bub had gone too far, but he couldn't stop himself.

"*That's not true and you know it. Take it back. And well.. at least I have friends.*" Harry mopped up tears of anger.

"*What's that supposed to mean?*" Bub screamed although her tears were cooling his temper slightly.

"*Oh, you know. You know. You're unlovable. Totally unlovable and I hate you. I really hate you! You dick.*" Harry spitefully shrieked.

"*Ditto, bloody ditto, sweetheart!*" at that Bub slammed the door, taking it clean off its hinges.

Thirty seconds later Bub came storming back into Harry's room, *"And Devil Keith, get my bloody office wall back. NOW. I won't ask again. And put down the popcorn. We are not your fucking entertainment!"*

# CHAPTER SIXTEEN

Harry's room minus a door…

Harry came out of the shower to find a duvet fort in the middle of the room. She smiled despite her low mood and tears. She was happy that Devil Keith had gotten over his dislike of forts as they played an exceedingly, and unusually, large role in his life.

*"Devil Keith, remember when you got trapped inside that duvet cover because you wanted to see if it was the same colour on the inside as on the outside."* Harry sighed and gave a small smile, as she was shaking her head.

*"Totally terrifying Harry! I was starving by the time I courageously rescued us."* Devil Keith puffed out his chest.

*"Mmm. You were inside the duvet cover first so I think I came in to rescue you. We were only in the cover for ten minutes, tops. What I want to know is why did you go to all the effort to button yourself into it?"* Harry quizzed as she towel dried her hair.

*"I wanted the full effect, duh."* Devil Keith threw a hairbrush at Harry.

Harry and Devil Keith crawled inside the spacious fort. *"You know he doesn't mean it, Harry. He got such a scare, and he's putting on a brave face. He'll say he's sorry, and it will be all right again. You need to say sorry too. Bub is loveable. Very loveable, and you are a bit of a Harpy. You sometimes boast about it."* Devil Keith adjusted his hairnet.

*"Devil Keith, I'm tired of always being the sensible one. I thought Bub might take that duty on for a wee while. He broke his*

*promise to me."* Harry sniffled.

*"I broke it too and you're not mad at me."* Devil Keith tightly tucked the sleeping bag round his knees.

*"Devil Keith, earlier today I shouted at you for a full thirty minutes straight. Of course, I was mad at you. What did you think I was doing?"* Harry untucked the sleeping bag, as Devil Keith would frequently wake up screaming that he was being murdered by a huge tribe of torch wielding marshmallows.

*"Harry, I thought you were doing your usual flirting and I didn't think any of your swearing, cursing and death threats were meant for me. I am, after all, a delight."* Devil Keith pulled the fluffy sleeping bag back. He had brought a thermos of cocoa so he could threaten the marshmallows to stay back.

*"You are that."* Devil Keith didn't register the sarcasm and went to sleep believing that he was, indeed, a delight.

Harry didn't have any more fight left in her, so she cuddled up in her cosy penguin pyjamas and hoped it would all be better in the morning.

# CHAPTER SEVENTEEN

I t wasn't better in the morning....

Harry felt like she had been dragged through a hedge backwards. Then forwards. Then back again. Her face bore the evidence of a night of tears, snot, and regrets.

Dippit barraged into Harry's room. Harry thought, *"I won't bother getting that door re-hung. It makes no difference. I have no privacy. I have no rights. I have no life."* She'd had a terrible night and was feeling very sorry for herself.

*"Harry? Devil Keith? Are you in there?"* Dippit kicked the side of the fort just to make sure she had their full attention. *"Neville's gone a bit weird. Well weirder than usual. Can you come have a look? I think it's pretty serious?"*

Harry sleepily dragged herself out of the fort, and looked around for her furry slippers.

*"Harry. Harry, I think it's been snowing in here. Harry, Harry. It's been snowing. The tent is full of snowflakes."* Devil Keith screamed in utter delight. He was tossing the snow in the air then began forming it into tight snowballs.

Dippit bent to look in the tent. *"Erm, I don't think that's snow you're licking. I think that could be Harry's tissues."*

*"Oh, they look so lovely."* Devil Keith giggled merrily and threw them in the air.

One, two and three...

*"Ahhhh. They're used tissues. Tissues. Oh, oh no, no. Used tissues. Get them off me. Ohhh, moist tissues. They're burrowing*

*under my skin. Help, help me, I'm dying in here."* Devil Keith belted out of the tent and lay gasping on the floor. He threw his empty thermos at the offending *"balls".*

Dippit had heard Harry and Bub's argument. All Hell had probably heard the shouting. She knew it was really bad when Harry didn't join in with her laughter.

A few snotty minutes later...

Harry dragged herself down to the kennels. *"Don't bad things come in threes? Bub, then Neville, what's next?"* she thought.

*"Nice pyjamas. Tres sexy."* Dave, the kennel master, laughed. Harry thought there's a reason some men are single, and she glared at him. Fudger.

*"Only saying, Harry. Don't bite my head off. I get enough of that here ha, ha, ha."* Dave mistakenly thought he was hilarious.

*"So, Dippit, what am I fixing this time?"* Harry sighed. Her head and throat were killing her.

*"Well before you get all mad at me. In my defence, I thought you'd already spoken with Neville and Carmen about the puppies."* Dippit was backing towards the kennel door, then held herself tight. She braced herself for a bollocking.

*"Don't tell me. I can guess. You thought you'd cheer me up by collecting a puppy? Am I correct?"* Harry just wanted to go back to bed. She was exhausted and very emotional. And feeling very violent. Very violent indeed.

*"Yeah, good guess,"* Dippit gulped and stepped away to allow Harry to see Neville.

Harry saw Neville...

*"Hells, bells. What's happened here?"* Harry gasped and raced to the front of the kennel.

Neville was wearing a red bandana on his large, squarish head. And what appeared to be heavy fake gold jewellery, the greenish tinge gave it away, around his chunky neck. He was also wearing a chequered shirt buttoned only at the neck, with a body-hugging white vest underneath. Harry looked closely. Well as closely as she was willing to risk, considering all the growling that was going on. She silently queried, *"was that a tattoo of a pistol on his paws?"*

*"You'll need some pee for this one."* Laughed Dave: whistling and heading off to get a China teacup. Silly cookie-bun!

Harry quickly drank the horrible pee concoction, and gently asked Neville how he was.

*"Donde esta la biblioteca?"* came the gruff response followed by an ominous growl and nose, wrinkling sneer.

*"Oh, that is so awesome. Neville has a little Spanish accent. Oh, I love it. Oh, you're such a precious little bundle of wire wool fur and multiple razor sharp teeth. Aren't you, oh yes you are? A Spanish accent? Who would have thought? Dave, what did he say? Go on, what did he say?"* Harry chuckled.

*"You do know that Hounds of Hell originated from Chihuahuas, right?"* Dave mumped.

*"Yes, but a little Spanish accent? Who would have guessed?"* Harry chuckled again. She couldn't wait to tell Bub this one. She stopped and realised that she wouldn't be telling Bub anything.

*"Mexican, Chihuahuas?"* Dave sarcastically stated. He also did a particularly elaborate eye-roll.

*"Yes, yes, but cute. So, so, cute. So, what did my clever little doggie say? What did you say? Oh, what did you say my little doggie?"* Harry was bent double and gently patting her thighs. She was also cooing in a very disturbing baby type voice. A sort of weird *"thingy"*, was happening to her. The *"weird thingy"*, that even a hard-hearted thug adopts when faced with a puppy or kitten. You know the one, you probably did it recently.

*"He said 'Where is the library?' I'm not sure why but that's what he said."* Dave was scratching his head and looking very perplexed.

*"Neville, what's in the library? What can I get for you? What do you need? What does my wee doggie, woggie need?"* Harry cooed.

*"Estas naranjas son frescas?"* followed by another deep,

rumbling growl and a spit onto the floor.

"*What did he say?*" Harry looked up at Dave.

"*He said 'Are these oranges fresh?' again I'm not sure what this is about,*" Dave was as puzzled as Harry.

"*Neville, you don't get oranges from the library, silly.*" Harry wanted to pet his head, but thought better of it. The snarling and all the savage biting through the bars of the kennel was a bit off-putting, to be honest.

"*Donde esta el salon de belleza?*" Neville barked and hit off the side of the kennel. It violently shook.

"*What did he say?*" Harry had stepped back towards a cowering Dippit.

"*Another strange one, Harry. 'Where is the beauty salon?' No idea what this all means. Neville might need wormed, again.*" Dave laughed and went to get the powder.

"*Carmen, what's going on?*" Harry was still delighted by the Spanish accent, but puzzled by the requests. Had there been a dog food incident again? Carmen tried to explain why her Neville was so upset. Harry was super delighted as Carmen, too, had a beautiful Spanish accent. Back to the explanation: calm it, Harry!

Carmen elaborated. When Dippit spoke with him about taking Hugo up to Harry: Neville was delighted, as Mistress Harry was one of his most favourite people in the whole wide Hell. As Dippit explained the request more fully, he realised that she meant she was taking Hugo away to be Harry's puppy, on a permanent basis. Neville then went completely ballistic: tearing the kennel apart, barking, biting, and generally cursing up a storm. When he finally calmed down, he said that he was joining a Mexican street gang called Los Zetas (The Zs) so that he could take a, "*hit out on Harry.*"

In order to join the gang, he felt he had to butch up his image, so he ordered the clothes and stick-on tattoos from a night-time shopping channel. He wasn't too happy because he couldn't understand why the postage for his few items was the same price as the postage for a full set of golf clubs. He was going to write a strongly worded letter about that.

Whilst waiting on the post to be delivered: Neville decided to learn some Spanish. All he could find was an old Spanish phrase book, left over from Dave's last holiday to the Costa del Sol. So, he'd been repeating the same phrases all morning. Carmen finished by saying that she was gravely disappointed in Harry, and her cavalier attitude. She thought that if Harry had wanted to adopt Hugo then she should have spoken with them directly. They would have considered it but, ultimately, they probably would have said no. However, being approached by Harry, rather than Dippit, would have been easier and less underhand.

Poor Dippit was crying and trying to explain that she had jumped the gun and it wasn't Harry's fault. Harry said that she should have spoken with them, and she tried to apologise. Carmen and Neville turned away: to tend to their family. They didn't acknowledge, the tear drenched, Harry leaving the kennel.

Can this get any worse? Simple answer...yes.

# CHAPTER EIGHTEEN

Devil Keith's room...

*"Have you seen Bub?"* Harry rushed in.

*"Don't you knock? Then wait for an audience with me? However, to answer your question. No, not since you were such a Harpy towards my sainted brother."* Devil Keith huffed. He was in the middle of a particularly difficult embroidery stitch.

*"Really?"* Harry infused that one word with enough sarcasm to choke a horse. Sorry Harry, won't mention H.O.R.S.E again, the authors promise.

*"Yes, sainted. You have a sharp, blistering tongue on you. Hmmm, I'm forever having to apologise to people on your behalf. You woman, you Harpy."* Devil Keith went to flounce off. He so loved a dramatic exit. Nearly as much as he loved a dramatic entrance.

Harry just couldn't be arsed responding to that load of nonsense. *"Wait a minute. Have you checked his room?"*

*"Have you?"* Devil Keith questioned.

*"I asked first, you fudger."* Harry snatched up his embroidery ring and held it behind her back.

*"Oh, you asked first did you, Harry the Harpy? And give that back this minute, you lady."* Devil Keith held out his hand. He hated when folks messed with his stuff.

*"Seriously Devil Keith, have you seen him?"* Harry dropped the hoop into his hands.

*"As a matter of fact, I haven't? Are you happy now? Pleased that he's nursing his emotional wounds? He's nearly as sensitive as I am."* Devil Keith cradled the embroidery, and stroked it as he

whispered words of comfort to the colourful threads.

Harry was very, very far from happy. She was an emotional wreck. She couldn't believe how quickly everything had spiralled out of control. She was also still hacked off at the Harpy comment, but she knew she and Bub had to have a *"talk."*

Ten minutes later and the embroidery was all happy again...

*"Well Devil Keith, he's not in his room and there are definite signs of a violent struggle. The room's a disaster."* Harry had rushed into Devil Keith's room again.

*"Aaahhhh, Bub's room might be in a tiny bit of a mess due to his wall mysteriously moving and even more mysteriously, crushing all his possessions."* Devil Keith hesitatingly said. He was surprised that Karen hadn't noticed all the missing wall rollers.

*"Ok Devil Keith, so there's probably not been a struggle and he's just off in the huff then?"* Harry let out a relieved breath.

*"Well...no. He normally tells me, and gives me a contact number in case of any problems or emergencies. He knows that I need to be there to rescue him. Quite regularly, as it turns out, and I don't even cast it up. Not ever. Harry, have you ever heard me tell you about a time that I've saved Bub? No need to answer that, because I have never said a word about that subject."* Devil Keith assured her.

*"Yeah, Devil Keith, that's totally why."* Harry sarcastically responded.

An hour later...

Devil Keith and Harry thoroughly searched Bub's rooms, but they couldn't find anything out of the ordinary. However, he did have an unusual set of cufflinks that Devil Keith sneakily purloined. Purely for scientific reasons and not at all because they would match Devil Keith's new, emerald green and orange striped tuxedo.

*"Devil Keith, I think we need to speak with Neville. Do you think he still has a hit out on me?"* Harry worriedly asked.

*"Probably Harry, I would."* Devil Keith sagely nodded.

Back at the Hounds of Hell kennels…

Harry felt very vulnerable and sad when she went to visit Neville and Carmen for the second time that day. Vulnerable because she hated asking for help, and sad because she feared that their relationship had permanently changed.

Neville had added a studded collar and flick knife to his ensemble, but Harry knew she had to persist. She was also getting quite use to the taste of the smelly tea.

*"Neville, I'm so sorry about earlier. You and Carmen had every right to be angry with me. I should have taken the time to speak with you. Please, can you forgive me?"* Harry pleaded and placed a dog treat on the top of the kennel.

Neville responded, *"Donde esta la biblioteca?"* followed by, *"Estas naranjas son frescas?"* and finally, *"Donde esta el salon de belleza?"* this was said with a pointed sneer and grunt. This was quickly followed by Neville miming the use of a gun, to blow off Harry's head.

*"Oh Neville, please can you help me? Bub's missing and I'm worried sick."* Harry sobbed.

*"Oh, you should have said. I'm a good doggie. Of course I'll help you, Seniorita Harry."* Neville rubbed off his tattoos and dumped the gold chains in the corner of the kennel. *"Come on Carmen, we have some work to do."*

Neville searched through Bub's room for over an hour but came up empty handed, or empty pawed to be more precise. Carmen thought she might try and three minutes later she dropped a blood stained, small slug like object into Harry's outstretched palm.

*"This is it, Seniorita Harry,"* smiled Carmen. Oh, that delightful accent!

*"What is it?"* enquired Devil Keith.

*"Chainmail,"* Karen and Harry said together.

# CHAPTER NINETEEN

Twenty minutes later in Harry's room…

*"I think it's safe to say that Bub has been abducted. After checking the Hell manual, it looks like it's probably the Medieval Hell that has him. That Hell has a two horns rating so that's less frightening than Hell number ten. That's a plus. I really hope he's alright. I can't believe that he's gone."* Harry sniffled as she said the word abducted. She was trying to stay strong but couldn't hide how devastated she was. Arguing then taken. What if they never have an opportunity to mend their relationship? Say they were sorry? Fix things?

*"Do you think it's due to the Drill?"* Karen could feel Harry's pain, but she felt that they couldn't focus on it; rather they had to try to work on a viable plan.

*"Yep, I think it's highly likely that someone has taken umbrage at Devil Keith and Bub's recent exploits. God did say there would be consequences."* Harry crossed her fingers when she said God, but no one appeared in a frilly apron smelling of pine disinfectant.

*"We're getting him back now."* Devil Keith was furious and feeling something else: something utterly new. He wasn't sure what that something else was. He had explained his feelings to Karen, and she told him that it was probably guilt. He decided that guilt was a terrible emotion and should be banned. Karen had nodded and agreed.

*"We need to prepare and do this right. We probably only have one shot at it. We need Dippit and Stan."* Harry firmly stated.

The War Room aka Harry's office…

"*Stan meet Dippit. Dippit meet Stan.*" Harry was keen to move things along. Social niceties were out the window as far as she was concerned. Bub was the only thing that mattered.

"*What do we know? I say, what do we know?*" the gorgeous Stan enquired.

Harry explained that the cockroach walking pavement had recently been sabotaged so they were going nowhere. The cockroaches were currently devouring the world's largest frittata. A sinister bribe that not only kept them focused on munching through the delicious treat, but the cockroaches were crippled with heartburn so they were having to take frequent breaks in order to chug down copious pints of Gaviscon. Whilst tag-team eating the frittata the cockroaches were also spending an extraordinary amount of time composing a reply to Devil Keith's one vulture review of their services.

So, in short, the Hell clan could only access Falkirk via Hitler's Bunker. As they had to use the entrance and exit from Hitler's bunker they were limited in the amount and types of weapons they could access. They were very lucky that they could get Stan in that way.

Regarding weapons, well slim pickings was the order of the day. This was deeply concerning as someone had to be working inside of their Hell. Someone who could get to the cockroaches, but who didn't know about Hitler's bunker? They queried. Since there were very few of the residents who did know about the bunker that wouldn't help them identify the collaborator.

They debated ordering weapons on Nile, but they didn't want anyone or anything alerting the collaborator and pre-warning the other Hell.

"*So, Harry what do we have?*" Dippit enquired.

A number of mildly threatening items sat on the coffee table...

Baseball bats, knives, lengths of rope, an embroidery hoop, hammers, jars of acid and a flamethrower nestled in the centre of the table. Devil Keith had also added an assortment of hats, gloves, and scarves. Just in case they all got cold. Harry was impressed, until she realised that the hats were elaborate fascinators, the thin gloves were purely decorative, and the scarves were little more than hair ribbons with tassels. *That guy has way too many tassels at his disposal.*

*"My items of clothing have infinite uses, but this lot of weapons just won't do. We need guns, or crossbows, or machine guns. Tanks. We need tanks. And bombs. Lots of bombs. Do you think we can get a military, grade helicopter in Falkirk?"* queried Devil Keith, whilst miming throwing a whistling grenade.
Tumbleweed was the response…

Dippit had been researching Stan's Moonshine Stills and their application in modern medicine and disease control. Could a diluted Fornication concoction help in the treatment of impotence? Could a dab of Greed be an organic stimulant to help students focus and study? The applications could be endless.

She had distilled small packets of red dust that contained Fornication and packets of green dust that held Greed. She didn't want to confuse those little suckers.

*"They're only samples but they might come in useful. I'm not sure how they would be useful, but they're small and easily carried. I'd say that we should use them sparingly until we know more about the side effects. However, what we do know is that they do impact on Devils."* Dippit said rather nervously.

*"Okaaay,"* Harry wasn't entirely convinced but she'd try anything and everything.

*"I have this, I say, I have this."* The *"this"* was small vials of Sloth's wax mixed with odds and ends from the bottom of Stan's tool belt. *"They'll put folks to sleep, I say, to sleep. Might be handy, yes might be. They're an antidote for Fornication and Greed. I say, Fornication and Greed so if we make a mistake we can fix it. We can fix it, I say."* Stan was his usual repetitive self, but Dippit was hanging on his every word. She was dazed by his intelligence and ingenuity. Her ovaries were plumping up with his every

word. A strong reaction that had taken Dippit by surprise.

*"Yes, I can see a lot of applications for that. Sorry, forgive the pun,"* Dippit giggled and pushed a lock of her dark, curly hair behind her delicate ear. Harry rolled her eyes at Karen, but Karen was too gobsmacked to react. Is Dippit subconsciously flirting with the bizarre guy?

*"I have Devil Keith's ear wax too. I say, Devil Keith's ear wax. I've changed it a bit. I say, changed it a bit. I think it will work on other animals. I say other animals, but not overly strong. Not like the pandas. The pandas, I say."* Stan popped the tubs of wax on the table. Dippit was now licking her lips and frantically batting her eyelashes. She may have been salivating, but just a little. She was a lady after all.

*"I think. I say, I think Dippit, that you have something in your eyes. In your eyes. Harry, can you have a look? I say, have a look Harry,"* Stan was clueless.

*"What else do we have?"* enquired Devil Keith whilst stuffing a fascinator into his rucksack and refusing to make eye contact with Stan. Devil Keith was still a bit scared of the ear wax concoction, and he was fed up with picking his earrings out of animal secretions. The saltiness was wrecking his rhinestones.

*"I have these,"* and Harry put a small bag on the table. It splodged as it hit the surface.

*"Oh, my tear ducts. Yeah, I've been looking for them. They are mine, so I'll just take them, right? They're mine. All mine. Just for little old me."* Devil Keith quickly snatched up the gloopy mess and pushed them into his eyes, pleased that no one had tried to lay claim to his moist *"things".*

*"I'm so reluctant to give you these back, but needs must,"* smirked Harry. Time for a bit of revenge, she thought. Nearly a woman? Ha?

A few minutes later...

*"Ouch, ouch...stop that. Stop it. It really hurts. You don't have to enjoy it so much."* Devil Keith squirmed and arched away from

the fiends.

Harry and Dippit were taking turns poking Devil Keith in the eyeball, then gathering the subsequent tears in small test tubes.

*"But they suit you and you're so brave for carrying them for us. Your tee-shirts tell everyone about the real you: and the real you is the bravest little soldier, who's keeping the ducts safe from all our enemies."* Harry managed all this this with a straight face but Dippit was hiding her smile behind her hand.

*"All true Harry, but the screwdrivers are really sharp and a wee bitty vicious. Please take the crowbars away. I don't know why, but I think you and Dippit are enjoying this a little bit too much now."* Devil Keith looked for some support from Stan but he was busy screwing the lids on small jars and admiring Dippit's creations.

*"Oh no, not us,"* Dippit was pleased that Harry had a distraction and Devil Keith could be a really silly cookie-bun at times.

*"There isn't much in the manual about Hell number three. Just a small review. There are Peacocks of Hell instead of Hounds of Hell. Can't imagine that's good, but I can't quite imagine that it's all bad either. Peacocks such are splendid creatures, but they might be a bit cocky.*

*Oh, the Devil is called King Adrian. According to the manual he's King Arthur's great, great cousin twice removed. If he has modelled himself on the mythical King Arthur and the round table, we might be fighting well trained Knights. And lots of them,"* Karen was taking notes and trying to build a strategy. *"Any suggestions anyone? Devil Keith, please put your hand down. I have no intention of ever picking you."*

*"Guerrilla warfare might work. A quick in and out."* suggested Dippit as she looked coyly at Stan.

*"What, kill gorillas? What have they ever done to us? Well, they might make a lovely snack, but I don't think we have time for that Dippit. Duh!"* Devil Keith stuffed a bottle of diet barbeque sauce in his bag. He thought he might share the charred gorilla

with Harry, but only if she used the low fat sauce. He couldn't spare **that** amount of fabric for her wedding dress. Devil Keith made the authors add that last sentence.

*"No Devil Keith, **guerrilla** warfare."* Dippit clarified and took the sauce out of his bag.

*"Yes, that's what I just said."* Devil Keith took the sauce back, and pretended to yawn so he could sneakily drop the bottle back in the bag.

*"No, I'm talking about a small group of us infiltrating, then quietly sneaking Bub out of Hell number three. We won't succeed if we take them on as a full frontal, force."* Dippit clarified and wondered how Devil Keith managed to breathe without significant help.

*"I have just the thing,"* Devil Keith ran off to gather *"the thing."*

*"Right while he's away and can't distract us. Any suggestions. Anything else?"* Karen quickly said and pulled them into a tight huddle.

*"I have some special translation teabags, and a flask of hot water. Dave gave me them after I promised him some industrial waxing strips for his holidays. He says he likes the smooth look. Yuck."* Harry added them to the pile. *"It means we can talk to the animals without all the pre-peeing nonsense."*

*"I'd like to volunteer. You'll need my help."* Karen looked at the teabags. She wasn't keen on just anyone talking to her lovely wee Hounds. They could be sweet talked into all kinds of problems. The wee snookums.

*"Sorry Karen, you need to keep running our Hell. You also need to hide all evidence that we've gone and finally, find that fudging collaborator. It's a big ask. Dr Riel, I know it's an imposition, but can you possibly help Karen?"* Harry slipped the teabags into her rucksack.

*"I'll help and I'll pack you a medical field kit too."* Dr Riel was tickled pink. Uninterrupted time with his cool calm crush, what could be better? Well, Bub not being abducted would technically

be better.

"*Thank you. So, it will be Dippit, Devil Keith and me. I was going to ask Gab but he's so busy when he visits. And, to be honest, things aren't great with us just now. He's colder than ever. He's been like that since the Hell number ten incident.*" Harry was irritated by his attitude as the visit to Hell ten had been an accident, afterall.

"*I want to come. I say come. Yes, I'd like that. Like that. Bub's a decent sort. I say a decent sort and I have another gadget we could try. I say another gadget.*" Stan sort of assertively said.

"*Oh, do tell Stan.*" Dippit had started gushing and was imagining being swept off her feet by the glorious Stan. Harry thought this won't end well and why isn't Dippit repulsed by Stan's voice? What is wrong with her? Has she been sampling her own fornication wares?

"*Rightyo. I say rightyo. Now, I've knocked us up some utility belts from my spare tool belts. I say, utility belts. They're prototypes but they should be ok. Yes, ok, I say. Harry, can you whistle? I say, whistle Harry, please.*" Stan gave Harry a tiny nudge and held out a toolbelt.

Harry whistled and tiny metal legs, with rubber soled red boots, dropped out of the bottom of the tool belt. The belt then zigzagged across to her. "*Oh, that's a creepy caterpillar, dog thingy but it could be really useful. Add a few to the pile, please.*"

"*Fill the rucksacks with the bigger items. The weapons will go with Harry, Stan and I. Devil Keith can fill the rest of his rucksack with bits and bobs. The powders, potions etc. should fit in the belts.*" Dippit added some lip balm and mascara to her belt. Plus a push-up bra. Well, a girl could have fluffy, wuffy dreams. No, obviously not that girl, her thoughts were purely salacious and X-rated. Afterall, she was a McTavish with a super big crush and a crisp copy of the Kamasutra at her disposal.

Devil Keith rushed in, looking extremely pleased with himself. He did a pretty nifty pirouette.

"*What have you got there?*" Dippit enquired.

"*Duh! Bananas.*" Devil Keith pointed at the fruit and did a sideways head nudge at Stan. As if to say, "*and she's meant to be the brains of the outfit.*"

"*Why do you have bananas?*" Dippit missed Devil Keith's insulting gesture and Stan's answering frown.

"*They're easy to transport, nutritious and they should help to bribe the resident gorillas.*" Devil Keith pointed at the fruit again and did another sideways head nudge at Stan. As if to say, "*and she's meant to be the brains of the outfit.*"

"*The gorillas? Well, I suppose that explains your outfit.*" Between Devil Keith's ear wax and his gorilla onesie he might get more than he's bargained for, thought Harry.

"*Yep, something wrong with you hearing? Dippit said we should employ gorilla warfare.*" Devil Keith was getting a bit moody.

"*No... Guerrilla warfare. Guerrilla warfare.*" Harry clarified.

"*Same difference. We just need to get going and rescue my brother. Move it. Come on, move it.*" With that parting shot Devil Keith began stuffing the rest of his bananas and his hats into his rucksack. Harry thought, on the off chance that we do find some gorillas, it will make for some smashing photos.

"*I might get a wee bit bored. I say a wee bit bored. So, Devil Keith, chuck in those knitting needles and wool. I say, needles and wool. Oh, wait while I pick Karen's dead skin off first. I say, get the skin off first.*" As Stan was rubbing it off Dr Riel was slyly scraping it into his pocket for his "*Karen collection.*"

"*What have you got there Stan? Is that a Tupperware box?*" Karen checked.

"*Yep. Just a few pork pies from my ploughman's lunch. And a steak-bake. I say, from my lunch. Might get peckish. Yes, peckish, I say.*" Stan sat the box of pies at the top of his rucksack.

The team were, mainly, decked out in camouflage gear as Harry held the beaten Drill to the wall and waited on the portal appearing. The eye appeared, then began changing colour until a sun dappled forest began to emerge in the viewer.

*"Off to the Medieval Hell. Well here goes nothing,"* whispered Harry and she stepped through.

# CHAPTER TWENTY

The wrong Hell...

*"Devil Keith, I think we're in the wrong Hell."* Harry stage whispered and pulled him down beside her to hide. *"Why's that, Harry?"* Devil Keith poked his head up.

*"Someone just threw a tomahawk at me. It's imbedded in the tree, just above my head. Didn't you see it?"* Harry stage whispered again.

*The words, "**TOMMY TALKS!**"* were quickly followed by two more lethal looking tomahawks thrown at Harry's head.

*"Scrub that. No, we're **definitely** with the Brownies, instead. I think the Drill's playing up and sent us to the wrong Hell."* Harry sighed and pulled Devil Keith down a second time.

Hell number two, the Brownies Hell...

The Brownies Hell was a clearing carved out of an ancient forest with tall redwoods and oak trees dwarfing the ferns and hydrangea bushes below. Harry noticed a dozen miniature tree stump stools, a smoky campfire, and a bedraggled washing-line in the centre of the clearing. The washing-line was sagging under the weight of dozens of small Brownie uniforms. Uniforms that were patched and roughly torn, then unevenly pegged to the fraying rope. The line was further tested with an assortment of socks that may have started off their life as bright white, but they were now scrubbed into varying shades of grey and full of darned holes. There was a surprisingly large section of the rope that appeared to contain lengths of bandages and, if Harry was seeing correctly, used sticking plasters.

*"Brownie Lynette, Brownie Lynette. Please stop that. We have guests. Look. Come and meet them.*

*She's a bit shy, but she'll come out when she's a little less skittish. I think you gave her a bit of a fright. Although, she's quite good at giving the other Brownies a bit of a warning regarding the axes now. That's such an improvement and a lot less messy. So just duck when you hear her screams, and you might be ok.*

*Hi, I'm Brown Owl, but as you're not my little Brownie pack you can call me Mac,"* said a smiling, but clearly exhausted young woman wearing a sorry looking excuse for a uniform. *"Welcome to my Brownie camp and clearing. But to be precise, they're actually ambitious pre-Brownies. So this is Hell number two: a Pre-Brownie Camp. The wee poppets and I are at your service."* Mac finished her speech with a salute and a clumsy curtsy.

Harry, Devil Keith, Dippit and Stan made their introductions. Mac was staring at Stan until he started speaking, then she turned her gaze to Harry. Harry could nearly hear Mac's thoughts of, *"gorgeous but wow, when he starts talking."*

*"Not to be rude, and to be clear I'm glad of the adult company, but why are you here? We don't get many. Actually, we don't get **any** visitors in our Hell."* Brown Owl Mac asked while strenuously pulling the axe from the tree. It was well imbedded this time, the stubborn little sucker.

At that a small walking bruise, with red hair stood in front of Harry and Mac. *"I's want my kitty. I's love my kitty. Where's I's kitty, Mac?"* The little walking bruise began silently crying and wiping her runny nose on her sleeve.

*"Oh Brownie Nelli, sweetheart. Come here and sit on my knee."* Neli scrambled up and looked at Mac with tears and wonder in her big eyes.

*"I's want my kitty. I's love my kitty. Where's I's kitty, Browns Owl?"* Brownie Nelli repeated, snuggling in, and resting her head against Mac's chest. The little girl was sobbing quietly.

*"Brownie Nelli, you can't have a kitty just now. The mummy*

*mountain lion has to look after the kitties until they're big enough to maul people on their own."* Mac was quite new to looking after the Brownies so she wasn't entirely sure how much they understood. Maybe maul was too direct?

*"But the mummy kitty is sooooooooooo busy. I's wants to help. I's sooooo good at looking afters a kitty. I's be goods."* Brownie Nelli rubbed her face across Mac's chest. The glistening trail, on Mac's uniform, shone in the sunshine.

*"I know sweetheart, but you keep getting hurt, and do you remember last week? The mummy kitty ate you all up. I was sad and you were really, really sore. You don't want to scrap poo out of your hair again. Do you, sweetie?"* Mac brushed Brownie Nelli's hair from her sweaty forehead.

*"I's knows buts she likes Brownie Nelli nows, so I's be better. I's really wants my kitty. I's love my kitty. I's loves you Browns Owl too, but I's love my kitty too. I's have twos bestest friends. Yous and my kitty. That's be good for I."* Mac cuddled the little girl and stroked her damp hair back from her sweaty brow again.

Mac was relieved when a small brown-haired girl, with baggy socks and a torn brown uniform, barrelled into the camp shouting, *"clears a space. I's bestest friend Brownie Mary Jo has a big, big 'prise. Big 'prise. Yous be sooo happys."* The little girl pushed over a few tree stump stools and stomped back towards the oak trees.

*"Oh, that's Brownie Hilary. She likes to sort things. That can be useful at times, but at other times it's a bit of a disaster. It's a surprise not a 'prise' Brownie Hilary, sweetie."* Mac corrected her.

*"Comes on. Clears a space for Brownie Mary Jo's SUURRRprise. Oh, it's a good 'prise. Yous like 'prises. Shoooo! Goes on, shoooo!"* Brownie Hilary stamped her little sandal clad foot, and waved the Brownie pack away from the centre of the clearing. She adjusted her crooked bunchies and tightened her hair-baubles then scowled. *"Nows, do it nows. Go, go. Nows."*

Brownie Mary Jo came into sight puffing and panting,

whilst dragging a rather portly, brownish Grizzly Bear behind her. He was lying on his back, twiddling his thumbs, and sighing.

"*Brown Owl, please tell Brownie Mary Jo that I don't need saved, and I don't need to go into her animal shelter either. Every time I sit down to eat my morning porridge and listen to a bit of excellent Phil Collins. He's my favourite, you know. Brownie Mary Jo appears with rope and her need to rescue me. And I know that Brownie Hilary and Brownie Hazel just want to practice on me for their first aid badge.*" Trevor softly growled.

"*Mac is that a 600-pound grizzly that tiny girl has there?*" gulped Harry, amazed at the strength of the little strawberry blonde.

"*Yep, can you take Brownie Nelli, please?*" Mac got to her exhausted feet.

"*I can. I say, I can.*" Stan picked up Brownie Nelli and balanced her on his hip. Brownie Nelli gazed at Stan with wonder and batted her eyelashes before sticking her grimy thumb in her mouth.

"*Hi Trevor. Here again I see. This is becoming quite a habit.*" Mac laughed.

"*Funny. Yep. Me, again. I don't mind all the kidnapping, but I do have one request. Please keep Brownie Rachel away from me. My uncle-in-law is taking the 'you know what' out of me because Brownie Rachel keeps putting ribbons in my fur. I can't get the pink and yellow hair dye out either. It's getting really embarrassing.*" Trevor showed Mac the patches of dye caught under his armpits.

At that a tiny girl, with dimples on her knees, screamed with delight "*I's loves my Teddy. My Teddy. I's love you...mostest in the whole wides world.*" With that Brownie Rachel leapt on Trevor and started cuddling him, or throttling him, depending on your point of view.

"*Now's Teddy. Yous need a haircut ands a biiig tidys up. I's has blue ribbons and I's has yellows ribbons today. I's sooooo want mys hairdressing badge. Eh Brown Owl, I's get my hairdressing badge* today?" Brownie Rachel looked so hopeful as she eyed her victim, eh client.

"*Erm, yes?*" Mac mouthed "*sorry*" to poor old Trevor.

Harry felt a tug on her shirt and looked down at yet another little girl. Wow, they breed them small and cute here, she thought as she looked at the pile of auburn curls. "*Yes pet, can I help you?*"

"*I's Brownie Hazel. Cans yous open I's box?*" with that, Brownie Hazel pushed a hefty first aid kit into Harry's hands.

Harry staggered under its weight. "*Oh, it's a lot heavier than it looks. Of course, I can. I'm Harry, this is my sister Dippit, and this is Stan. I seem to have lost Devil Keith but he's here with us too. It's nice to meet you all.*"

"*TOMMY TALKS!*" a tomahawk sliced through the air. Mac threw out her arm, and caught it mid throw.

"*Wow, good save Mac.*" Harry was feeling slightly picked on by the pint-sized hellion.

"*Brownie Lynette, please come and say hello properly.*" Mac firmly stated.

"*I's nos wants to. I's want my tommy talks back. They's mine. All mines.*" Brownie Lynette scuffed her toes into the patchy grass.

"*Brownie Lynette, we've talked about this. You can't just throw a tomahawk and expect to get your survival badge. You have to do other things too,*" with that Mac attached the axe to her belt. The belt was straining as there were four other axes hooked into the belt loops.

"*I'll give these to Brownie Kat and Brownie Louise. They love a project and are currently doing their orienteering badge, so they should be able to hide them for a while. Well at least until I can get some of the mud off Brownie Lynette and get her to do a less dangerous part of her badge. Wish me luck.*" Mac started to walk off in search of the elusive pair.

However, Mac was distracted by. "*Ouch, ouch not so tight.*"

*Brown Owl, Brown Owl, tell her. The Plaster of Paris is pulling off all my delicate fur."*

"Brownie Hazel, sweetie, try the normal plasters first, then we'll see if Trevor needs a bandage. And please try the full body plaster-cast last." Mac gently explained.

Brownie Hazel looked up with sparkling tears in her big eyes. *"I's fixing the boo-boos. I's kiss thems' alls first thens I's puts on 'ages and plasters."*

*"I know. You do such a good job, Brownie Hazel. Brownie Rachel, Brownie Rachel please don't shave Trevor again. He gets awfully cold."* Mac made a grab for the open cut-throat razor.

*"Oh, I's makes a wig for mys Teddy. He's so cold. I's love my Teddy,"* with that, Brownie Rachel squashed Trevor's cheeks tightly together and kissed him on the nose.

There was an almighty bang followed by, *"ta da!"*

*"Oh, that'll be Brownie Gillian and Brownie Lisa back from their early morning run. They're doing really well with their fitness badges."* At that, they saw two little blonde girls do eight backflips and a cartwheel, before racing off into the trees again.

*"Be careful Brownie Gillian, Brownie Lisa. Watch out for the low branches."* Mac turned to Dippit. *"One of the wee poppets impaled herself on a tree yesterday and a few days ago the other one flipped into the campfire. I'm really quite worried about them both."* Mac started ticking items off on her fingers. *"Now that's Brownie Hazel doing her first aid badge, Brownie Rachel doing her hairdressing badge and Brownie Hilary sorting out the camp. Oh no, where's Brownie Mary Jo? I have to find Brownie Claire before Brownie Mary Jo gets to her."* Mac took off at a sprint with Harry by her side. *"Dippit, Stan can you hold the fort?"*

A teeny, weenie wee girl with the most amazing ball of blonde, curly hair was sitting at the far end of the clearing. Brownie Mary Jo was sitting beside her crying and picking off a grotty scab. *"Browns Owl, shes eats mys birdies. Her, I's nos likes her no more. I's birdies gone…poof. All gone."*

"*Brownie Claire. Spit it out. I said spit it out. Now, all of it. Oh Harry, if I'm not quick enough I have to clean up puddles of vomit. And trying to get it out of her hair is terrifying.*" Mac explained whilst turning Brownie Claire upside down and vigorously patting her little back.

Mac puffed out. "*Brownie Mary Jo likes to feed the hummingbirds. Unfortunately, she's so caring that they frequently burst due to overeating. Brownie Claire spends a lot of her day in a world of her own, meditating. So, when she sees the ruptured birds she just thinks that they're her lunch, so she quickly eats them. The raw birds play havoc with her digestive system, but Brownie Claire so enjoys them and can't seem to stop.*"

Brownie Claire was dazed and dizzy as she was turned the right way up, but she immediately reached for another squishy bird.

"*No's mys birdie. Is sleeping now. No's, Brownie Claire. No eats my birdies,*" Brownie Mary Jo was still crying, shooing Brownie Claire away and shoving the smashed birds into her pockets. Mac winced at the thought of the next pile of laundry, and the "*treasures*" she would find later.

"*Brownie Claire, can you and Brownie Mary Jo get some water? Teddy so needs a drink.*" Mac gently pushed them towards the tap.

Off they trotted, bestest friends again, "*That sick was sooos gross buts fun. I's like the colour. Do's it again.*"

"*I's try,*" said Brownie Claire. None the worse from her ordeal, her puffball hair already gaining back its vast volume.

"*Right, I have nearly all of them occupied. Is that your friend Devil Keith over by that tree? I think we should check on him.*" Mac pointed to the far end of the smoky clearing.

Devil Keith was looking decidedly odd. Well more odd than usual, so all in all that was pretty bad. Harry thought he looked dazed and concussed. And he had a massive bruise appearing on the side of his head and along his jaw.

"*What happened to you?*" Harry gingerly touched his jaw.

"*Smmmmirtitsss.*" Devil Keith opened one eye, and tried to concentrate on the four Harrys in front of him.

"*Brownie Lesley, what happened to Devil Keith?*" Mac pointedly asked the blonde haired tot.

"*We's makes necklace fors Nora. Eith's girlfriend,*" Brownie Lesley nudged Brownie Margaret and Brownie Jacqui, then they all giggled. They then rolled on the ground, and held their tubby tummies.

"*So why does Devil Keith look so funny?*" Mac enquired of the jolly tots.

"*We's no enuff teeffs Brown Owl, so I's hit Devil Keith on the head wif as tree and we's have enuff now.*" Brownie Lesley proudly held up a tooth and bone necklace. It was dripping with fresh blood.

Harry had the awful feeling that the teeth and bones were human… and Keith's. But she figured that if Mac was alright about them then she'd better not comment.

"*Oh, Brownie Lesley. You shouldn't hit people with tree trunks to get their teeth. I've told you that before.*" Mac scolded the wee one.

"*Before?*" enquired Harry.

"*Yes, it happens surprisingly frequently.*" Mac responded with a shrug of her shoulders.

Devil Keith groaned then began to focus. "*Harry, it's yourself. It is. Brownie Lesley, Brownie Margaret, and Brownie Jacqui have helped me make the most smashing necklace for my Nora. Think she'll like it? They're going to show me how to make bracelets from the intestines of ruptured birds later. Seemingly I just have to trade Brownie Mary Jo and Brownie Claire for some of them.*"

"**TOMMY TALKS!**" the axe landed at Devil Keith's feet. He picked it up and lobbed it back at Brownie Lynette's head. "*Bloody good throw, young Brownie Lynette. A bit more of a twist and you would have severed my foot clean off.*"

"*Devil Keith, please don't help Brownie Lynette with her aim. She already uses little Brownie Jill for her target practice. Talking of which. I wonder where the teeny chatterbox is. If you hear the names Joey and Chandler, then Brownie Jill won't be far away."* Mac looked around and under a smallish bush.

They found Brownie Jill struggling to remove a rather large, plucked and un-cooked turkey from her head.

*"Oh, come here blossom. Just follow my voice. Harry, can you help me? I have to get this off before Brownie Hilary tries to organise a rescue party."* Mac coaxed.

*"What's so bad about that?"* Harry asked.

*"It usually involves the use of a hacking tomahawk, or Brownie Hazel uses her bandages to fashion a throat tourniquet. Either way, it's not pretty."* Mac shuddered.

Luckily, Mac removed the turkey before being spotted by Brownie Hilary. *"Brownie Kat, Brownie Louise can you re-orientate the turkey into a bin please? Brownie Jill come here my wee blossom and let me have a look."* Mac began scraping the turkey offal out of Brownie Jill's ears. *"Just one more kidney to find and I'm all done here."*

*"I's just get Joey ands Chandler. They's gots sore bits ands kidneys too."* Brownie Jill waddled off.

Mac explained that they were Brownie Jill's imaginary friends and they usually kept her entertained until they discussed either lobsters or Thanksgiving. Then mayhem usually ensued.

*"I think you're all better now,"* Mac kissed her on the head and sent her back to play.

*"Ah, about time. They're late."* Mac checked her sundial wrist watch.

Three, obviously inebriated, tots came stumbling into the camp clearing. Holding each other up and pronouncing their love for each other.

*"I's love you mores."* Brownie Kirsty slurred.

*"Nos, I's love you mores."* Brownie Liz hiccupped.

*"Nos, mes. I's do."* Brownie Mirka giggled.

*"Nos I's do. Hic, hic, hic."* Brownie Liz hiccupped.

*"Brownie Kirsty. Brownie Liz. Brownie Mirka. Have you been eating the over ripe apples again? Afternoon drinking? Again?"* Mac sternly asked and waved her index finger at the wee headbangers.

*"No's."* Brownie Kirsty slurred.

*"Yesssss."* Brownie Liz hiccupped, again.

*"No, no's,"* said Brownie Kirsty whilst nudging a gleeful Brownie Liz. *"No's Brown Owl. We's no do that. No's more. We's listenings. We's goods, hic, hic, hic."*

*"Yous gots the i-cups, ha, ha, ha."* said Brownie Liz, and then promptly fell over, onto her face. Brownie Mirka and Brownie Kirsty began giggling until they too fell over. Then they all farted.

*"Harry, can you see if Brownie Claire and Brownie Mary Jo have brought the water? These three rapscallions. They're gonna have one hellava hangover."* Mac pointed over at the water tap.

*"Ohs, Browns Owls, yous said a bads word."* Brownie Kat's lips made a perfect O, as she scuffed the toe of her sandal in the dirt and stuffed a worm in her pocket.

*"Wow, where on earth did you come from?"* Harry couldn't believe how quiet they were, and how good they all were at sneaking up on people. They could teach a ninja a few tricks.

*"Brownie Kat, I'm a grown up and sometimes grown-ups say bad words but you're so little so you're not to say them."* Brownie Kat walked off you, but you could see her little brain trying to work out how to add *"hellava"* to a sentence, and not get in trouble.

*"Harry, I have to be so careful about what I say. Brownie Kat can and does swear like a sailor on shore leave if I'm not careful. Right, to get the little drunken toerags sorted out."* Mac rubbed her hands together.

*"Yous said a bads word, agains."* Brownie Kat was back? Harry was so impressed with her stealth.

*"Brownie Anne, Brownie Anne put that brick down please. Put*

*it down now. Don't you dare throw that."* Mac went racing away to stop another catastrophe. Harry thought: is this what it's like to be a parent? Surely, not.

Mac shouted back at Harry, *"Brownie Anne throws bricks at Faery doors and their houses. I've tried to get her to stop but so far it hasn't work. I've tried giving her rubber and foam bricks, but she quickly gobbled up the rubber and spat out the foam. She then munched through the wooden boxes that they were stored in."*

A few minutes later and Brownie Anne was sitting on Mac's knee, *"I's sorrys Browns Owl. I's justs want mys badge ands I's want the Faeries to haves news houses. I's really like the Faeries buts they's mean to me. They's call me names."*

*"Blow your nose wee one. How about you make a tent for Harry? Harry would you like Brownie Anne to make you a tent?"* Mac enthusiastically nodded at Harry.

*"Mmmm, yes?"* Harry responded. Not at all wanting a tent from the Faery vandal.

Brownie Anne ran off smiling, delighted with her new badge opportunity.

*"Thanks Harry. The Faeries were getting a bit threatening there. I still don't know where she gets the bricks. I think Brownie Margaret and Brownie Jacqui may make them in the crafts corner, but I have no proof yet."* Mac decided to investigate as soon as possible.

*"Ta da!"* the two pretty blondes were back and had fashioned exercise weights. Well, that's probably being generous. They were throwing Devil Keith back and forth in the air. Strong little bits thought Harry: not at all concerned by Devil Keith's pleading looks, yelps and recent concussion.

*"Off to see Brownie Liz, Brownie Kirsty and Brownie Mirka. Harry, can you grab the orange juice for me? It's so good of Dippit and Stan to look after Trevor, but I think he's probably ready for his counselling session about now. His uncle-in-law really gives him gip over the girls and the things they do to him. Brownie Rachel*

*completely shaved him last week, but a wee guy from your neck of the woods saved the day by making him a dust and fluff coat. Ever so grateful to Chick for that.*" Mac nodded then took a slug of the juice.

"*Wow, he fairly gets around.*" Harry said then promptly forgot that piece of information.

"*Brownie Arlene, Brownie Arlene sweetie. Can you come see Trevor, please?*" Mac shouted into a purple buddleia bush.

A smiling, miniscule girl skipped over to Trevor and threw her little arms around him. "*Rights Teddy. Whats yous need todays? Coulds yous alls go overs there so's I's can chats with Teddy?*" Brownie Arlene proceeded to shoo the Brownies away. Then she got to work removing some of the ribbons and brushing out Trevor's fur, whilst she listened intently.

"*Trevor will be as right as rain once he's had some time with that little sunbeam.*" Mac softly smiled.

"*Well one last thing to do before I can sit down. I hope Brownie Mirka has sobered up, as Brownie Claire and her are leading the yoga class today. Then it's blessed, nap time.*" Mac breathed a sigh of relief.

"*Brownie Lynette, honey, can you please slice the oranges? No, no, use the knife not your tomahawk. No, I said the knife. You might lose a hand again.*" Mac instructed.

"*I's haves a porpoise. I's haves a porpoise,*" Brownie Lynette was singing and dancing in a circle, whilst tossing a lethal looking machete in the air.

"*A porpoise?*" Harry enquired with raised brows.

"*Oh, sorry you get used to their strange ways and I forget that they have some creative vocabulary. It's a purpose. Although to be fair, a porpoise is just as likely.*" Mac nodded and lifted her brows.

"*Yeh Mac, I meant to ask. What's with the eighty-foot giraffe hiding behind that oak tree?*" asked Harry and pointed at the shy giraffe.

"*Now that's a tale. Brownie Nelli, Brownie Hilary, and Brownie*

*Mary Jo so want either a cat or a dog as a pet. So, Brownie Louise helpfully suggested that they get a cow in order to attract the cat or dog. I think it was so we could milk the cow, but it could just as easily be to slaughter the cow in order to entice the beasties with a slab of freshly, dripping meat. The delightful wee savages!*

*Well Brownie Angela heard all of this, and thought she'd help. She then did the oddest thing: she wished it into being, but instead of a cow she got a giraffe. She still insists it's a cow and I'm terrified to say otherwise."* Mac said this as if it was all totally normal.

"*Yep, that definitely rates as odd. Has she done anything like that before?*" Harry also slugged down some juice.

"*No, never seen the likes. I just keep in her good books and hope no one wants a pet hippo, or we're all doomed.*" Mac laughed but did look a little frightened.

Mac got back to sorting her troupe...

"*Brownie Jill and Brownie Anne, can you please organise the sleepy blankies?*" Mac instructed.

"*Brownie Hazel, can you put away the first aid box? Hopefully, we won't need it again today.*" Mac looked around. "*Brownie Mary Jo, Brownie Mary Jo. Oh no, where's Brownie Mary Jo gone?*"

"*I's here. I's has aa kitty fora Brownie Nellis.*" Brownie Mary Jo was dragging a very angry mountain lion, by the tail, into the centre of the camp.

"*Oh kittys. Mys kitty. Brownie Mary Jos, yous sos clevers.*" Brownie Nelli ran at the furious lion.

"*Brownie Nelli, please take a step back.*" Mac whispered and crept towards the lion.

"*Buts I's loves my kitty.*" Brownie Nelli pouted and crossed her chubby wee arms in a pronounced harrumph.

Stan grabbed the lion's tail as Harry, Mac, Dippit and Devil Keith scooped up the young Brownies and ran. Fast.

# CHAPTER
# TWENTY-ONE

T en minutes later...

Stan sat in the middle of the clearing with his adoring, wide eyed Brownies covering him in sticking plasters and trying to pick off his scabs. Dippit also looked very adoringly at him, although she left his scabs well alone.

*"He's a good man to have around. Really lucky too."* Dippit was happily picturing their children and making a referral for some Speech and Language Therapy. Stat.

*"Yep Dippit, he's really lucky. Those pork pies really did the trick."* Harry nodded and blew out a breath. She couldn't believe her eyes when Stan had grabbed the pies, from the top of his rucksack, and offered them to the roaring lion. By the time the mountain lion had finished three pork pies and a steak-bake she was Stan's bosom buddy, and wandered off in the most delightful mood. But not before giving him a full body cuddle and some non-shredding kisses.

Brownie Hilary got up from the circle and stiffly walked over to Stan. *"Oh, this can't be good,"* Harry thought. The purposeful Brownie squatted down in front of him with her elbows on her chubby, dirty knees. She stared at him: then using her thumbs and index fingers she opened his eyes to stare some more. She touched her nose to Stan's and stared yet more. When she was content that she had his attention and he was listening, she said. *"I's want a puppy. I's a goods girl ands I's wants a puppy.*

*I's calls him Harris. Nos, Jack. Nos, Ian. I's calls hims Harris. Rights? Yous gets I's one, 'k?"* with that Brownie Hilary went back to her place in the circle whilst Stan looked positively horrified.

*"She's like a mini-Mussolini,"* Harry mumbled to Mac.

*"You could be right. Can I ask a last favour? Can you look after them whilst I collect Wee Brownie Murphy and Brownie Leanne?"* Mac rubbed her hands on her uniform pockets.

Stan and Dippit quickly offered to collect the last of the troupe instead so that Mac could have a rest and Stan could keep out of Brownie Hilary's way. Harry persuaded Brownie Mirka and Brownie Claire to do the yoga class badge despite their hangover and food poisoning. Kids are so resilient, she thought.

*"Sorry, but I have to ask. How can Hell number two be inhabited by Brownies? They're a danger to themselves and others. I just dislodged Brownie Lisa and Brownie Gillian from a tree. And you've saved them several times today. But they're also amazing and curious, and well, great. Oh, and very, very tiring. What could they have done to deserve all this?"* Harry queried as she pointed at the clearing.

*"Ah, I should have explained. They're not here to be punished, I am. Yes, they are all those things and I love them dearly. My punishment is to love them and keep them safe, no matter how bad things get.*

*I hate seeing them being mauled or eaten by a tiger, a mountain lion, a bear, a giraffe, or a wolf. Or in Brownie language: a kitty, a teddy, a cow, or a puppy.*

*I worry about Brownie Hilary getting a stress induced ulcer. I hate seeing Brownie Claire choke and vomit all the time. Or Brownie Lesley and the other crafters get fatal gingivitis because they've played with too many rotten teeth. I hate seeing Brownie Jill suffocate in a turkey, or Brownie Hazel have an allergic reaction to latex, or Brownie Rachel stab herself... repeatedly. I really hate seeing Brownie Lynette being so brave and injuring herself. Making her go into hiding yet again.*

*I'm always worried about the non-identical triplets, and their alcohol consumption. Their livers are getting mighty big now. I'm scared silly that the Faeries will change Brownie Anne into some sort of, well... changeling. And Brownie Lisa and Brownie Gillian, well they have all manner of injuries and near misses as they pursue their dreams.*

*You've yet to meet Wee Brownie Murphy and Brownie Leanne but they're equally wonderful, strange, kind, and brave. I worry for them too."* Mac signed and wiped away a tear. She really loved her tearaways and their wild ways.

Harry understood Mac's dilemma because she felt like that about Devil Keith. Oh damn, she had forgotten about Devil Keith. Oh, it's fine he's doing yoga. Oh, not so fine...he's tied himself in knots. Going by the sinister laughter it looked like Brownie Gillian, Brownie Louse and Brownie Lisa helped...a lot.

Ah well, one of the other Brownies must have a knot tying or untying badge. He'll be fine, she decided.

*"So, this has all been set up for you?"* Harry said, as she subtly moved away from Mac.

*"Oh, no. You don't need to watch your back. I'm not that bad. This Hell seems to have pockets of Brownies. When I walk too far, I find myself back here. In this clearing. I'm presuming that the other Brown Owls go through this too. Unfortunately, I've never met any of them, but I sometimes hear their voices in the distances. Well shouts and screams, so I think it must be them."* Mac patted Harry's knee.

*"So, Mac, how did you come to be here?"* Harry moved Mac's hand away from her knee. She reasoned that no one came to Hell unless they were out and out baddies.

*"I may not look it now, but I was a bit of a petrol head and a speed freak. I was forever getting cautions, tickets, and court summons. I couldn't be bothered dealing with them, so I stuffed them all into a cupboard at work. There were a lot. I mean a LOT. One day my colleague opened the cupboard door and the tickets tumbled out. Falling on her and burying her.*

*She was instantly crushed to death. I tried to save her. I really did. I was scraping the tickets from her squashed body. It was no use, and I was getting badly injured. The last thing I heard was the paramedics say that they had never seen anyone bleed-out due to that number of paper cuts. So here I am.*

*Oh, as it turns out, my colleague fostered children and ran the local Brownies troupe, so this is my punishment. Here I am."* Mac spread her arms and indicated the smoky camp.

*"Harsh."* Harry shook her head.

*"No, I deserve it."* Mac smiled sadly.

*"So how do you know how this Hell works?"* Harry was intrigued by Mac's knowledge of her punishment.

*"Ah, well. When I arrived here there was a pamphlet attached to a tree. It told me that I had to look after the Brownies. It also said that if there were too many injuries and/or fatalities then I would have more Brownies added. I was scared and not very good at it, so I ended up with yet more Brownies. Brownie Leanne and Wee Brownie Murphy were the last to arrive. Within a few minutes of their arrival a French restaurant appeared. I'm not sure if they did a 'Brownie Angela' and made it appear, or if it's just part of the tableau."* Mac shrugged. Those early days were brutal.

*"We can't just make things appear in our Hell. Do you think it's because we only have one horn? Maybe the higher up the more the non-residents can request?"* Harry took out a pen to write the answer on her hand.

*"Not sure Harry, it's a possibility,"* shrugged Mac.

*"My turn. So why are you lot here? Not that I'm not enjoying the adult company."* Mac turned and gave Harry her full attention.

Harry explained about Bub going missing and the role of the Drill. She became a little tearful.

*"I know this sounds blunt...How do I say this tactfully? Harry, I would have expected you to be a bit more upset."* Mac was genuinely puzzled.

*"I know what you mean, but our Dippit is a genius. I mean*

*really clever. Off the charts clever. Stan's bizarrely lucky, and Devil Keith hasn't killed himself yet. A miracle in itself. I suppose I have faith in them. They'll help me sort this."* Harry smiled over at a twisted Devil Keith.

Harry looked over and noticed that Brownie Arlene had Trevor by the hand. The little girl was walking the huge, smiling bear back home. She was glad he was feeling better. Maybe Brownie Arlene could help her sort out her life and make her smile again. Where was Bub, and was he safe? Would he talk to her again?

Stan and Dippit walked back into the camp with an ecstatic pair of girls.

*"Looks, looks. Stans made thes froggies betters."* Screeched an excited wee blonde bundle.

Dippit explained that they had gone to collect Wee Brownie Murphy from the local French restaurant. Wee Brownie Murphy had been practicing for her embroidery badge by sewing the legs back onto the disabled frogs. Unfortunately, despite the tight French knots and impeccable chain stitches, the poor frogs would hop no more.

While there, they had noticed that Brownie Leanne was maniacally destroying sockets and stealing microwaves to turn into a Dr Frankenstein re-animation type machine.

Despite Brownie Leanne continually shrieking. *"Theys be poorly, makes thems alls better".* That appeared to be her version of, *"they're alive! They're alive!".* The unfortunate frogs were still poorly, and not at all alive. So, Stan being Stan, had helped Brownie Leanne modify her macabre microwave-ish device. So now the girls had pockets full of embroidery thread, pins, and thimbles. Plus, an armful each of very much alive, highly decorative, and ever so slightly smoking frogs. Frogs who were plotting a second French Revolution, and trying to work out how to get Stan to make them a guillotine large enough to despoil a lardy chef.

Brownie Leanne raced over to Mac, *"Browns Owls, Browns*

*Owls. Thats mans mades the froggies alls better. I's gonna marrys him,"* and with that profound announcement Brownie Leanne used her knuckle to push her little spectacles up her button nose.

*"The man of the hour?"* grinned Harry and stretched to rub Stan on the head.

*"Just helping Harry, I say just helping. I think we should go. I say go."* It was clear that Stan was becoming attached to the cuties and Dippit was becoming attached to Stan. Harry had spied them briefly holding hands whilst trying to corral the girls along the leafy path.

*"I think you're right. Let's hit the road and all that, chaps. Ah, where is the road?"* Devil Keith was obviously still a bit wonky.

*"Mac, how do we get to Hell number three, from here?"* Harry asked.

Thirty minutes later...

*"Thank you, Lady Catherine, we wouldn't have made it without your help."* Lady Catherine was the majestic snowy owl that looked after the Brownies to allow Mac to have short breaks. The day in the Brownies Hell never turned into night, so the Brownies never slept. Apart from very short naps. So, Brown Owl never really slept either. A cruel and disorienting punishment.

Lady Catherine had led them past the poison oak and around the killer salmon river. They had waved at Trevor and made rude signs at his uncle-in-law. They then scarpered, before being eaten by an immense, angry grizzly bear. Lady Catherine had also distracted the enticing redwood trees so that Devil Keith didn't get sucked in and burnt, yet again.

*"Thank you for all your help. Please, tell Mac we'll come back and see her soon."* Harry waved at the beautiful bird.

*"I want one."* Devil Keith assertively announced.

*"Devil Keith, you want a child? A Brownie?"* no fudging way, Harry thought. They'd break him, roast him over an open fire and eat him in the blink of an eye.

*"Nooo, nooo. Yuck. Yuck. I want a kitty, duh."* Devil Keith gagged then smiled.

# CHAPTER TWENTY-TWO

**H**opefully the correct Hell…

After tentatively placing the wonky Drill against a tree and very, very carefully selecting Hell number three, they stepped from the sun dappled forest clearing into a darkened landscape. It appeared to be late afternoon or early evening. The shadows were lengthening, and the light drizzle of rain obscured their view. The trees were so tall that very little light could penetrate the gloom. It was clear that this ancient forest lacked the warmth and welcome of the previous Hell.

They could hear shouting, laughter and screaming in the distance. *"That would have to be their guide,"* thought Harry. She was zipping up her jacket and wishing that Devil Keith had brought woolly hats instead of fascinators. It was chilly in them there woods.

*"Here Gorilla. Here gorilla, gorilla."* Devil Keith enticingly screamed into the trees and under rocks

*"Devil Keith what are you going on about now? We need to be quiet. We're using guerrilla warfare tactics. Remember?"* Harry put her finger to her lips and hushed him.

*"Duh, how do we attract gorillas if they don't know that we're here? Think Harry. Think. Ha, I thought that you were the clever one here. My bad."* Devil Keith lifted an insolent brow and rattled a rhododendron bush.

*"Shush, you fudger. Why can't you retain information in that thick skull?"* Harry put her finger to her lips, again.

*"It's too full of wonderful ideas, stunning designs and kind thoughts."* Devil Keith smiled sweetly and patted his chest.

Lady Catherine assured them that all possible paths led to the castle, so although they could feel lost, Hell number three was designed to always lead them in the one direction. So the small team stumbled and squelched through deep puddles and shallow streams. Filling their boots with stagnant water and other things that they were glad they couldn't see. However, they could hear and feel the things crunch, then turn to mush against their sodden woolly socks. Harry slipped and fell into a fast-flowing river. The strong current dragged her rucksack away. Harry had the awful feeling that the stream meant to take her rucksack. Meant to take away her weapons. Meant to take her away, too. Dippit and Stan yanked her out and brushed her down. She was a wee bit shaken and she held onto Devil Keith's hand for the remainder of the journey.

They narrowly avoided some savage looking bear traps and hoped that old Trevor never strayed into this Hell. Dippit scraped blood-filled leeches from Harry's shins then wiped the subsequent sick from Devil Keith's chin. They were wet, cold, miserable, and thoroughly disheartened.

The striking castle came into view…

There was an imposing grey, stone structure carved from the very rock it sat upon.

**No, no, no there wasn't. Yes, there was. The authors are arguing. Give it a minute. Ah, and they're back.**

The team stepped from between the trees and looked up, up and up further. A magnificent citrus yellow castle filled their vista. The perfectly rendered walls soared into the stunning, bright blue sky. The four tall corner turrets peeked out of the perfectly formed clouds. The clouds slowly gliding across the sky; forming puffs of fluffy sheep, or mimicking the dance of a lazy sun-drenched bumblebee, or the flutter of an elegant butterfly. The rows of mullioned windows gleamed and were surrounded by an abundance of pale pink, stencilled flowers. The stamen of the flowers sported cheeky smiles or winking eyes.

The air was soaked with the scent of blooming summer roses and fields of scented jasmine. There was gentle, calming music moving in the wind, soothing the very soul. Small, brightly coloured birds sang as they gobbled up the fruits from the miniature cherry trees.

Harry had seen many examples of medieval castles, but few had left her with feelings of such...nausea. Where were the decapitated heads; displayed on stakes? Where were the crumbling, dangerous walls that fall on folks and squash them like pesky beetles? Do they even have a resident dragon here? Doesn't look like it. Amateurs!

Like any castle worth its salt, it was surrounded by a moat that guarded the majestic King's Gate. However, this moat had plates of water lilies and serene black swans, gliding on water so clear it looked like delicately blown glass. Harry wanted to see bits of old bicycles and dead shopping trolleys poking from the greasy water. She sighed; it was not to be.

*"Pretty. So pretty. How do we get in?"* enquired an entranced Dippit. The romantic castle would make an excellent wedding venue. The photographs would be lush.

*"I'll just go ask the gargoyles over there?"* Devil Keith went to walk off.

*"Whow, boy. Hold your horses. Oh, so sorry, Harry. Hold your H.O.R.S.E.S. I heard about the Kelpies, and old Duke being really upset. You're not going near statues ever again."* Dippit said this as she was being dragged across the ground. But there was no way that she was releasing the back of Devil Keith's fleecy outfit.

*"Jonathan said I should provide some much-needed feedback to the shiny guys. And suddenly I'm the villain of the story. He suggested that they're just lazing around and wanting to be famous*

*without doing a jot of work. Suddenly, I'm the bad guy for telling them the truth. Jonathan told me that the Kelpies could have gone off on one at any time. But no, poor old Devil Keithie boy is being blamed yet again."* Devil Keith slowly shook his head. He picked Dippit up by her shoulders then put her to the side. He then indicated that Harry should give him a hug.

*"I knew there was more to that incident than you were letting on. Why couldn't you have had some compassion? If you knew Duke was feeling low and lonely, why did you have to make it worse? Devil Keith, doing nothing would have been better than making unnecessary comments. Why did you listen to Jonathan? He's a twit. A nipple less twit?"* Harry stage whispered yet again. She really needed to go somewhere where she could shout and kick his ankles.

*"Harry, you forget that I am the Devil. I enjoy a bit of misery and mayhem. An odd word, said at the right time, can be so much more effective than a physical injury. Just look at Jonathan and his gossiping ways. You're welcome by the way. Anyway, the pen might be mightier than the sword, but a word said at just the right time, ah bliss,"* Devil Keith smiled and tried to walk towards the gargoyles again.

*"I'll go. Dippit, don't let him go this time. Devil Keith, thank you for reminding me. And to think I actually felt sorry for you. That the Kelpies running amok was just a coincidence. I should have known that you and Jonathan were behind it."* Harry was fuming and a little sad as she walked away. Is Bub right? Do I treat Devil Keith like a child? Harry wondered.

The gargoyles…

The gargoyles were tucked around the side wall of the castle, and the racket they were making did not sooth the soul. Not one little bit. They appeared to be having a blast, and consequently totally ignoring Harry's request for assistance. There seemed to be some type of comedy show going on: with the castle gargoyles as the only acts. They were sporting polka-dot bow ties, wearing neon name tags, and repeatedly shouting that, *"every vote counts."*

*"What do you call a man with a spade on his head?"* Chortled Lum M., the first gargoyle. *"Doug. Get it. Vote for me or it's boiling rice pudding for you all."*

Despite the enthusiastic round of applause, a sea of greyish, lumpy rice pudding poured from his stone mouth and melted the first row of the *"audience."* The audience were the residents who were manacled to stakes or clipped into splinter, soaked stockades. Many had red earmuffs. No, Harry shuddered. They had scrapped off their own ears rather than listen to the jokes. There were earlobes caught in rusty nails, and chains gunged up with pieces of pus encrusted ear cartilage. *"This is like that fudger Nero all over again,"* she thought.

*"What do you call a man, floating in the sea, with no arms or legs?"* screeched M'Key, the second gargoyle. *"Bob. Get it. Vote for me or it's ice cream brain freeze for you all."*

Despite the enthusiastic round of applause (yep, again); a stream of tutti fruity ice cream erupted from his gaping mouth. Freezing their heads, then drowning the second row of the audience in a creamy, chunky river.

*"How does an elephant hide in a cherry tree?"* bellowed Pip, the third gargoyle. *"He paints his toenails red. Get it. Vote for me or it's cheese and biscuits for you all."*

Despite the enthusiastic round of applause (yep, yep, again); Pip opened his stony mouth. Cheddar, brie, camembert, and extremely sharp edged biscuits exploded from the gargoyle's cavernous mouth. They were catapulted through the air and beheaded the third row of the audience. At least they wouldn't have to listen to the show again.

A pretty fourth gargoyle was oblivious to the carnage around her. She appeared to have a honey scented liquid dripping from her stone mouth. Kerri, the gargoyle, closed her mouth then loudly belched, and giggled.

"*Ah, it's mead,*" Harry murmured.

Then Kerri stared shouting, "*Abracadabra, hic, hic, hic, ha, ha, ha. Great word.*" Followed by a ground shaking belch.

"*Open sesame, ah brilliant words.*" Belch and part of Kerri's left wing fell off, crushing a doddering dwarf to death.

"*Perambulate, ha, ha, ha, classic. A belter of a word.*" A belch, followed by a dab of vomit.

"*Oh dear. Philadelphia is so cheesy, ha, ha, ha.*" Another humungous belch and more sweet mead poured from her stony spout. "*I have £60 to buy a cat. Any takers. £60? Any cats in the audience?*" A final belch and she completely fell off the wall.

"*I'm alright. I'm alright hic, hic. No need to panic.*" Kerri giggled and slid into the bottom of the moat.

A man lodged in an Iron Maiden beckoned Harry over. "*If you scratch my nose, I'll give you all the information you need.*" Harry scratched his nose and narrowly avoided having her index finger gobbled up. Why can't anything be simple and safe? What sick person writes this stuff?

Harry joined the others. "*Right, so in order to cross the moat we have to answer a riddle.*" Harry noticed a sign and a small lever, carefully screwed to a man sized stretching rack. The sign said, "*Pull me to get over the moat, but only if you can answer a riddle.*" Harry came to the conclusion that none of the Hells have public relations, marketing, or advertising executives in their crews.

Harry pulled the lever. The person attached to the rack whispered, "*Thank you for your business.*"

A squishy, grumpy older man popped out of the moat. He was more a dollop of loose skin and wrinkles than an actual man. "*What! What now?*" he grumbled, smoothing down his leopard print leotard, and dislodging it from a body crevasse or two.

"*We want to cross the moat and get to the castle.*" Harry smiled her bestest smile.

"*You should have said.*" He brightly smiled back. "*Rightyo,* the riddle. What cheese is made backwards?"

"*Trifle!*" Devil Keith proudly shouted, and fist bumped the air.

"*Trifle? Oh, mate it's not trifle. I say, not trifle. Not at all. At all, I say.*" Stan was holding his head in his hands and rocking.

At that the moat filled with what appeared to be strawberry trifle. The hundreds and thousands were replaced by brightly coloured but lethal looking daggers. The cream had been replaced by yodelling polar bears, tentatively perched on dainty ice shelves. There were killer rubber ducks with maniacal grins instead of custard and... pints of strawberry jelly? If you have ever wrestled in strawberry jelly, you'll know that it's nearly as bad as fighting rabid polar bears. Harry and Dippit were horrified by the sight before them. Devil Keith wandered off to find a dessert spoon. He came back, but he quickly realised that he was gonna need a bigger spoon.

Stan ambled over to rest against a nearby cherry tree and began raking in his backpack. Pulling out knitting needles and balls of wool, he settled down at the base of the tree.

"*Knit one, purl one. I say, knit one, purl one.*" He mumbled to himself.

"*What's he doing?*" queried Dippit.

"*Knitting one, then purling one. Duh,*" with that Devil Keith tried to pet a polar bear and lost the front of his gorilla onesie.

"*Stan, this isn't the time to knit a jumper. We're cold but not that cold.*" Harry prompted.

"*Just give me a minute. I say a minute. Knit one, purl one. I say, knit one, purl one.*" Stan continued.

Dippit was speechless as Stan began knitting, and knitting, and knitting some more. The marvellous man was knitting a suspension bridge. How on earth did he know that he would need knitting needles and wool on this adventure?

"*Right, that's ready. I say, that's ready. Now how to get it over the other side? I say the other side,*" a completed bridge sat in front of Stan.

Dippit checked her utility belt. *"How about this?"*

The polar bears were positively purring as they carried the knitted bridge over to the castle entrance. Devil Keith's adapted ear wax had done the trick and beguiled the scary bears. Harry couldn't understand why they hadn't just used the ear wax to begin with. The polar bears would have just carried them all across.

Maybe Stan just liked to knit?

# CHAPTER TWENTY-THREE

A cross the moat, but stumped…

They had walked around the walls of the castle, twice, and still couldn't find any other openings. The walls were perfectly smooth so they couldn't find any hand holds in order to scale the walls. Reluctantly they agreed that they could no longer pursue their guerrilla warfare approach. They decided to use the front door and blag their way in to the castle, and just hope for the best.

They all looked at the rhinestone, bedazzled front door…

*"Do we knock and wait?"* enquired Dippit. She had inspected every inch of the door and couldn't find any way of opening the massive door. The wood was expertly crafted and there wasn't even the width of a fingernail between the sparkling wooden panels.

Stan knocked. The door opened and they were greeted by a Knight, in full armour, hugging a glorious plump Peacock. The Peacock's fanciful feathers were iridescent in the bright sunlight

*"Good day to you all. This is Sir Ian of the Crescent, and my name is Brian,"* said the beautiful Peacock with impeck-able manners. Sorry, Lum M., M'Key and Pip's terrible sense of humour appears to be catching. Between understanding Trevor and now Brian, the higher Hells must have some sort of animal to human translation app, Harry decided.

*"We are coming in, and you can't stop us. Now bird, get a move on. We want to partake in some refreshments. A haunch of venison and a few pints of that mead the gargoyle was guzzling. That's for me. This lot can have some gruel. It is normally gruel that you give to the minions and serfs? Yes? Jolly good,"* with that Devil Keith pushed past the Knight and the Peacock, and entered the bailey. Harry wasn't sure whether it was his arrogant attitude that got them in, or the fact that he was wearing a bedazzled suit of armour. How much did he cram into that rucksack? When did he change his clothes? And why, o why didn't he pack some woolly hats? Harry silently fumed.

*"Please enter. You're very welcome. However, I'm awfully sorry but the King won't permit visitors looking the way you do. Also, I need you to remove your weapons. Please follow me."* Brian's really, really polite, thought Harry. Devil Keith wondered how he would taste; fried up with chopped onions, a teaspoon of lemon drizzle cake and a sniff of blanched Brussel sprouts.

The team were handed objects that, on first sight, looked like large umbrellas. When pulled and stretched out they were, in fact, hats that fitted over the head (duh), via a forehead band. They were then instructed to pull the cord and the sides extended down to their feet.

So, the four intrepid adventurers were reduced to four walking beach huts; Devil Keith strongly protested as he felt that his armour was rather splendid. Brian responded with a raised bushy eyebrow, and then arched his tail in order to display the tips of the feathers. The tips which were curved scorpion stingers.

*"Absolutely correct, this old armour needs binned right away."* Devil Keith pulled his cord. Once in his tent he muttered and began soothing his armour. *"You know I didn't mean it. You **are** splendid but that overinflated turkey wannabee is a bully. I'll give you a lovely oiling later, and we'll all be friends again."*

The team were instructed to walk on the path of

newspapers and led, crocodile style, through the castle. Harry had so wanted to see the inside of the castle. Not to ooh and aah, but to give them some much needed constructive criticism and coax them into adopting a mangy dragon.

# CHAPTER TWENTY-FOUR

**H**ell number three's inner sanctum…

They were ushered into King Adrian's throne room. An ornate throne sat on a dais at the far end of the colossal room. Well, less a dais; more like a full set of sweeping, marble stairs. The solid gold throne was surrounded by elaborate rose-gold candle sticks and jewel encrusted vases that were stuffed with bouquets of singing flowers. The air was heavy with the scent of dripping beeswax candles, and Chanel Number 5 perfume. Devil Keith felt right at home there.

Etched crystal sconces were filled with flickering candles and illuminated the myriad of paintings and tapestries that adorned the walls. The subject of the paintings appeared to be one man, in many different poses and flamboyant settings. As the Dashing Hunter or as the Dashing Fencer or as the Dashing Woodsman or as the Dashing Pirate or as the Dashing Soldier. The authors haven't run out of adjectives or adverbs…those was the actual names on the plaques attached to each of the paintings.

Each painting was framed with yards of gaudy silk swags and raspberry red velvet curtains. There were strings of seed pearls laced across the vaulted ceiling and culminating in a chandelier of dazzling delight and epic proportions.

The centre of the throne room was dominated by a huge triangular oak table. At the apex of the table sat another highly decorative throne. The throne appeared to have been carved from a single deep blue sapphire. Around the table were small, plain wooden stools. It was obvious that the other diners would barely be able to reach the table, whilst the person at the head of the table would loom over them. Dominate them. *"So much for a round table, and equality,"* Harry whispered

They were asked to remain standing, as the Peacock didn't want them touching the furniture and corrupting it with their filth. They were permitted to open a small gap in their walking tents, and told to wait at the table as the King would be in shortly. Stan ignored the rude bird and picked up a golden plate. Around the rim of the plate was engraved the words, *"Nikad ne možeš biti previše mršav ili pre bogat."*

*"What's that?"* Dippit enquired and leaned over.

*"I think it says. I say, I think it says. 'You can never be too thin or too rich'. Thin or rich, I say."* Stan ran his fingers over the plate and it emitted a deep ringing tone.

*"I thought a family motto normally said something about honour or gallantry. Something positive to live by."* Dippit was puzzled, but thrilled that Stan spoke Bosnian Latin so well.

At that they heard repetitive, short, sharp clipping.

*"Ahem."* Then a small, discrete cough and yet more clipping.

*"What the fudge?"* Harry turned and stared.

Introducing *"what the fudge"*…

*"Ah, an audience for little old me? Well tickle me with a feather duster and call me a Chippendale sideboard. Well floss my front teeth with a sturdy rope and call me a Spanish Galleon. Well scrub my back with a sponge and call me the lost city of Atlantis. Ah maybe a shade too much explaining for that one. Dear Hearts. For me? You're here for me? Haw, haw, haw."* A high pitched squeal emitted from the creature.

*"What the fudge?"* Dippit also gasped and stared.

*"Ah, I see that you're struck dumb by my very presence. I am…*

126

quick, you there, give me my line. I am, oh it's so worth building up the sizzling anticipation. I am King Adrian Pentupdragon, at your service." With that, the eight and a half foot talking *"thingy"* made a flourishing bow. And there may have been a small fart in there too.

"*Devil Keith are you two related?*" whispered Harry as she nudged Devil Keith.

"*No, no. How dare you? We're nothing alike. Absolutely nothing alike. At all. He's vain. Vanity itself. I'm what you would call... the salt of the earth. Well maybe not salt. Mmm, that cripplingly expensive one? Ah, saffron. I'm the saffron of the earth. Yes, I like that. I'll have that one, instead of the inventor of non-stick frying pans and the red squirrel name. Mmmm, on second thoughts. I think I'll have both names. Throw caution to the wind and all that palaver.*" Devil Keith decided that new business cards were urgently required.

"*Ahhem. Dear Hearts, I was expecting you earlier. I am aware of your names and I know a little about you. There have been rumours flying about that Hell number one is getting grandiose ideas. That you're visiting other Hells, and stealing their ideas. I would have thought that you would have been at my Hell first. It would have saved you a lot of time and effort. Go for the best first, I always say. Haw, haw, haw.*" Then there was another discrete cough from the *"thingy."*

King Adrian, aka the *"thingy,"* was dressed in highly polished, golden armour. So highly polished, that Harry was looking around for some much-needed sunglasses. Her eyes were stinging, and she looked away; rapidly blinking in order to re-hydrate her eyeballs.

"*Ah, startled by my beauty? Dear Hearts. I get that a lot. Serf, my cloak. Haw, haw, haw.*" With a click of his fingers King Adrian was draped in an orange, ermine edged, floor length cloak.

Devil Keith stared in wonder. "*Harry, when we go home, I want one of them?*"

"*A cloak?*" She enquired.

"*A serf.*" Devil Keith assertively stated with a crips nod of his head.

King Adrian's skin was stretched tightly over his cheek bones; with every ridge on his facial bones and the gaps in his teeth clearly visible through the paper-thin, blue veined skin. The King liked his minions to constantly see, and be amazed by his sluggish blue blood. Harry was convinced that he was using trowel loads of gold highlighter on his cheeks and ringing his eyes with a thick coating of black Kohl. With eyelashes as thick as camel's lashes, she was sure that multiple sets of false eyelashes were also nail-gunned in situ.

He was smelling of ripe strawberries, as his permanently pouting lips were dripping in pints of the greasy lip balm. The pout contributed to his exceedingly posh accent. His lack of back molars contributed to the pout.

"*Where are my manners? Haw, haw, haw. I am such a poor host, Dear Hearts. No please, don't all rush at once to correct me. You must be so peckish, and you appear rather travel weary. And positively shabby. Let me offer you some assistance. Brian, take them to a bedchamber and assist with their toilette.*" King Adrian flicked his fingers at the prostrate bird.

King Adrian clicked his skinny fingers and a serf helped him turn around. He walked away, and for the first time Harry noticed his feet. His boots were peep toe in order to allow his yellowed, long curling toenails to tap and click on the parquet floor.

The King turned back. "*Ah, I see you admiring my pedicure. I'm thinking of making it all the rage, Dear Hearts. It so matches my shiny locks. Haw, haw, haw.*" With that King Adrian removed his colossal golden helmet and tossed his midnight, black hair. All eight and a half foot of tightly coiled ringlets, interspersed with precious stones and topped with a rose-gold coloured tiara, settled perfectly around his painfully narrow shoulders and fell to the floor.

"*Ah, it's so refreshing to know that little old me can still impress an audience into silence. Haw. Haw. Haw. Don't be shy, Dear Hearts. You can all touch my crowning glory. Well obviously not you, red headed female. Your hands look like you moisturise them with wet cement."* King Adrian finished his invite with a snarl at Harry.

I do not use cement, thought Harry. Huffing and mumbling under her breath. *"Never wanted to touch it anyway. I've no time for moisturisers or face packs. Too busy having a life. A great life. You fudger."*

*"Is that table moving? I'm sure that table is moving,"* whispered Dippit as she did a double take. The table was indeed moving.

*"Oh, I see you've noticed Mr Hamhands. Mr Hamhands can you come over here? Haw, haw, haw."* The table waddled over, and Dippit was amazed as King Adrian removed the silver tray from the table's head.

Introducing the one and only Mr Hamhands…

There stood a man: less than thirty inches tall, with truly massive hands. Hands that were trailing on the ground. He was a rather portly chap with a chubby belly and skinny little legs. He was wearing snug denim dungarees under a mud coloured brown jacket. The type of jacket that is usually worn by hard-wear shop employees. He had a completely flat head, with a precise crew cut that could only have been achieved whilst using a spirit level and exceedingly sharp scissors. A well-used pencil stub was tucked behind his ear, and black rimmed spectacles attached to a silver chain completed his look. He was smiling angelically with round, chubby, red cheeks. His head was broader than its length which gave him the appearance of an exceedingly cheerful toad.

*"You use people as pieces of furniture?"* Dippit was horrified, but desperate to investigate the little man further.

*"Why yes, Lady Dippit. Haw, haw, haw. Well, in truth, there*

is only one Mr Hamhands table. He is uniquely mine, Dear Hearts. Although if I patented it, I'm sure that they would be exceedingly popular. I think they'd be very cheap to make, but I would have to investigate his one, small design flaw. He does so love a large mixed grilled. Lamb chops, steaks, pork loin, grilled tomatoes, and mushrooms. With a sneaky side of baked beans. The lot.

He can be choking on the stuff, and he'll still shovel more in. Won't you Mr Hamhands? Won't you? It's hilarious. He goes the most marvellous cerise colour when he chokes. I liked the colour so much that I commissioned a pair of curtains in the same shade. Haw, haw, haw." King Adrian pinched the rather full cheeks. The exceedingly sharp pinch dislodged a full block of square sausage, which Mr Hamhands quickly sucked back into his mouth.

"Doesn't he complain?" Dippit was concerned for his general welfare and his regular choking fits.

"Oh no. Not at all. Not a word, Dear Hearts. He is unable to speak, but he does sometimes use sign language. Always thought it might be useful to know a smattering of it, but I can't really see the point now. He's only here to serve my every whim, afterall. Haw, haw, haw." The King then kicked and slapped Mr Hamhands, as the wee chap passed on his way to collect some glassware and crockery.

Cue back story...

Mr Hamhands could speak, but he chose not to. When Mr Hamhands first met King Adrian he was asked if he could talk. Mr Hamhands was sucking on a particularly tasty lamb chop, so instead of answering. He had said, "mmnnyaya." The King had taken that as a no, and had gone on to say that if Mr Hamhands was able to speak then the King would have had Mr Hamhands tongue removed. The King is a thoughtless jerk, and paranoid as fuck.

Mr Hamhands would be forever grateful for that delicious lamb chop. He decided there and then to never again sully another piece of lamb with cheap mint sauce.

Just after the job interview, Mr Hamhands moved in with Mrs Hamhands, his widowed sister-in-law, and his four footstool nephews. Mrs Hamhands was well-meaning but spoke incessantly, so he found it easier to tune out most of the conversation. He then pretended that he *"forgot"* how to re-start speaking, and then found that he couldn't get out of the lie. Consequently he was hounded, by his rather loud sister-in-law, into attending Lady Waddell's excellent Sign Language School.

Due to the size of his hands, there was an unforeseen side effect of the sign language. His exceedingly large hand movements led everyone to believe that he was aggressive and constantly shouting at them. He tried Lady Waddell's kind suggestion of making a duck's beak sign at his mouth, to indicate when he was really shouting so that people could tell the difference. Unfortunately or fortunately, depending on your taste buds, people kept filling his hands with soft fried egg butties. So he had to stop the duck beak practice as his dungarees were getting a bit tight, and he didn't want to lose his sculptured bottom. After all, he was a bachelor with aspirations of marriage. He eventually wanted little footstools of his own.

So Mr Hamhands was gainfully and painfully employed. And he had unlimited access to carbonara pasta, but he could never sing karaoke again.

Back to the throne room…

*"Chop, chop. Dinner and entertainment soon. Haw, haw, haw."* King Adrian smoothed out his hair and wedged his helmet back on top of his pointed head.

# CHAPTER TWENTY-FIVE

**A** rather drafty room in the castle...

After a thorough and rather invasive toilette, the team stood in front of the large mirror to admire their transformations.

*"Can we carry any of the weapons with us?"* Dippit patted down her sides and measured her waist with her hands. She didn't think that it had ever been so small.

*"No, I can barely breathe, and I'm scared to sit down. These seams are working double time to keep me in as it is. Nothing else is going in here."* Harry was pleasantly surprised that she looked so feminine. So graceful. She never thought she could pull it off but robust Rosie, the dresser, had been fantastic. Painfully enthusiastic, but fantastic.

Harry was wearing an evening gown. A pale green silk sheath that fitted to the knee then gently flared to the floor. She loved the matching dancing slippers and miniature diamante studded clutch bag. Dippit was wearing the same ensemble, in rose pink, to highlight her lightly tanned skin and dark curls. They had both agreed to leave their hair tumbling down their back, so they resembled delicate wood nymphs. Admittedly, wood nymphs that ate to excess, drank until nearly unconscious, laughed until they peed a little, and partied hard, but wood nymphs all the same. A squirt of perfume, a fluff of their shiny locks and they were ready. The guys were in short faux fur capes and snug silver amour, that left little to the imagination. The buxom Rosie had used a crowbar and a couple of pints of oil to stuff them into the barely, man sized cans. Rosie had left a can opener so they could get out of them later.

Stan stood still and stared. He coughed and stared some more. He blinked a couple of times too. *"Ah, he's finally realised that our Dippit is a female. A beguiling female,"* thought Harry. This should get a bit more interesting; she giggled behind her hand and hid it as a delicate cough. She also wondered if Bub would ever give her the same adoring look. That look of a snuffling hedgehog, hit a glancing blow by a muddy Range Rover.

There was a loud knock then Stan answered the door to a very unusual sight.

The unusual sight…

*"Good evening, we are Sir Muckle of Nursingerton, Sir Fergus of D'Fries and Sir Alan de Aloha. Such a pleasure to meet you at last. We are here to escort you to the Banqueting Hall."* This was followed by a very messy bow and a fair bit of elbowing.

*"No, Sir Muckle of Nursingerton, you are mistaken. I was to do the introductions tonight. You did it last time."* Sir Fergus of D'Fries elbowed Sir Muckle of Nursingerton out of the way.

*"I think you'll find that you are both wrong. It's my turn, Sir Muckle of Nursingerton and Sir Fergus of D'Fries,"* and with that Sir Alan de Aloha pushed them both. They fell into an undignified, clanging heap in the middle of the corridor. They immediately started trading blows and using bicycle pumps to beat the living daylights out of each other.

*"Dippit. Harry. I say Dippit. I say Harry. There's an unusual sight. I say, an unusual sight. Can you come here? I say come here."* Stan called to his team mates.

*"You're an unusual chap. Do you always repeat yourself? Sir Muckle of Nursingerton, do you think he always repeats himself?"* enquired Sir Alan de Aloha. They stopped fighting long enough

to ask the questions, then they went right back to biting and giving each other savage Chinese burns.

*"Do you mean the way you just did, Sir Alan de Aloha?"* Sir Muckle of Nursingerton made no attempt to hide his sarcasm. Stan slipped in a quick kick... or two. Afterall, he was known for repeating himself.

Stan helped them rise from the floor. It was a messy task as the three young guys appeared to be joined together. One set of feet would be on the floor, then yanked back as another set of feet touched the ground. There were bony elbows, skinned knees and the occasional heavily bandaged hand trying to gain purchase on the floor. Their armour was so bent and broken that Stan thought they looked like they had been playing tag with a steamroller. The steamroller clearly won, and often.

*"Dippit. Harry. I say Dippit. I say Harry. Can you come here? I say come here please."* Stan asked again.

*"What? I'm trying to find my other earring...Oh,"* Harry looked out of the door to an unusual sight.

The double unusual sight was the three conjoined triplets. They were wearing identical, poorly fitted armour. And numerous bruises, at what appeared to be, various colours of recovery. The triplets looked to be around seventeen or eighteen with feet and hands they were still growing into. A tall, young lad with exceedingly long blonde hair introduced himself as, Sir Alan de Aloha and added. *"Great bit of totty you have there, Sir Stan."* He then shook his long golden tresses back into place.

The red-haired fellow with a magnificently wild, orange beard introduced himself as Sir Fergus of D'Fries. *"Sir Alan de Aloha, sees himself as a bit of a ladies' man. I have to agree though, great bit of totty, Sir Stan."*

*"I already said that Sir Fergus of D'Fries,"* and with that, they started squabbling again. Stan had to prise them apart. A difficult task, as they were joined together via skin tags on their shoulder blades. From above they looked like a struggling,

heaving, fleshy triangle.

The third young chap, with close cut black hair shouted, *"quit it, or I'll give you both such a hard nipple twister that we'll all feel it. Sorry for those two. Can't take them anywhere, but as you can see, I must bring them with me. I am the delightful one of the bunch. As I previously said, Sir Muckle of Nursingerton at your service."* He bowed and slipped in a couple of sly, stinging slaps.

*"Sir Fergus of D'Fries, you owe me £10. I told you Sir Muckle of Nursingerton would call himself 'delightful' within the first five minutes of meeting our charges. Cough it up."* Sir Alan de Aloha rubbed his hands with glee.

*"No, Sir Alan de Aloha, you said he would call himself 'adorable.' Sir Muckle of Nursingerton said 'delightful.' So, you cough it up."* Sir Fergus of D'Fries was trying to dance with delight. They all fell over again. Another enthusiastic battle ensued.

*"What's the deal, I say what's the deal?"* Stan was getting fed up as he had caught a couple of thumps too.

The deal was...

Sir Muckle of Nursingerton, Sir Fergus of D'Fries and Sir Alan de Aloha were conjoined triplets. An unusual occurrence made all the rarer as they had the same mother but three different fathers. The biology wasn't completely clear, but what was abundantly clear was their competitive natures. They bet on everything they could. From how often they could burp to a Brittany Spears' song, to the number of stones they could shove up each other's noses. They also did longer challenges such as:

The *"chopstick challenge"*, where over a three-month period every item of food had to be eaten whilst only using chopsticks. They all did reasonably well until they purchased the sandwich and soup combo at a local cafe. Unfortunately, they were banned following the flood of gazpacho and flying corned beef on rye. In their defence they were severely dehydrated with low blood sugar at the time.

The *"grow a chilli"*, plant challenge ended due to flagrant cheating. They drip fed alcohol and washing up liquid into each other's plants. How they did this and kept it a secret, whilst attached to each other, is in itself a puzzle. So, the poor plants died due to the puddles of alcohol, clouds of bubbles and someone may have hacked off the plants at their roots. Eh, Sir Alan de Aloha?

The *"let's just wear the elastic waistband of old boxer shorts"*, was a particularly difficult challenge. Oh, for clarity's sake they wore other clothes too. Those three bumbling around naked? Perish the thought. The elastic band was from old ripped, boxer shorts and it was to be worn at all times, even in the shower. However, they were permitted to repair the bands when they became threadbare and scabby. After three or four months they all got drunk one night and consequently lost their bands. They said they lost them in the bed of wenches but, well really, what were the chances? Just as well though, as according to Sir Muckle of Nursingerton, the bands were beginning to smell decidedly *"ballsy"* by then.

The only thing the triplets agreed on was their fear of having the minor surgery required to separate them. They said that they didn't like needles or blood or gauze or pain. That made no sense as they were always sporting blood, gauze and were rarely pain free due to their incessant arguments and fisticuffs.

Back to the present day and the castle...

*"We are here to escort you to dinner. Follow us, please."* Stan didn't care who said what, but he was intrigued. How did they get to and from places?

The triplets *"got to places,"* via a bright green tricycle. The three bike seats rotated clockwise so that they each had a turn at steering, pedalling, and complaining about the other two siblings. To give them any chance of reaching their destination they adapted their bicycle helmets. Attaching oversized wing mirrors to the front, back and sides of the helmets.

It was still a bit tricky and very bruisey.

# CHAPTER
# TWENTY-SIX

O n the way to the Banqueting Hall...

One very careful traverse down the stairs for the Hell number one team. One almighty clatter and an A&E visit for the squabbling triplets. Then an exceedingly long walk along gleaming marble corridors and the Hell team entered the Banqueting Hall. The triplets were still lying at the bottom of the stone stairs, arguing over who had the greatest number of bones protruding from their punctured skin and who would organise the ambulance.

The Banqueting Hall was even more ornate than the throne room. There were glowing spotlights highlighting classic scenes of war, acts of bravery and righteous crusades. The faces of the combatants were all obscured, with the exception being the exceedingly detailed drawings of a triumphant King Adrian.

There was a collection of large paintings and tapestries along one wall. They were titled, *"Just a normal day, you too could be a King."* This collection started with a painting of King Adrian wearing an eye mask and lying in bed. The next painting depicted him getting out of bed (he sleeps in the nude), and stretching (still nude) and then there was the King in the bath (oh, nude again, how novel). Harry could have done without ever seeing that wizened arse ever again. His bottom was utterly repulsive too. Roughly, two hundred boring paintings later and he was bent over getting back into a gaudy bed (nude apart from an eye mask and a black beauty spot)

Between each painting and tapestry were cherubs playing harps, lyres and blowing trumpets. Harry looked again: the cherubs all had King Adrian's face, and his greatly exaggerated hairy bits, carved into the blush marble. *"The figures must have some mighty big artistic licence going on there,"* mumbled a repulsed Harry.

Talking of arses. King Adrian had forgone his golden armour and decided to go with a full-length lilac cloak instead. Open to the waist, it allowed his subjects to see every protruding rib and admire his bony sternum. Harry was convinced that he was so emaciated that she could see the outline of his heart, spleen, liver, gall bladder and kidneys. Her knowledge of anatomy isn't too hot, but she knew there were liquids swishing away in there. She could see them slosh about.

The King continued to wear his peep toed boots, but had added silver toe rings decorated with miniature bells to the mix. His ringlet festooned hair was loosely flowing, but it was now blonde with teal green highlights. Perched on his hair creation was a cavalier's hat complete with a five-foot, red ostrich feather.

*"Devil Keith, sure you're not related?"* Harry enquired, again.

*"Positive Harry. Peep toes are so out just now."* Devil Keith responded.

*"Oh, my Dear Hearts. You scrub up rather well. Haw, haw, haw."* King Adrian laid his bony hand over his heart and looked across his left shoulder. Leaning back, he looked like he was going to swoon. He was attempting a classic old Hollywood, leading man pose. He was really terrible at it.

Harry produced a small smile and thought, this is getting really old really quickly. She wasn't sure that she would be able to stop herself from screaming in his face, *"where is my Bub? You twit."*

*"First order of business, Dear Hearts. I want an increase in guards around my paintings. I've noticed that a few of them are*

*being defaced by scoundrels who are jealous of my beauty."* King Adrian went from gracious host to snarling beast then back again in a blink of an eye. Harry had seen that face before. Oh, a touch of the Deadly Sin of Vanity was alive and well, and living in Hell number three?

*"Dear Hearts, we have visitors. I would have introduced you to them earlier but they were rank, and would have offended your eyes and other senses. Now they look a little better. May I introduce, well of course I can. Haw, haw, haw. I am the King, afterall. We have Lady Harry, Lady Dippit, Sir Devil Keith, and Sir Stan. Now for my favourite Knights. You've already met Sir Ian of the Crescent and my trusty Peacock."* The King casually pointed at each of them in turn. Although he did do a double take when he saw the transformation of Lady Harry. Rosie would be getting a visit later that night, whether she wanted one or not, the King decided.

Sir Ian was still carrying the Peacock, so his bow was a little clumsy but well intentioned. *"Oh, Sir Ian of the Crescent, I see you're still embracing my little challenge, haw, haw, haw."*

Sir Ian of the Crescent was an excellent musician and all round good guy. His bagpipe playing was hauntingly beautiful and much admired. Unfortunately he had made the mistake of winning the daily talent contest. Following the unlikely win, King Adrian suggested that Sir Ian should carry around the King's favourite Peacock so that he could increase his endurance. Endurance to what, no one was quite sure, but Sir Ian accepted the challenge and sadly laid down his bagpipes. There really was little choice in the matter.

*"Oh, who do we have here Dear Hearts? Haw, haw, haw. Ah, it's Sir Andrew de Lardites...creator of pies and Mr Hamhands best friend. Aren't you, Sir Andrew de Lardites?"* King Adrian forcefully prodded the Knight in his stomach. *"Now for one or two of your famous poems."*

Sir Andrew reluctantly stood, made a small bob, and offered an awkward smile to Harry and the audience. He was clearly embarrassed by the unwanted attention.

*"There once was a woman from Dubai,*
*Who baked the most marvellous pie,*
*She used chicken and gravy and crispy bacon bits,*
*She made my pastry rise with her big..."*

*"Naughty, naughty, now there are ladies present. Haw, haw, haw. Another one, if you please."* The King spitefully giggled and soundly punched the Knight in the stomach.

*"There once was a young lady who made pies,*
*She was very easy on the eyes,*
*Her sausage rolls were laid out in tubes,*
*They were golden and bouncy just like her..."* the Knight stopped and gratefully sunk back into his seat.

*"Ah a new poem. Still naughty, naughty, though. Haw, haw, haw. Sir Andrew of Lardites adores pies. He even swapped his sword for a pastry crimper. Didn't you my podgy friend? I'll introduce the rest later, Dear Hearts. Now time for dinner and a little snifter of brandy. Then it's the talent show. I bet you can't wait for my internationally renowned show. Well, you're in luck, a couple of exclusive tickets having just become available. Haw, haw, haw."* The King clicked his skeletal fingers and the atmosphere changed from grovelling and anger, to one of anticipation.

Harry was ravenous. She was convinced her stomach was kissing her spine and she could eat a scabby heided wain (A popular Scottish saying that means; Harry would happily cannibalise a small, unkempt child). She smiled, then smiled some more as the waiting staff staggered under the weight of the silver serving dishes. Breathless with exertion, they arrived at the long table with trays of golden skinned crispy roast chickens, steaming gravy boats and mounds of creamy mashed potatoes. However, the centre piece of the banquet was a full roast boar, garnished with a shiny red apple and surrounded with heaps of crispy roast potatoes. There was an assortment of vegetables in heavy cream sauces, but Harry couldn't stop salivating at the thought of the crackling and the soft, buttered rolls. The table was groaning, and yet more food was added. There were creamy Black Forest gateau's squashed next to plates of decadent chocolate éclairs, heaped bowls of fresh exotic fruit (for the strange people who don't like chocolate), mounds of raspberry jam tarts and pots of warm crème caramel.

*"Now dig in, Dear Hearts. Dig in everyone. Don't stand on ceremony, not on my behalf. Into the breeches and all that. Haw, haw, haw."* The generous King gleefully announced to the masses.

*"It's the breach, you twit,"* mumbled Harry raising her eyebrows and leaning towards the bowl of creamy mashed potatoes. The bowl was whisked out of her reach and the contents were being shovelled into the mouth of one of the Knights. Harry looked around the table and was shocked by the rabid squabbling over the food. *"There's more than enough..."* she started to say, when she happened to look over at King Adrian.

He had a heavy, cut-crystal bowl of grapes in front of him. He slowly stirred the bowl clockwise then anticlockwise with his long, bony index finger before carefully lifting out a plump, dewy grape. The black grape glistened in the candlelight. The King lifted his snowy-white linen napkin and gently removed the moisture from the grape. He then brought the grape to his right eye and examined it. Turning it left and right then back again. He brought the grape to his left eye and followed the same performance.

When he was completely satisfied, that it was indeed perfect, he placed it against his red rouged, pouting lips. He took a breath and using his long ragged fingernail he carefully pushed the grape through the pursed orifice. Harry was fascinated as she watched the outline of the un-chewed grape slide from his mouth and down through his digestive tract. She thought she saw the shape of the purple grape resting inside his collapsed stomach.

*"Extra-halibut, now Dear Hearts. Haw, haw, haw."* The King

dabbed his lips with his monogrammed napkin and sighed in utter contentment.

Two of the harassed servers rushed to the table with the legendary-ish sword clasped in their hands. *"My that's a big knife. I wonder if it's for a humungous block of cheese and some salty biscuits."* Devil Keith pondered.

*"I'm stuffed, serfs. Clear the table, minions. Haw, haw, haw."* The King announced and boxed a servers ear; just for the fun of it

The frightened servers cut a swath through the loaded table. They were smashing dishes, pulverising puddings and toppling cakes onto the floor. The Knights were making a last-ditch attempt at saving some of the plates and serving bowls, but King Adrian was having none of it.

*"Sir Derek of the Var, Dear Hearts. Step away from the trencher of curried baked beans, and while you're at it take that whole roast chicken out of your helmet. Haw, haw, haw."* Sir Derek scooped out the fragrant chicken, then rammed the chicken skin into his mouth and furiously chewed. Sir Andrew was doing his level best to wrestle the dish of sage and onion stuffing from one of the emaciated servers. He lost, and due to the Knight's loss the waiter would eat that night. *"Sir Ian of the Crescent do not reach for that tankard of ale. I won't have fat little sausages around me. Haw, haw, haw."*

Harry nearly cried. She was so busy watching that fudging twit King Adrian eat a single grape that she had missed out on all the grub. She then realised that someone had dropped some jam in her hair, so she licked it off and starting looking in her locks for some more. The hungry Knight sitting beside her was also casting longing looks at her jammy hair.

*"The talent show, Dear Hearts. Give me a hooray or else. Haw, haw, haw."* The King surveyed the empty table with satisfaction. He then made sure that he, and the waiting staff, stood then stamped on all the food piled up on the floor. He then indicated

that his trusty Peacock, Brian, should despoil the remaining food. The Peacock happily pecked and pooped across the roast boar and spat on the jam tarts.

Harry did cry a little at that.

# CHAPTER TWENTY-SEVEN

The talent show...

"*That guy's smoking,*" whispered Harry as she pointed to the far side of the Banqueting Hall.

"*Terrible, truly terrible. My poor brother is away for the briefest of seconds and you're ogling other men. Do tell, which one has Harlot all of a twitter?*" Devil Keith barked and threw her a dirty look. Devil Keith was definitely adding her preposterous comment to his hidden diary.

"*You silly cookie-bun. That guy is literally smoking, as in smoke is coming out of his fudging head.*" Harry pointed at the steaming, swearing Knight.

"*Ah Dear Hearts, I didn't get round to introducing you to Sir James de Spark. I have him harnessing lightning bolts. I need it for my many spotlights. He has permanently lost his eyebrows, but I feel that it's his small price to pay. His singed fingers are ever so slightly gangrenous, but he insists on completing his courageous work. He is so in awe of me and my simple dreams. He would do anything for his beauteous King. Ahhhhh. Hee, hee, hee.*" King Adrian rested the back of his hand against his forehead. He so enjoyed a dramatic, tragic act of his own selflessness.

"*Sir James de Spark, Dear Hearts. Put down that flagon of beer and cigar. You don't want me sending Brian around again, now would you?*" even in a singsong voice there was no mistaking King Adrian's threat. Harry heard the murmured rumour, from one of the poor servers, that Brian had bullied the resident dragon out of the castle. Cecil, the Downtrodden, was still receiving counselling following Brian's incessant gaslighting.

*"Attention, attention. Now, Dear Hearts, I have some bad news. Sir Daniel of Foxtine can't make it tonight. Someone cut the strings on all of his guitars. It may have been self-inflicted due to the amount of cheese he stole from the royal kitchen, then greedily consumed. We all know that cheese gives one nightmares. Our thoughts and kind wishes go out to him. We will, of course, **not** be doing a collection to replace the strings.*

*But don't be disheartened. The marvellous Sir Derek of the Var and Sir Ougie of the Muir will, of course, provide the closing act tonight. Following their excellent run as the two ugly stepsisters in the pantomime 'Cinderella', they are going to perform in a tribute to Black Beauty. The two absolute hoots will, of course, take the joint role of the stunning horse. I think you'll all agree that this new comedic show will so benefit from their breadth of emotions and talents.*

*Afterall, we can't have them wearing their watermelons and brassieres all the time now, can we? Haw, haw, haw."* The King cupped his hands in front of his chest and gave the scowling pair a saucy wink. He then pointed at Brian until the pair of Knights produced a thin smile.

*"Why did you ban the pantomimes?"* a voice from the back heckled.

*"Please come closer and say that. Dear Hearts, I didn't hear your question. Haw, haw, haw."* The King smirked then shrieked.

Tumbleweed was the reply.

# CHAPTER TWENTY-EIGHT

**N**ow for the first act...

*"We have a new contestant, Dear Hearts. Please make her feel welcome. Haw, haw, haw."* The King announced and fell back into his cushioned chair.

A staggeringly beautiful, tattooed lady sashayed into the middle of the room. She was sensuously dragging a chair. Yep, seemingly you can indeed sensuously drag a bloody big chair into the middle of a Banqueting Hall. She nodded and the hypnotic music filled the night. She moved seamlessly to the beat and lilt of the ballad: precariously balancing on and around the chair. She was slowly stretching in order to create silhouettes and gravity defying body shapes. She was using her white boa and trilby, as props, to entrance the appreciative audience. She was mouth-wateringly mesmerising.

Devil Keith's eyes were nearly out on stalks. *"Forget the kitty and the serf. I want one of those."* Devil Keith jabbed at the air.

*"Attention, attention, thank you Jayne-Jayne. Don't call us, we'll call you, Dear Hearts. Haw, haw, haw."* The King arrogantly said, as he indicated that the servants should chuck the talented lady out and lock the door behind her.

The stunning Jayne-Jayne was ushered out of the Banqueting Hall, whilst protesting that she hadn't finished her set. She hadn't seen her scores either.

The second act of the night...

*"Now put your hands together for an old favourite. An exquisitely beautiful and talented favourite. Our very own Lady Van de Burgh. Haw, haw, haw."* The King gallantly announced whilst slowly and softly patting his heart.

A gorgeous, delicate lady with glowing, golden skin and gleaming black hair was highlighted with a powerful spotlight. Her ruby red and jewel encrusted dress was clinging to her sensuous, hourglass figure. She softly smiled, and the whole room seemed to sigh in contentment and delight. Devil Keith was crossing his fingers and hoping that she too could dance and fling her legs about. She was graceful perfection. *"As delicate as China and twice as precious as gold,"* he whispered. A perfect lotus blossom.

The stunning lady gently nodded, and delicate music filled the air. Devil Keith was sitting forward in his chair, holding his breath. He had warmed up his hands so that they were ready to give a rousing round of applause. The dazzling Lady Van de Burgh began singing. Oh, my goodness. It was bad. So, so bad. The tapestries were unfurling in fright. And the wool was trying to squeeze under the door and through cracks in the walls. Trying to get away from the wailing and cackling that emitted from the Banshee. The audience were filling their ears with hot wax and Brian, the Peacock, was having a hard time keeping the scorpion tails under control. They wanted to blast the racket away.

At the last screech, the audience fell silent.

*"Wooed into silence, every time. Excellent performance, as usual, Dear Hearts. Scores please for our favourite lady. Haw, haw, haw."* The King hollered and impatiently clicked his brittle fingers.

The four judges were shaking as they held up their score cards: 7, 8, 7, and 9.

*"Twenty points. What? Oh, thirty-one points, Dear Hearts. Sorry, your lowest score so far my Lady, but a true songbird,*

nonetheless. *Haw, haw, haw.*" The King indicated that the judge, who corrected him, should be removed and executed. Brian merrily hummed as he dragged the protesting judge from the Banqueting Hall.

"*She was robbed.*" Devil Keith said as he enthusiastically applauded and whistled.

"*Devil Keith, what did you just say?*" Harry gawped in utter amazement.

"*She was robbed.*" Devil Keith said, again.

"*Did you just nip outside for a good taste removal? She was very, very beautiful but a terrible singer. Truly terrible.*" Harry questioned the strange man and his stranger taste.

"*Jealous much?*" Devil Keith smirked.

"*Fudger much?*" Harry responded. There may have been a small skirmish and someone was aggressively poked in the eye.

The third act of the night..

"*Our very own master of mystery, Dear Hearts. Our triumphant trickster. Our magical Magician, Dear Hearts. My very own twin brother, Dearest Hearts. Drum roll please for Melvin the Marvellous. Haw, haw, haw.*" The King jubilantly stated. He scowled at the glum audience until they stamped their feet and threw small pairs of rolled up socks onto the stage.

"*Oh no, not two of the silly cookie-buns. Two?*" Harry groaned and hit her head off the table.

Melvin the Magician was the mirror image of his conceited brother, right down to his flouncy lilac cloak and the yellowed, ragged toenails. He closed his bony fist and pulled out a line of brightly coloured handkerchiefs. Handkerchiefs that were badly hidden in Melvin's top right, inside pocket of his cape. The audience went wild. Harry wondered why they were throwing lacy underwear and flowers at the terrible Magician. She then noticed that Brian was using a pair of binoculars to study the audience's reactions.

Melvin then reached behind the ear of one of the members

of the audience and pulled out a lump of white, flaky dandruff. *"Surely, they'll chuck him out,"* whispered Dippit, whilst casting a puzzled gaze at Harry and Stan. Another raucous round of applause ensued.

*"I will now pull a dove from this top-hat. Be assured there is nothing in the hat and no doves were harmed during this trick. Hee, hee, hee. Sir Devil Keith, as our honoured guest, can you check that the top-hat is completely empty?"* Melvin the Magician flashed the hat towards Devil Keith.

*"Yes, it's empty. I pinkie swear to that fact."* Devil Keith solemnly stated.

*"Thank you. Now with a wave of my magic wand and a few mystical words, the top-hat will now contain a white dove. Hee, hee, hee."* Melvin waved the wand, whispered and reached into the hat. He removed his hand and cupped a dove. *"Voila, an invisible dove, for your pleasure and amusement. Thank you, I thank you. Hee, hee, hee. I'm here all week."*

The audience were on their feet as Devil Keith whispered, *"Stan that hat was empty. I checked. He's amazing. A dove, **and** he made it invisible. Wow. He is good."*

Harry had a bruise forming on her forehead.

*"And for the lovely ladies,"* Melvin handed Dippit and Harry a small, bunch of bashed up plastic flowers. Flowers that had spent most of the night blatantly poking out of the front pocket of his cape.

*"Now for one of my most famous acts. And back by popular demand, hee, hee, hee. I give you...balloon animals. What animal would you like?"* the Magician gleeful exclaimed.

*"A gorilla,"* shouted an excited Devil Keith. He looked at Harry and nudged her in the side.

*"A snake, you say. He wants a snake, folks. Hee, hee, hee."* The Magician hollered into the silent audience.

*"No, a gorilla,"* Devil Keith bellowed back.

*"Then a snake you shall have, my friend. Hee, hee, hee."* Melvin, blew up the long balloon and handed it to a very

disappointed Devil Keith.

"*Dippit, I'm not sure if he heard me.*" Devil Keith sulked and moved his thumb close to his mouth.

"*Oh, he heard you alright.*" And Dippit patted Devil Keith's slumped shoulders.

"*Oh well done, Dear Hearts. A winner I'm sure, but I may be a little bias. Not because you're my brother, but because you are such a rare talent. Haw, haw, haw. Scores, please.*" The King finished his simpering speech with a threatening snarl.

The three remaining trembling judges held up their new score cards. They read: 10, 10, and 10.

"*Three hundred points, Dear Hearts. How wonderful. Let's hear it for tonight's winner. Four thousand and twenty-three consecutive wins. A record surely, Dear Hearts. Haw, haw, haw.*" The King preened on his brother's behalf.

"*What the fudge?*" then Harry noticed that there were now tiny zeroes hand-written on all the score cards.

"*Encore. Encore, Dear Hearts. We must see some more. Haw, haw, haw.*" The King blatantly encouraged the audience to scream and stamp their feet.

"*Well, if the audience insists, hee, hee, hee. I have a new trick that I was practising during your bountiful and delicious dinner. Bring in the box. Hee, hee, hee.*" The Magician happily announced and bounced on the balls of his withered feet.

Two harangued serving staff wheeled in a four foot long, wooden box. The box had a hole at each end and an oozing, black stain in the middle. The air was saturated with the smell of particles of iron. It was sickening.

"*Bring in my willing assistant. Hee, hee, hee.*" The Magician was positively sizzling with energy.

A bundle of squirming rags was dragged into the hall. The woman beneath the rags was pleading and crying. The servers ignored her pleas.

"*Put my assistant in the box and make sure there's no gag. We want to see and hear it all. Bring a bucket of water for her. They'll be no fainting during this act. Not this time. Hee, hee, hee.*" Melvin grinned menacingly. He produced a dull edged, blood drenched saw. A saw designed for hacking and torture, rather than a single, quick cut. The audience went wild. Cheering for blood, guts and gore.

"*No, no, no. We have to stop this,*" Dippit and Harry cried at once.

Stan jumped on the table, and grabbed a partially filled bowl of congealed macaroni cheese. Harry was so distressed that she hadn't even noticed it sitting there. Stan began running his finger around the rim of the bowl. The baying audience turned towards Stan as he pulled a beautiful melody from the copper kitchen appliance.

"*Ooh, pretty. So, so pretty,*" Dippit dreamily sighed. She rested her head on her cupped hand and stared at Stan. Oh, she had it bad.

"*King Adrian. King Adrian, he's stopped my encore. He can't do that. No hee, hee, hee from me,*" Melvin had a petted lip and was stamping around in a small circle.

"*No he can't, Dear Hearts. Guards! Haw, haw, haw.*" The King gleefully shouted.

# CHAPTER TWENTY-NINE

T he Banqueting Hall exploded...

The Knights leapt into action. Harry ripped open the side seams of her tight dress. She jumped on the table then began throwing bits of pottery and cutlery at the Knights' heads. She was sliding through the remains of the buttery mashed potatoes and then squelching in the blobs of stodgy jam roly poly and custard. Dippit tripped over the carcass of the roast boar and quickly picked herself up off the sticky floor. That damn Peacock. She tore through her dress. Then she started charging at the Knights with two colossal candle sticks gripped in her hands. She turned then charged again. Harry savagely ripped off a particularly unluck Knight's arm, and began hitting him with the appendage whilst shouting, *"where is my Bub, you fudger?"* That was interspersed with, *"I wish I'd brough a can opener, you oversized tin of tuna flakes."*

Stan was still balanced on the slippery table. He had converted his musical bowl into a makeshift, metal boxing glove. He was swinging left and right, catching helmets, and crunching through cartilage and bone to break the Knights' noses and jaws. A pile of dazed and groaning Knights lay at his feet.

*"Harry, I want to see the encore. I wonder what was in the box? Don't you want to know too?"* Devil Keith was sat at the table, staring at the bloody, box.

*"Devil Keith, fight you fudging fudger?"* Harry screamed and narrowly avoided being choked with a soggy lump of poop infused Black Forest gateau.

*"Okey dokey."* Devil Keith readily agreed.

Devil Keith stood, and he immediately went into full fighting mode. There were fists ploughing through breast plates and tearing at the gleaming armour. Powerful kicks resulting in jaws dislocating and cheekbones crumpling then turning to fine dust. Arms wrenched from their sockets amidst screams of pain and please for mercy. Teeth were exploding from skulls, but it was no use: the Hell number one gang were outnumbered. The Knights just kept coming and coming. They were clambering over their fallen comrades and charging the poorly equipped clan. *"How can we lose?"* Thought a breathless Harry. Stan's always so lucky. She never, for a moment, thought they'd be in this predicament. This much danger.

An exhausted Dippit did one last roundhouse kick and sent Sir Andrew to his back. His decorative armour split open, revealing rusty broken chainmail. The skin beneath the chainmail was covered in pus, old scars and open sores. His highly polished armour also hid his concave stomach and the devastating extent of his starvation.

*"You, it was you. You fudger!"* Hollered Harry, trying to land a couple of kicks. Still no swearing from our feisty lass. The etiquette training was still paying off. Just.

*"Off to the hanging tower with the lot of them, Dear Hearts. Haw, haw, haw."* The fight was over. The Hell number one team were quickly surrounded and restrained by Sir Andrew, Sir Derek, Sir Daniel, Sir Ougie, Sir James and Sir Ian, who was back to carrying the smug Peacock under his arm.

*"Erm, that's being redecorated."* Sir Derek informed the livid King.

*"Then the east wing of the dungeon. Haw, haw, haw."* The King responded with a smile and a giggle, but he was clearly

154

furious with the brave Knight.

"*The east wing's full after the last talent show. How about the west wing?*" Sir Ougie helpfully suggested.

"*As I was saying before I was so rudely interrupted. To the west wing. Please don't spare the kicks and occasional stabbings as you go. Here, I'll get you started. Haw, haw, haw.*" King Adrian tried to kick Stan, but he missed and fell on his bony bottom.

Off to prison with the lot of them…

The Hell number one team were violently pushed through a side door and down worn stone stairs into the murky subterranean passageways. "*This is what a castle should look like,*" Harry whispered to Dippit. They side stepped a group of hungry rats and brushed against the green, dank walls. The path went on, deeper into the bowels of the castle. The smell of rotten wood and long dead corpses were burning through their nasal hair and making them all gag.

"*Devil Keith, why do you still have that fudging balloon with you?*" Harry enquired.

"*Damn good snake Harry. Fellow's a certified genius.*" Devil Keith responded as he lovingly stroked his snake.

"*Stop. No talking. This is the end of the road for you lot.*" Sir Jim barked. They stood before a heavily fortified cell door.

"*In… Now. Mind, no funny business.*" Sir Ian said. Then the Knights opened the door a smidgeon and roughly pushed them through. The Knights abruptly retreated, locking the door as they left and clunked back up the narrow corridor.

"*We'll never find Bub,*" thought Harry. Oh, there he is!

# CHAPTER THIRTY

And there Bub was...

"*Oh, Harry, Dippit, Stan and Devil Keith.*" Bub grabbed and then hugged a surprised and delighted Harry. "*You made it. Harry, I've missed you so much. Are you alright? Do you know that you've got something in your hair? It's either some jam or a gooey finger? Your dress is torn too, are you warm enough? Devil Keith, mate, your rucksack's in the corner. There's others there too, but they're empty. Great to see you all.*

*This gallant gentleman, cluttering up the corner, is Sir Mark de Butcherine. My guard.*"

"*What's up?*" said Sir Mark, through a mouthful of crispy bacon, thick velvety butter and soft, soft bread.

"*Baconnnnn,*" drooled a starving Harry as she walked towards the ginning Knight.

"*Now, now I'm a rainbow. I don't eat spam, bacon, or pork.*" Sir Mark added, whilst carefully tucking the remains of his sandwich in his mouth. Sir Mark started laughing at the look on Harry's face. His laugh started somewhere round his feet and rumbled through his entire body. Harry couldn't help herself and joined in, until tears ran down her cheeks.

"*How do you do that?*" Harry was amazed and puzzled, as Sir Mark didn't really say anything funny. No, not funny at all.

"*A gift?*" and Sir Mark started his full body laugh yet again.

"*Please, you have to stop, or I'll pee myself,*" gasped Harry, leaning on Dippit for support. Dippit nearly dropped Harry, as she too was overcome with mirth.

"*Oh, he's a right tonic. He doesn't know what it means, and*

*I can't fathom it, but that comment always cracks us up. He's a laugh a minute, that one. But he's not strictly funny, in the Saturday night at the Palladium sort of way. It's normally pretty obscure, or sometimes a bit naughty, or sometimes it's due to his quirky bartering. And I think he'd beat our Fachance at the old haggling game. He's brutal when it comes to getting a bargain.*

*A word of warning though, you have to be careful because the laughter comes on quickly and it becomes highly addictive. I saw a scruffy rat laugh himself to death earlier today. His sloppy lungs hiccupped right out his twitching nose. Messy business... but it so reminded me of your haggis, Harry. I stopped laughing because I became homesick and depressed. I missed you so much. Those Highland beasties probably saved my life,"* added Bub, and he now regarded Sir Mark and his laughter as a clever weapon.

An astounded Harry turned to Bub. *"Well, that's just fine. Really useful to know, and I'll get back to you re the whole missing me and why. So how are you? You look well. They've not tortured you? Put you on the rack?"* Bub looked very healthy. In fact, Harry noticed the beginning of a small double chin on her beau. *"You look really healthy. They have been looking after you? They have been feeding you, right?"*

*"Erm, yes,"* Bub looked decidedly guilty and hid a family size crisp packet down the side of his chair.

*"Don't 'erm, yes', her. Aileen the Cook and Alanagh, her daughter, have absolutely loved having him here. He's been spoiled rotten. Has them eating out the palm of his hand, he has. Forgive the pun. Ha, ha, ha."* And the body laugh started again. The Hell number one team covered their ears and looked away.

Harry took the time to look around the cell and take stock of the cosy environment. There were multiple stacks of books and board games piled at the side of Bub's plush chair. Plus, there were thick woollen rugs on the floor and tucked under a huge four poster bed. A bed covered in soft quilts, snowy-white sheets and plump pillows. And she spotted a door to an en suite, luxury bathroom in the corner. She could be doing with that just about now as she had just pulled half a dozen mushy broccoli florets out of her tangled hair. She had also scraped a smear of dried potato from her left buttock. She really needed a shower, a cuppa and a change of clothes.

There was a blazing fire in an open hearth with a jug of steaming mulled wine and a tin of biscuits on the side table. A plate piled high with black-pudding and fried egg sandwiches sat next to it. Where are the rushes full of animal bones and faeces? Where is the thin gruel and greasy water rations? Where are the thick window bars? Are they stained glass windows over there? We're in a dungeon, how is that even structurally possible? What the Hell? Harry could feel her relief at finding Bub being replaced with cold, brutal anger. This was less a prison cell and more a luxury hotel suite.

There was a particularly large, plump grey cushion on a chair in the corner. *"Oh, that's just old Periwinkle. He's a bit of a brute, but Sir Mark thought I'd appreciate the extra company. I haven't been able to bond with the bruiser yet, but it's rather nice having the rats dealt with. Without all the laughter and warm offal exploding up the walls."* Bub was oblivious to the tension in the room and Harry's tick in her left eye.

Periwinkle opened a sleep drenched eye. He slowly leaned over, and scooped up an eight-pound, chocolate covered rat out of a nearby wicker basket. The cat opened his mouth, dislocated his jaw and delicately dropped the rat on his pale pink fuzzy tongue. Then, with obvious relish, he slowly sucked in the thin, hairless tail. Harry was so hungry that she wondered if people would find it gross if she licked the chocolate off one of the rats. Obviously, not eat the rat. Just eat the chocolate covering it. Sheesh.

*"A cat? You have a fudging cat? You have food and wine? You have company in case you get lonely? You felt homesick because you saw lungs and thought of me? You have a fudging double chin? You saw wet lungs and then you missed me? You have a fudging cat? Explain, and it better be fudging well good."* Harry screeched. Then

she repeated herself so often that Stan wondered if she had spent too much time with him. He's such a gentleman.

# CHAPTER THIRTY-ONE

**H**arry is still fuming and muttering...

At that they heard a familiar clip, clipping coming down the corridor. King Adrian, Melvin the Magician, and the Knights appeared at the door. Sir Ian was cradling the vicious Peacock and avoiding a good old eye pecking.

*"Well, what do we have here? This is a mighty fine prison cell. Is that one of my rugs I see before me? Haw, haw, haw. Sir Mark is that a black-pudding sandwich I see before me? Fried eggs, I see before me? Haw, haw, haw, Dear Hearts."* King Adrian sneered at the jolly guy. The King was reading a children's simple guide to Shakespear, age three plus. So, he enjoyed adding the words, *"I see before me"* to as many of his sentences as possible. He believed that it made him sound ever so clever and important.

Sir Andrew dived past a startled Sir Mark and stuffed three egg sandwiches in his mouth. The other Knights looked mightily pissed off. They weren't quick enough and the plate was now empty.

*"An explanation, Dear Hearts. Don't you think, brother? Haw, haw, haw."* King Adrian was making no attempt to hide his contempt.

*"Nothing to do with me. Hee, hee, hee. But I think this place is too good for the likes of them. They need to be moved. Hee, hee, hee."* Melvin the Magician grinned, but he was furious as his luxurious bed had been stolen and was sitting in the corner of the room.

Sir Andrew menacingly pulled out his favourite yellow pastry crimper and hit it against the palm of his hand. Sir Mark pulled out his non-stick frying pan and began swinging it in the air. He was limbering up, and working off his many bacon sandwiches. Sir James withdrew his new roll of duct tape and stretched out a length of it. Sir Daniel pulled out a battered song book, as his guitar was currently in the shop. Sir Ougie pulled out a greying slingshot brassiere, from his Cinderella days, and a large bag of neon green tennis balls. Sir Derek pulled out an i-pad, showing a game of FreeCell. Sir Ian then threw a startled Peacock at an equally startled King Adrian.

*"What! What! What! Dear Hearts. Do I see a mutiny before me? How amusing, Dear Hearts. Haw, haw, haw."* King Adrian batted away the squawking Peacock.

*"Appears to be brother. Hee, hee, hee."* Melvin laughed and held his bony sides.

*"You need to take this seriously. We've got you surrounded, and we have a plan to replace you with a Devil that will take this place seriously. Someone who'll take us seriously. Someone like Bub, over there."* Sir Derek said all this whilst moving his Jack of Spades to a free space. Maybe a rapier sharp sword would have been a better part of the plan? Just saying, like.

*"Oh, someone **like** Bub? It must be me that they want then."* Devil Keith smiled and put out his hand so they could kiss his ring.

*"Devil Keith, not exactly what they mean. Give it a minute."* Harry hushed him and waited.

*"I'm ignoring that oaf completely. Seriously... you said seriously thrice in one paragraph? That sounds sooo desperate. Are you desperate, my traitorous Knights? A jolly, little mutiny just for me? Little, old me, Dear Hearts? So, what are your terms? Haw, haw, haw. We'll wait, won't we brother? Melvin, aren't you just the tiniest bit intrigued? A chair. Now."* King Adrian clicked his fingers, then arranged his flamboyant cloak across the most comfortable

chair in the prison cell. Harry grimaced and wondered why the King and his brother couldn't have a fixation on underwear. Actual just wearing some would be good. Really good. Especially when considering her current red and wrinkly view.

*"Everyone comfortable, yes? You may now begin, Dear Hearts. Haw, haw, haw."* The King crossed his spindly legs and the view just didn't seem to get any better.

# CHAPTER THIRTY-TWO

T he Knights took turns explaining why they had lost all confidence in the current regime and why they had kidnapped Bub...

"So, Sir Ian, you no longer feel up to the challenge of looking after the royal Peacock? Such a pity, Dear Hearts. You look quite dashing with him under your arm. Well, if you must. Feel free to go back to your bagpipe playing. Dishonouring your King, for a quick blow now and then? Pitiful, haw, haw, haw. What says you brother?" The King shook his head and sighed in dramatic disappointment. His talentless brother copied him.

"Quite, quite pitiful. Laughable really, but so little that one really should agree. Hee, hee, hee." Melvin laughed at a squirming Sir Ian.

"My faithful and loyal brother agrees, Dear Hearts. You may start your little band thingy. Oh, silly me. You won't have a band as no one else plays that bizarre, banshee-like instrument. Haw, haw, haw.

Now, onto smoky Sir James. You want the feeling back in your fingertips? Do you? Even your little, tiny pinkies. Well one does need electricity, but I'll ask the masses and see if they can live without it. I fear you may be very unpopular, but if you wish to stop being the royal engineer then please feel free to abandon the common folks to their fate. Shameful really. Not what I'd expect from a Knight. Haw, haw, haw." The King rolled his eyes and gave a sad little tut.

"No, no. You're twisting my words. I'm not objecting to people *having electricity, I just don't want to get burnt any longer. It's the huge spotlights. They're unsafe."* Sir James spluttered.

*"A bad workman and all that...Plus one must sacrifice for one's art. That brings me onto Sir Ougie and Sir Derek. I had no idea you took dressing in women's clothing so seriously. Of course, I'll cancel all of the planned productions and bring back non-stop pantomimes. If you want to be type cast, then who am I to stop you, Dear Hearts?"* The King gazed at them in pity.

*"That's not..."* Sir Derek started to say.

*"Now, now. You had your say so I'm now having mine, Dear Hearts. Haw, haw, haw."* The King barked at the reluctant thespians.

*"Wow, he's manipulative,"* Harry whispered to Dippit. He's made their complaints sound so trivial, but I don't think they are, are they?

*"Sir Mark and Sir Andrew now to your complaints. I was only thinking of your health when I ordered the table cleared of all temptations, Dear Hearts. I thought I was looking after my poor subjects who lacked the willpower to stop gorging themselves. Also, correct me if I'm wrong, but Sir Andrew aren't you vegan?"* The King actually appeared concerned about their health.

*"I was vegan, but now I have to eat whatever I can get my hands on. You're making us all sound so greedy. But we just need to eat. We're here as part of the set dressing for this Hell, and not here to be punished. Our job description does not include starvation. You forget. We aren't residents here."* Sir Andrew assertively stated.

*"Ah, you are correct, Dear Hearts. Your job description does include bed and board. You do receive both, now, don't you? It doesn't specify how much food, so long as you get it. Haw, haw, haw.*

*Now to Sir Daniel, Dear Hearts. You did steal from the royal larder, so must be punished. I must make sure that there's no favouritism towards my Knights or there would be an uprising. So many people harmed because of your inability to follow simple rules. Cheese? Is it worth hurting others? Pitiful, really."* The deceitful

King pretended to have a petted lip.

*"You deliberately wrecked my guitar. You enjoyed cutting the strings on my guitar because you didn't want me to enter the talent contest and threaten your talentless brother's success. And it was only a sliver of cheese. I was starving!"* Sir Daniel cried in outrage.

*"Yet you had the energy to cook up this little plan. Now, didn't you?"* The King hissed. There was a district lack of *"haws"*.

*"What about the Human Resources department? We tried taking our complaints to them, and they were sent back."* Spluttered an outraged Sir Ougie.

*"But are you really human? You said it yourselves, Dear Hearts. You're 'set dressing', not residents. Not human at all. Demons to the core. Haw, haw, haw."* The *"haws"* were back as the King knew he saw defeated Knights before him.

The Knights began turning on each other with exclamations of, *"you said it would work. I thought this was a done deal."*

*"Ouch, something bit me. Ouch, there it is again. Ouch, ouch. Stop it. It nips."* Devil Keith was leaping around and frantically shaking out his clothing.

*"Devil Keith, what are you on about now? Are you alright there."* Harry was pulled back from the squabbling Knights.

*"Harry, something just bit me."* Devil Keith checked his elbow for teeth marks.

*"No it di.... Ouch. What is that?"* Harry looked around and realised that they were all flinching and trying to brush down their arms and legs.

King Adrian, Brian, and Melvin the Magician had used the Knight's arguing as a distraction to sneak out of the cell. Melvin was maniacally laughing as he scooped items out of his top-hat and shoved them through the grate in the door.

*"See Harry, I told you he made invisible doves appear."* Devil Keith nodded over at the magician, then flinched as he was brutally nipped on the nose.

*"You didn't tell me they had false teeth with oversized incisors."* Harry gasped and slapped a couple of invisible doves off Devil Keith's back.

Devil Keith grimaced, before taking a denture wearing, invisible dove to the face. His eyebrows were gone again. Where's furry Chick when you need him?

Sir Ian pushed a pile of books towards the wall. *"Help me make a cage for the doves. They're chomping right through my armour."*

*"The fudgers are trying to get in the biscuit tin. Stop them. I need those shortbread rounds,"* Harry squealed and dived at the table.

The team grabbed books and made a very rough, square shaped dwelling against the wall. They carefully shoved the denture wearing doves into the cage. To ensure air holes, they topped the cage off with the empty wicker basket; the basket which had previously housed the rats. After all, no animals were hurt whilst writing this book. Well except for the rats but they were dead, and chocolate coated before entering the cell. Supposedly.

*"Cooeeee, just to be clear. All deals are off. I only made them under coercion. Enjoy your new living quarters, Dear Hearts. Brian, tell the cook that if one single morsel of food enters this cell, she and her daughter will go to the gargoyles live show. Haw, haw, haw."* The King giggled and linked arms with his brother.

# CHAPTER THIRTY-THREE

I n a cramped but stylish prison cell…

*"So, to borrow that old, fudgers phrase. 'Correct me if I'm wrong,' but all of this, including abducting Bub, was to get new Hell management? Am I correct?"* Harry slumped onto the dove book cage then jumped back up. They're nippy wee sods.

*"Yes, it used to be a right smashing little Hell. It was on its way to a three horns rating when those two plonkers discovered reality TV and talent shows. Since then, all the jousting has been stopped, the melee was too expensive to run and even the Punch and Judy shows were cancelled."* Sir Mark was hunting in the biscuit tin for more jammy dodgers, as he explained their problems.

*"Never, the Punch and Judy shows?"* Harry sarcastically questioned. She looked up from chewing on her one, stale garibaldi biscuit.

*"Ok, laugh at us, but we're at risk of losing one of our horns and we don't want to be one horn losers. No offence."* Sir Derek had devised most of the plan and was heartily sick that it had gone array.

*"Eh, offence very much taken."* Huffed Bub.

*"So, what was the plan?"* Dippit could feel the tensions rising and thought she'd attempt to cool the room. She had watched the movie Roadhouse and fancied herself as a bit of a bouncer. Or as the delectable Patrick Swayze had said, *"a cooler."* Mmm Patrick Swayze, yummy.

The plan…

The plan was to make Bub feel so comfortable and needed, that he wouldn't want to go back to Hell number one. They figured that as Karen ran that Hell and was very loyal to her domain, Bub had no purpose there. No reason to return. So they were schmoozing him into submission with a comfortable cell and a purring cat. Well, the cat wasn't exactly purring but he hadn't shredded Bub, so that was a start.

*"Whoa there. I am the eldest brother and I run my Hell number one with accuracy and efficiency."* Devil Keith had finally put down the balloon and was now, sort of, paying attention.

*"We heard a rumour. Didn't Eva Braun take over, and you didn't notice? Not even with the German accent?"* enquired Sir Ougie.

*"The accent was very faint, and no one noticed it. I'm not convinced that it was even there."* Devil Keith was squirming and hoping that Bub would take over this conversation.

*"We heard that she gave Schwarzenegger a run for his money; 'I'll be back.' So, is that a yes to the accent?"* Sir Ougie was barely stopping his laughter.

*"Well technically, yes. But I was busy trying to secure a queen to rule as my consort. My baby momma."* Devil Keith hotly protested.

*"For over ten years? She had been swapped over for over ten years? You do know that?"* scoffed Sir Ian.

*"No. It's too complicated for 'set dressing' to understand,"* Devil Keith began raiding the biscuit tin and lifting it out of Harry's reach.

*"We have time, don't we boys? And what's with the balloon?"* laughed Sir Ian.

*"It's a snake, duh. Stop laughing. In my Hell we respect each other, and even though I'm clearly in charge, I delegate. Fairly."* Devil Keith huffed.

*"So, Karen runs your Hell and you all sort of help? Is that*

*correct?"* enquired Sir Derek.

*"No, I'm the boss,"* spluttered Devil Keith.

*"Are you sure?"* Sir Derek questioned.

*"Yes!"* Devil Keith shouted.

*"Who has the keys?"* Sir Daniel politely enquired.

*"Karen has the keys."* Devil Keith muttered.

*"Who has the keys when Karen goes on annual leave?"* Sir Daniel asked, whilst writing notes in the margin of his songbook.

*"She takes them with her,"* mumbled Devil Keith.

*"What was that?"* Sir Derek cocked his ear.

*"I said, she takes them with her!"* Devil Keith shouted out.

*"So, being really generous. And I mean really, really generous. You have a democracy in your Hell. You have a figurehead, or three, but you all help out. All have a say in how it's run? Is that right? Well, we want one of those,"* and with that Sir Derek had the last word on the subject, and went back to his engrossing card game.

*"So how do we get out of here? Anyone happen to have included having a set of keys in the plan? Oh, I can see by the look on your faces that is a firm no."* Harry looked around the cell and blew out a breath.

*"Harry, sarcasm isn't helping."* Bub responded with a sigh.

*"Oh, Bub and what is helping? You filling your belly, and living in luxury? You enjoying yourself and being gifted a cat? A cat? You and Sir Mark bonding over sandwiches and laughter? Tell me, what have you done to help while we've been nearly drowned? Starved and had to fight our way here to save you."* Harry accused the relatively innocent man and the kidnappers.

*"We kept him locked up. He couldn't escape. We were the ones that gave him no choice."* Snarled Sir James.

*"Come on, even a child could get out of here."* Harry scoffed.

*"Show us then."* Sir Derek indicted that Harry should lead the way.

# CHAPTER THIRTY-FOUR

The locked prison cell…

An hour later and they were no further forward. Stan and Sir James had checked every inch of the cell and they couldn't find anything to fashion into a key.

Dippit pulled Stan aside and they began whispering and nodding.

*"Harry, can you whistle?"* Dippit excitedly enquired.

*"Whistle? Whistle? Oh yeah, I can whistle,"* Harry began whistling and smiling, then whistled again.

A few minutes later they heard the scuttle of little feet and in bustled three utility belts. Harry was on the floor in an instant, greeting them as if they were her long-lost pets. *"Oh, you clever little things. Oh, you managed to get right through the mean old castle. Aren't you clever? Look how clever they are. Look at their little red rubber boots. They're just to die for."*

The utility belts were jumping at Harry and looking to be clapped and petted. Harry was tickling them behind their stud fasteners. *"Oh, you like that, don't you? Yes, you do. My little poppets."*

*"Wow, that's some broody sister I have,"* thought Dippit. Bub was entranced by Harry's childlike glee and thought she'd be a great baby momma.

They spread out the contents of the utility belts and began planning.

Twenty minutes later...

*"So, we knock the guard out with Sloth's wax?"* Dippit asserted.

*"Dippit, it doesn't matter how many times you say it, we've tried it twice already and all we have are three guards who've fallen asleep just out of our reach."* Harry stated.

*"Three guards?"* Dippit checked.

*"Yep, the last guard fell over the other two and smashed his head in. One last go then, wish me luck. No, no better yet. Stan, can you do the honours?"* Bub handed over their last packet of Sloth wax.

Stan called the fourth and last guard over. The guard wasn't the sharpest tool in the toolbox and didn't seem to notice his slumbering colleagues. A quick dab of the powerful wax and he was snoring too. Stan dragged him over and snatched the keys. Stan looked at the jumbled key ring and selected one key; put it in the lock, turned it and the door opened. Why is he so lucky? Most folks would fumble about and try each key at least three or four times. Swear then start the process all over again. Then they'd kick the door and break a toe or two, then maybe find the key when they came back from a visit to A & E.

They were out and hurrying up the dark passageways. They had agreed to sacrifice two packets each of the Fornication and Greed powder in the Banqueting Hall. That left one of each for the rest of their plan. They hoped that four packets were enough to distract the occupants of the Banqueting Hall without having them going *"all out Devil Keith"* on them. Devil Keith thought that meant their dress sense would improve exponentially and no one bothered to correct him.

The teams reached the door to the Banqueting Hall. They covered their nose and mouth as best they could. Stan used the fire bellows, from Bub's mantel, to spread the potent powders throughout the room. The Fornication and Greed powders worked a treat as the Hell number three demons and residents flirted outrageously and pinched items to line their pockets. They never noticed the prisoners successful escape. Although, the Hell number one team and the Knights were now dragging golden candlesticks and several of the serving wenches with them.

# CHAPTER THIRTY-FIVE

F resh air and released wenches…

The teams braced the doors closed, as they went through the castle, until they reached the bailey. How do they get across that open courtyard without being seen? Thought Bub. He was surprisingly breathless. Maybe the fried breakfast, fried lunch and roasted dinner were a mistake. However, the sumptuous afternoon cream tea was a must. Best not complain though, he had clocked Harry looking hungrily at the rat basket and she did one of those stretches that meant she might have had a go at wrestling with the malicious cat.

Harry poked Devil Keith in the eye and shoved him violently towards the stables. Devil Keith quickly ran back out. *"No, I'm not going in there. There's giant, bloody crocodiles in there."*

*"Yes, I know. Sir Daniel told me. King Adrian rides them instead of you know whats."* Harry confirmed.

*"Whats?"* Devil Keith looked confused.

*"You know. 'Whats'. Those things."* Harry mimed riding a horse.

*"No, idea what you're on about woman. Have you got jumping beans in your pants, again? I'm not fishing them out again. They were all sweaty and swampy the last time."* Devil Keith scowled and twisted his lips in disgust.

*"Go. You're wasting your tears. Hypnotise the overgrown handbags and get them to stampede. Stampede away from us. Away from us, mind you."* Harry began pushing him again.

*"We have test tubes full of tears in those toolbelts. Bub can do*

*it. Can't you bro."* Devil Keith patted Bub's shoulder.

*"Bub's gotten slow and fat."* Harry snapped.

*"No, I bloody haven't. Give me the tubes."* Bub ran into the stables and promptly ran back out again. *"I'm gonna need a bigger tube."*

Bub was loaded up with all the test tubes of Faery tears. It was super risky, and he didn't really want to do it, but Harry's rude comment needed an answer. A brave answer. A stupid answer, but brave too. They so needed to talk and clear the air. Bub did feel slightly guilty that he'd just sat in the prison cell and enjoyed the pampering, but he also felt that Harry needed to calm down.

Armed with Stan's punching/singing bowl and a swing of urine infused tea, he entered the crowded stables. He stopped and poured the tears into his eyes. Bub blinked then looked at the largest crocodile. *"Look into my eyes. You are under my control. You will run away from me and the people around me. Run away. Not, I repeat, not towards us. Also, don't eat us. Equally important. The no eating part."*

*"Alright matey. While you're here can you help our Petunia to stop smoking? She's hacking away all night."* The crocodile politely requested.

Bub quickly glanced at the female crocodile, *"Stop smoking, Petunia. It'll make your skin wrinkly and your breath bad. Erm, well worse than it is. Right, that should do it."*

Bub walked out of the stables feeling pretty good about himself and his act of bravery.

*"So, smoking makes you wrinkly?"* Harry tried to keep a straight face but began laughing.

*"Harry, I think it does."* Devil Keith defended his brother.

*"Devil Keith, no one asked you,"* huffed Bub. His display of courage was reduced to a giggly story that those silly cookie-buns would never let him live down.

*"Oh, why can't anything be simple? Why can't we just use the Drill to get outta here?"* Dippit moaned. Her push-up bra was

pinching her something awful.

*"No, sorry Dippit the Drill is on the fritz, so we need to go to the same spot where we used it before. The wall between the dimensions should be thinner there. It's more likely to work and get us back to Hell number one or even Hell number two. Anywhere but here. Plus, Bub needs to do a bit of running to lose a wee bitty of his double chin. Lastly, the authors need extra pages so they won't just let us get outta here too quickly."* Harry, the ever sarcastic, growled.

They had reached the main castle gate and were faced with the trifle moat. The adapted ear wax had worn off and the polar bears were tearing the suspension bridge apart whilst yodelling. There were chunks of wool missing. No darning needle could fix this.

*"Harry, the polar bears are big."* Bub nodded at a bear who was chewing on a ball of wool then making a Cat's Cradle.

*"Yes, I can see that, Bub. I'm not blind."* Harry tutted.

*"No, I mean they're big. Big males. Males! Look woman!"* Bub shouted. He was getting fed up with Harry's sarcasm and huffing.

Harry started ripping the bottom off her dress and pushing the wadded-up fabric at the Knights and the male team members. *"Cover your ears. Cover your ears. Block them with this."* And then to the amazement of Stan and the Knights, Harry began swearing. And swearing and swearing some more. Harry thought that Brownie Kat would be equally horrified, amazed, and chuffed at the display.

The polar bears began fanning themselves and swooning. One bear managed to drag a fainting couch onto his ice shelve and then dramatically draped himself over it. Ah, the ability to create items at will was available here too, Harry thought.

*"Run, run. Harry keep swearing."* Bub screamed.

The team jumped and dived over the decaying woollen bridge. Tripping, falling, and twisting ankles. They made it to the other side. They clattered onto the grass, gasping for breath, and feeling more than a tiny bit smug.

Over their heavy breathing they heard. *"Oh, my lovely bears. You've broken my lovely bears. Don't you worry my cuddly Dear Hearts. We'll let you play with them. Well bits of them. What's left after I've gotten up close and personal with them. Haw, haw, haw."* The King happily announced.

# CHAPTER THIRTY-SIX

T he stand-off…

A preening King Adrian was in his full golden armour and mounted on a huge grinning crocodile. His peep toe boots had been replaced by two giant slippers. You know, the slippers that Billy Connolly refers to. Each individual slipper is big enough to take two feet or in King Adrian's case one foot plus curls of horny, yellow toenails.

The humungous crocodile looked at Bub and mouthed, *"sorry, call me."* King Adrian was surrounded by heavily armed castle guards who were baying for blood and guts. The guards were pulling levers and old leotard attired men were popping out of the moat. As each riddle was correctly answered a wooden bridge slowly formed over the moat.

The teams had seconds before they were overwhelmed by a raging hoard of tinned up soldiers.

*"What do we do?"* Dippit mouthed to Harry.

*"Ah, don't think about trying that parlour trick again, Dear Hearts. The wind will dissipate the powders and tears before they reach us. Your unladylike voice won't reach us either. You fishwife. You're on your own this time. Haw, haw, haw. However, it has been most entertaining to watch you squirm. Please don't surrender, Dear Hearts. Run and we will catch you. Tallyho... to the hunt. Haw, haw, haw. Release the Peacocks of Hell."* The King giggled and flicked his hair out of his eyes. All the better to witness the carnage and all those gooey bits.

The guards groaned, but they did their duty. The snarling, spitting Peacocks were unceremoniously chucked over the moat.

The air was filled with the squawking brightly coloured birds. It was a magnificent, if deadly sight. The teams looked around in panic and despair. They needed shelter and some weapons. It also might have helped if Devil Keith had brought his utility belt rather than the rucksack full of fascinators and sparkly junk. The fascinators!

"*Stan, can you do something with the feathers on those fascinators?*" Dippit squealed and pointed at Devil Keith's bulging bag.

"*Good idea. Dippit, I could try. I say, I could try. Sir Ian, I could use you help. I say, your help.*" Stan grabbed Devil Keith's extremely heavy rucksack and tipped out the feathers and ribbon covered hats. He and Sir Ian were frantically winding feathers together, whilst the other two teams were wrestling with the vicious, biting birds.

The second fight of the day...

Devil Keith was trying to hypnotise the Peacocks with his tears, but the birds kept tipping their tails over their eyes and swiping at him with their scorpion stingers. His tears were drying up fast and he longed for some optrex eye lubrication. He picked up his rucksack and rummaged inside. He tried to distract the Peacocks with the golden tassels on his scarves. Two Peacocks grabbed a tassel each and began corralling Devil Keith towards the moat and the ravenous killer rubber ducks.

Sir Daniel had created a funnel with the pages of his song book. He had the funnel shoved in a Peacock's mouth and was risking his fingers trying to stuff stolen cheese down the throat of the squawking bird. The soft and waxy brie was working really well, but the more robust cheddar was proving too hard to mould. A frantic Sir Daniel was getting desperate as he tried to soften the hard cheese with a dab of apple and fig chutney.

Sir Mark assumed a tennis player stance and was playing

a fantastic backhand; a technique that Andy Murray (fabulous player) would be so proud off. He was batting the Peacocks back over the moat, but he was fast running out of energy and the birds just kept a coming. His frying pan was running out of resilience, and its non-stick coating was badly scratched. He feared that it had fried its last sausage sandwich.

Sir Ougie was using his brassier slingshot to fire balls of watermelon seeds at the screeching Peacocks. Unfortunately, the elastic was old and much used. The seeds went shorter and shorter distances until the elastic sagged and the brassier was no more. He then began swinging the remains of the old grey bra around his head and slapping the vicious birds to the ground. It was exhausting, but oh so satisfying.

Harry and Dippit looked around for weapons. Bub shouted, *"your bra, use your bra."* Harry and Dippit had to wait until the Peacocks were within striking distance then they began stabbing the Peacocks with their bra wire and ripping off the scorpion stingers. A dangerous dance indeed.

Sir Andrew had a Peacock pinned down and was running his pastry crimper over its neck. The pattern was really quite lovely but ultimately ineffectual. He then started lobbing the Peacocks about the head with the crimper. Less lovely, but much more useful.

Sir James was having the most success. He was using his duct tape to trap the tails and stop the stinging, but he was fast running out of tape and luck. Sir Derek's i-pad was long gone. One hit and it had crumpled. Maybe a great big bloody sword would have been a better part of the plan? Just saying, like, again.

Bub was swinging at the wicked birds with Stan's bowl and sending the birds flying back over the moat. A novel experience for the normally flightless Peacocks. He looked down and found some of the excited birds forming an orderly queue for their return flight. What the....

# CHAPTER THIRTY-SEVEN

The battle was lost until...

Sir Ian and Stan stood up, and the Peacocks suddenly stopped fighting. There, on the banks of the moat, was a perfect replica of a Peahen. It was completed with the help of Devil Keith's fascinator feathers, some ribbons and Dippit's mascara wand.

The nearest Peacock bowed to the Peahen and started squawking and giggling (?). Can a Peacock giggle?

*"Bub, what's going on?"* Harry was stunned by the change in the malicious bird.

*"Oh, he's pledging his troth. It's kinda sweet."* Bub laughed. He was delighted that he still had enough pee infused tea to enjoy the bizarre but adorable spectacle.

At that, the other Peacocks gathered around the Peahen. They too began squawking. Three Peacocks at the back of the pack pulled out notepaper and ripped off a tail feather in order to make a quill. They then began composing love letters and sonnets. Using their blood as ink.

*"What are they saying? I'm too far away to hear them clearly."* Harry called over.

*"'Never have I seen such a fine bird as you*
*You may be made of fascinator feathers and glue*
*But to me you are a Queen, the keeper of my heart*
*And cos you're not real I don't worry if you'll fart.' Needs some*

work Harry, but my, that was quickly pulled together." Bub was well impressed by the whole "lovers not fighters" malarkey going on.

The Peacocks began squabbling amongst themselves over the hastily constructed Peahen. King Adrian was screaming threats about using them in millinery projects, but the Peacocks were suffused with love and desire, so they felt it was an acceptable risk. They then began presenting the Peahen with elaborate gifts. "Where did they get all the hair tongs and the pitch perfect glockenspiels from?" shouted Harry.

"Dear Hearts, this just isn't cricket. What, what? Stand still and then be hunted. Tell them brother. I want a chase." King Adrian was no longer haw, hawing as he watched his elite force of Peacocks being brought to their knees by a mere female.

The crocodiles were smelling the blood and the adrenaline of battle; they wanted in on the action. The bridges weren't fully extended but the crocodile began crossing the moat. Their leathery tails smacking the polar bears in the face and sending them into the killer rubber ducks and jelly. The impatient crocodiles dived into the moat. Their excited riders were quickly trapped in the strawberry jelly and their drowning, gurgling screams filled the night air. As an aside: it was still bright daylight in Hell number three despite the late hour.

There was blood, feathers, and fur everywhere. The teams decided to make a run for it. It was their only chance. Bub swiped Devil Keith's rucksack from the ground then staggered under its weight. "What has he nicked this time?" Bub murmured. A cat's paw poked out and slapped Bub across the face; semi-blinding him. He staggered and knocked Dippit into the moat. Stan immediately dived in after Dippit and began punching lumps out of anyone and anything that came near his Dippit.

Exhausted, Stan and Dippit crawled out of the moat; covered in blood and gizzards.

"Devil Keith, you brought the cat?" Dippit gasped and

coughed up a hundreds and thousands colourful dagger.

"*Yes. He's mine now. Finders keepers. I have my very own kitty now.*" Devil Keith picked up the rucksack and realised that maybe bringing a rotund, rat filled cat on an escape mission wasn't his best idea. Devil Keith considered his best idea to be his multi-coloured play suits. This, on balance, may have been a mistake but he was committed so he shrugged his shoulders and RAN.

"*Run. Run!*" Bub belted out.

The teams scattered into the gloomy, dank forest. Their eyes were struggling to adjust to the change from bright sunshine to dismal darkness. They were falling over tree roots, banging into branches, and sliding into puddles. Still, they ran. Wiping a drizzle of rain from their eyes they jumped streams and careered into steep embankments.

They were covered in mud, leaches, and dead leaves. Still, they ran. Panting heavily and gasping they tried to duck around lethal looking spiked bushes and avoid the patches of razor-sharp nettles.

There was a blood curdling scream, "*Go, go, leave me. Run. Run.*" Sir Ian had fallen into the bone crunching, rusty teeth of a bear trap. Stan and Dippit surveyed the trap. Without specialist tools there was no way they could open the jaws to release his shredded leg. All of the Knights huddled around him, and the rest of the Hell number one team joined them.

"*We're not leaving you. You're not just our colleague, you're our friend. I'm staying.*" This sentiment was echoed by all the Knights. They were adamant. They proudly decided to stay and protect Sir Ian.

"*Go, please go. You are dishonouring me. Please, the Hell team need your help. You must go with them. Protect them.*" Sir Ian pleaded.

After much debate, or as much debate as they could afford, considering there were mammoth crocodiles and a few psychopaths after them; they decided to send Sir Mark and Sir Andrew to protect the Hell number one team, whilst the rest of the Knights provided cover and tried to get Sir Ian out of the jaws of the trap.

There was no time for lengthy goodbyes. The team started running towards the boundary between Hell number three and Hell number two.

# CHAPTER THIRTY-EIGHT

The boundary between dimensions...

*"The Drill. The Drill. Get the Drill."* Harry demanded.

The team had found a small glowing patch and realised that they had reached the boundary line.

Devil Keith pulled the beaten Drill from his rucksack and put it against the light filled patch. A stressed and exhausted Dippit kicked him in the groin, *"no way, just no way. We can't risk it. Stan over to you."*

*"Good call,"* groaned Devil Keith, from the muddy ground.

Stan put the Drill against the tree and carefully selected Hell number one. A portal slowly began to appear as they all heard, *"oh Dear Hearts, going so soon? You'll miss all the fun. Won't they? Haw, haw, haw. Brian, fetch."*

The Hell team and the two Knights were scrambling through the portal when Brian caught hold of Harry's hair and began dragging her back into Hell number three. There were clumps of hair, pulled from the roots, entangled in the spiteful bird's beak. Devil Keith held onto her hand, *"No! No way. No. Bub help me. That feathery beast has our Harry."*

They both pulled and pulled until a huge, grey furry paw reached out of Devil Keith's rucksack and belted Brian in the face. Brian shrilly squawked and fell backwards. Harry was frantically scooped through into Hell number one.

They were home.

# CHAPTER THIRTY-NINE

Hell number one and a warm welcome...

*"About fudging time."* Karen said before jumping over the jumble of bodies and grabbing Harry in a tight, bear hug. *"We were so worried. We've nearly walked a hole in your floor. Tell me all about it. Oh, look at you. You look like you've be shoved into a food processor and blasted. You've got something in your hair. So, a bath or food first? A shower then food? Possibly some sleep? I'm hoping you say no to sleep and a bath, I want to know what happened."*

Harry, Bub, Devil Keith, Dippit and Stan had bowls of steaming broth sat on their knees. They began talking all at once. It was a complex rumble of Peacocks, curly toenails and fainting polar bears. No matter how hard she tried: Karen just couldn't follow the story. So she produced a talking stick, well a blue felt tip pen, and instructed them that they could all have a turn at telling the sordid tale.

Obviously when the stick was given to Devil Keith, Karen snatched it from his hand and rapped him over the knuckles. *"No, not you. I can't take another tale from your point of view. No, you were not the hero. Yes, you probably ate something you shouldn't have. No, the heroine did not pledge undying love and yes, you probably caused most of the pain and distress. Does that cover it?"*

*"Actually, Devil Keith saved me."* Harry stated to the amazed group.

"*What? Dr Riel, can you check Harry over for a head injury?*" Dr Riel was rising from his chair.

"*No Karen, really. Devil Keith saved me.*" Harry confirmed.

"*Really? Like, really, really?*" this was the second time that Devil Keith had been heroic. Karen still couldn't get over him finding her in the filing cabinet. This was some strange mojo going on in Hell number one. Karen was concerned that another Deadly Sin had been released into the air conditioning. Was there a Deadly Sin of Totally Unexplainable Events?

The team explained what had happened and introduced Karen and Dr Riel to Sir Mark and Sir Andrew.

"*So, what happens next?*" enquired Dr Riel whilst surreptitiously checking Harry's pupils and searching for concealed bruises.

"*We've hidden the inter-Dimensional Lance, so King Adrian can't get into this Hell. Oh, yeah, meant to say... that's what we used to kidnap Bub. Our bad. You'll be safe here, but Sir Mark and I are going back to save our friends. I know that this is really cheeky, considering what we did, but can we borrow your Drill? We'll bring it back as soon as possible.*" Sir Andrew was intrigued by Hell number one. He could barely believe that everyone had been given the opportunity to speak. They were encouraged to voice an opinion and, most importantly, they were taken seriously. Well Devil Keith was the exception to the rule, but even so Sir Andrew could hardly believe this warm welcome.

"*Stan and Dippit, can you fix the Drill?*" Karen said whilst looking at the cracked casing.

"*No, Karen, I say no. It's broken. Really broken. Brian smashed it. I say Brian smashed it. In the last attack. I say, the last attack,*" Stan picked up the mangled Drill and passed the pieces over to Dippit. She shook her head as she tried to push them back together.

Sir Mark and Sir Andrew were devastated by this news. "*Is there no hope? None whatsoever? Stan, is this really beyond even your skills?"*

*"I'll speak with The Oracles. Maybe they could help. Harry don't look at me like that. I can visit The Oracles without something terrible happening. I am an adult. And believe it or not I can have a sensible thought in my head."* Bub made to leave, and Devil Keith followed him out. Harry let him go. Devil Keith had offered the Knights' space in his room as Bub's room still needed a wee bit of a stretch and a tidy.

During the catch up, the Knights had confirmed that someone had been spreading tales about the recent exploits of Hell number one. The gossip included how disorganised the management were and how every Tom, Dick and Harry seemed to have a say in the running of the place. On a positive note, the rumours also implied that Hell number one had some potential, hidden under all that messy management. Unfortunately, the Knights had never seen the person responsible for the stories but felt that if they could get back to their Hell they could find out more information. Then pass their findings over to Hell number one to action.

Karen and Dr Riel left to get some much-needed rest. They still hadn't found the spy, but they weren't giving up. Not yet. There were still some residents to interview and discount from their enquiries. However, they had repaired the cockroach walkway and thrown away the rotting frittata, so they could get out of Hell if there was a siege situation.

# CHAPTER FORTY

An hour later...

"*You two need to talk. This won't get any better until you talk. You're both still angry and miserable about the entire stupid situation. It'll fester and it will never heal properly.*" Dippit sat on the floor with her arm around Harry, whilst attempting to pick the Peacock feathers and dried in mash from Harry's mangled hair.

"*He had a cat. A cat!*" Harry exclaimed.

"*Why are you so fixated on that cat?*" Dippit looked at Periwinkle. He was smugly sitting right in the middle of the sofa, and no one was brave enough to move him to get a seat.

"*I was worried sick about him, and he transferred his affections to a cat. And he only missed me when he saw splattered lungs dripping down the walls.*" Harry sniffled.

"*That is the single most draft, crazy, and plain stupid thing that I have ever heard you or anyone else say. Ever. It's so bad that I'm gonna tell Will and Fachance. Actually, I won't tell them. You can tell them. They'll laugh their heads off, then hit you and Bub's heads off each other. Transferred his affections to a cat? Only missed you due to haggis? That man is besotted with you. He waited years for you.* **And** *he never put any pressure on you no matter how many scrapes you and Devil Keith got into. Do you know how many times he raced out of here to save your life? To rescue Devil Keith? To hide the evidence? To hide the bodies?*" Dippit shook her head at her naive sister.

"*The bodies? Plural?*" Harry stammered and started to count on her fingers. Oopsie.

*"Don't interrupt me when I'm getting mad. To be honest, I'm beginning to wonder why he bothered. He was so upset when you said that Devil Keith saved you. You should have seen his face. Bub did that too. Did you see the state of his hands? The claw marks? You're talking a load of fudging nonsense. You're scared and a you're a fudging coward. That's what you are. I'm embarrassed to be your sister. And you're making me swear, using those utterly ridiculous words instead of..."* Dippit exploded at Harry.

*"I am not a coward. I have never been a coward and I'm not an embarrassment. This is nothing to do with you. You're my sister; you should be taking my side. Supporting me. I'm going to see Devil Keith. He'll make more sense than you do."* Harry stormed off.

*"Ha, ha, ha. Good luck. Maybe Karen was right. You do have a head injury and Dr Riel needs to examine you for lumps and bumps. Fudging cat. Bloody haggis. Bloody stupid, that's what it is."* Dippit shouted after her retreating back.

Harry stomped to the door and turned to say something witty and amazing and original and cutting. Really just so that she could get in the last word. She realised that she didn't even have a door to slam, so her chance at a put-down was a bit limp.

*"Right Dippit. You beautiful, succulent wood nymph. Over here now. We've waited long enough, ma peachy girl."* Harry was shocked and stunned. Stan had said a full sentence, no, make that four sentences with no repeats. Harry was momentarily stunned by his handsome face and ripped body. Bow chicka...

*"Oh, ride em cowboy. Grrrr."* Dippit ran; full tilt at Stan's open arms. He lifted Dippit, slung her over his left shoulder and was purposefully striding towards the bed. Harry's bed.

*"Toodles, Harry. Just leave some food outside the door and get yourself some perspective. Ya silly cookie-bun,"* grinned an upside down Dippit. She was wiggling her fingertips and her eyebrows, then repeatedly pointing at Stan's bottom and kissing her fingertips.

Stan playfully slapped Dippit on her arse. *"Leave enough food for a couple of days, will ya Harry? Will ya Harry. We're gonna be busy. So busy."*

# CHAPTER FORTY-ONE

A bove. Way above…

God had walked around the tables four times now and was no nearer to finding a solution to her problem. She picked up objects, turned them over in her hands then sighed as she placed them back on the table. As she looked down, she realised that she had distractedly plucked, removed the giblets and de-boned four plump pigeons.

*"Gab I just can't find my spark. I'm not up to the challenge. Not this year. I give up."* God flung her hands in the air and was about to walk out the cloudy room.

*"God, you are proficient in all things but maybe you are, ever so slightly, burnt out. And in need of some down time. I know that you are still disappointed in Hell number one and their rank stupidity. This is exactly what you require in order to re-charge your batteries and forget about your responsibilities."* Gab was concerned as he had never seen God so low in mood. She was normally the life of the party and so full of brilliant ideas. Afterall, the duck-billed platypus was one of her bestest evolutionary suggestions ever. Her leadership was exemplary, so this current lack of focus and direction was a cause for concern.

*"Gab I've worked on this for nearly a year, and for that old reprobate to add an additional clause at the last minute is just a power play. I've a mind to just not bother, stuff the lot of it I say."* God huffed out.

The challenge was the highly coveted invite to the Faery Court's Annual Music Festival. This spectacular invite was dependent on the results of a rather cutthroat treasure hunt. God had furtively collected items all year. She had them proudly displayed, and carefully labelled, on five family-sized kitchen tables. The recently added clause; was the need to produce one fabulous item from all the *"acquired"* treasures. That item would have to bring a Supreme Being to their knees. God was stumped. She had nine days to create the *"item"*, and inspiration had completely deserted her.

*"Nine days Gab. Nine days! I don't think I can do it. It's impossible."* Lamented God as she nibbled the chocolate off a KitKat then bit into the crispy wafer. She really should have washed her hands between the pigeons and the biscuit. The KitKat was decidedly gamey and more squelchy than it should have been.

*"I would like to make a suggestion, and can you please give it some consideration before you say no? You could take all these provisions to Devil Keith. Give him the necessary mission details and see what he can create. He still owes you for all of your kind assistance and he would benefit from a constructive project. Idle hands and all that, as the saying goes. Plus, he normally makes some strange and wonderous things. I have been reliably informed that his tuxedoes are 'truly bizarre but amazing.' I thought I needed something more formal to wear, therefore I'm on the list for one from his next batch."* Gab handed God a wet wipe.

*"Hmm, well technically I'm not really talking to him and Bub, but I suppose they've learned their lesson by now. Let's go."* God produced a thin smile and rubbed the goop off her hands.

God, Gab, and the kitchen tables unceremoniously landed in Devil Keith's room. Crushing his mannequins and destroying all order that Devil Keith had previously made. Devil Keith hadn't actually tidied up anything yet, but he sure liked to moan about it. Moan a lot.

A minute or so later...

God explained her complicated dilemma. *"So, Devil Keith. Can you help me?"*

*"Nine days to bring a Supreme Being to their knees? I'm not sure. Oh, are those the washers from Stan's Moonshine stills?"* Devil Keith made to grab them, but God slapped his hands away.

*"Yes, I may have gathered those items during my many, many travels."* God clarified, although she was slightly embarrassed by her confession.

*"Oh, you wee tea leaf. Imagine pinching the washers that caused me to turn into a monster. I just knew that I was innocent. The victim of a nefarious plot. A patsy...."* Devil Keith babbled on.

*"Oh, Devil Keith? If you want to start the blame game, then go ahead. Bring it on."* God whispered. Devil Keith was a bit odd, but he wasn't that odd. Or, come to think about it, that courageous. Oh no, not that brave. At all. Ever. A moaner not a fighter; that's our Devil Keithie Boy.

*"Eh no. Let's call it quits and I'll put my thinking cap on. Wherever did I put that fudging felt hat?"* Devil Keith rummaged through a crowded shelf.

*"Good lad,"* and with that, God patted Devil Keith rather heavily on the head and permanently reduced his height by a good two inches.

Harry never knocks...

*"Devil Keith, can I stay here tonight? I know you have the Knights here, so I don't mind squashing into a wee corner. Dippit and Stan have stolen my room for some naughty, and apparently cowboy themed, business. Oh sorry, you have company."* Harry was about to leave when she realised that it was God. God was back!

*"Oh, I'm so, so glad to see you. I've missed you so, so much. I think Bub hates me."* Harry gave God a rather rough hug and started to cry. Big, fat, sore tears.

*"Yes dearie, and I've missed you too. Quite an adventure you've had yourself. Are you doing all right? I felt awful that I couldn't help out, but I had to make those boys realise that I meant*

business. *I'm only here because I'm in a bit of a pickle."* God gave Harry a tissue, then once Harry had used it God added it to her tables. Gab scribbled out a label and tied it onto the soggy mess.

Bub never knocks…

*"Devil Keith, Devil Keith. I'm all packed. I can't face saying goodbye to Harry. Tell her… actually I don't really know what to tell her."* Bub stopped when he realised that a sobbing Harry was in Devil Keith's room.

*"Bub, you're leaving? You weren't going to say goodbye to me?"* Harry hiccupped and rubbed at her red eyes.

*"Harry, I couldn't. I'm clearly making you miserable and I can't do that to you. To us, not any longer. Our latest misadventure showed that only too clearly. I knew one of us would have to go, and I thought I'd make it easier. I will come back, but not for a while. Give us a chance to heal and hopefully get over each other. Although I don't think I'll ever completely get over you…I love you. I have from the moment I first saw you, although I didn't realise until it was too late. I have to admit that I was angry when The Oracles predicated a human bride, but your laughter, honesty and courage won me over. I love you more now than I did then. So I have to leave. I don't think we can go on hurting each other. We're just too different."* Bub's voice broke.

*"Don't go. It will crush me."*

*"Devil Keith, it's not your decision. Sorry bro."* Bub rubbed Devil Keith's heaving shoulders.

*"Don't go."* Harry whispered and held out her hand. *"Don't go. It would break my heart. Stay with me…I love you too. Please give us a chance. Marry me, please."*

Bub stopped. He dropped to his knees and lifted the stolen Moonshine washers from Harry's outstretched hand.

*"If you're sure. Then yes. Yes I will."* He shyly said. There was a stupendous flash of light.

*"Dearies, I've brought a Supreme Being to his knees with one of my finds. **And** I won a ticket to the Faery Court Annual Festival.*

*Oh yes, congratulations by the way."* God punched the air and gaily danced around the tables with her gold trimmed hostess trolley.

# CHAPTER FORTY-TWO

A few days later and an exhausted Dippit finally emerged from Harry's room...

Harry still hadn't left Bub's room. Dippit knew there must be good news as the mound of dirty dishes in front of each room indicated a good time was had by all.

Much later that same day...

"*Oh, you little minx. Walk of shame, is it?*" Dippit was nudging and winking at Harry.

"*No actually. Walk of the recently engaged.*" Harry smugly stated and raised her eyebrows suggestively.

"*Engaged? You're engaged? When? Spill the beans.*" Dippit gushed.

"*Yep,*" and Harry showed her the washer ring. Dippit and Harry began laughing, hugging, and dancing around in a circle.

"*Harry, about fudging time.*" Dippit wiped away a happy tear.

"*Yep,*" Harry coyly stated.

"*Is that all you have to say? 'Yep?' Was it dreamy? Was it romantic? Spill girly. Details, details.*" Dippit jumped around some more and banged off the metal banister.

"*Not got the energy for much else,*" and then they both leapt around some more.

"*Finally Harry, some decent company. The Knights are a morose pair. I thought Sir Mark was a jolly type, but he can't stop talking about the Knights they left behind. All honour and justice. No fun at all. I'm soooo bored. Sir Andrew's worse... all pies, help me and 'don't break my pastry crimper'. Yawn."* Devil Keith was admiring his turquoise three-piece suit and shining his new cufflinks. Harry thought he looked nearly passable. Obviously for someone else, not her. Never her.

*"About that. Stan and I have an idea."* Dippit added and grinned.

*"You had time to have an idea? To talk? Girl you're doing it all wrong."* Harry was laughing and nudging the red faced Dippit.

*"It didn't take long. The talking I mean. We're just so clever and smug that we think we might have worked something out. We're leaving in a few minutes, but we'll be back soon. Hopefully with a solution to the Drill problem."* Twenty minutes later and Dippit and Stan left on the cockroach walking pavement. They were off to visit beautiful Ireland.

Ten minutes after that...

Harry was making breakfast and surveying her room. No she thought, this is my home. My apartment and soon to be Bub's too. because Devil Keith was never gonna give up that extra square footage. No siree.

*"Hi honey, how are you?"* Bub walked over and kissed the back of Harry's neck. She playfully giggled and tingled.

*"Better now that you're here."* Harry was blushing but so, so happy.

*"Wedding? Can we discuss the wedding? We are still engaged, right? I haven't imagined all this?"* Bub tried to smooth down his wild hair.

*"No, we're engaged and yes, we can talk about a wedding."* Harry blushed, again.

*"Well Harry, ma darling, what would you like? Place? Flowers? Harp? Cherubs?"* Bub munched through a slice of toast with a dollop of lime marmalade on the top.

*"You sound just like Dippit. Oh, she's off to Ireland with Stan. They have an idea regarding the Drill. Fingers crossed. It would be good to get the Knights home and I have a selfish reason for wanting*

*the Drill fixed. I would like us to be married in the Brownie Hell. If possible."* Harry blushed again.

*"I'm easy."* Bub nodded and pinched a second slice of buttery toast.

*"Oh honey, you certainly are that,"* and with that naughty pronouncement Harry dragged Bub back to bed.

# CHAPTER FORTY-THREE

A few days later...

An excited Dippit rapped at Harry's door. *"Harry, Harry. Put Bub down and answer the door. Come on. Come on. You don't know where he's been. Scrub that. I think you know exactly where he's been."* Dippit was laughing and bouncing on the spot.

*"Oh no. It's too early to deal with your madness. Go and annoy Devil Keith. He's in a right tid over the mumping Knights."* Harry went to shut the door in Dippit's face.

*"No, no. Look."* Dippit shoved her hand in Harry's face.

*"You're engaged?"* Harry excitedly asked.

*"No, look again."* Dippit waved her hand around until Harry grabbed it.

*"Is that a wedding ring?"* Harry gasped incredulously.

*"Yep, we're married. Stan's folks wouldn't let us stay together. Live in sin. Try before you buy. Make sure the furniture fitted the room. Bump uglies. You know? So Stan said that he wanted to marry me, and was going to propose soon. So, he did... there and then. We couldn't wait. Just couldn't wait a second longer."* Dippit squealed and sniggered.

*"No way. No fudging way. Congratulations. Bring it in for a hug. You're married and you're beginning to repeat yourself. Ha, ha, ha."* Harry cuddled Dippit and they jumped up and down.

*"Funny Harry, so, so funny."* Dippit chortled.

*"I thought so."* Harry smugly said. Then she cackled and hugged Dippit yet again.

*"Talking of repeating things. Do I have a story for you? We went off to Ireland to see Stan's 90-year-old mammy and his 92-year-old dad..."* Dippit started to say.

*"Brought up by his grandparents? Great-grandparents? Nice one."* Harry nodded.

*"Eh, no Harry. His actual 90-year-old mother and 92-year-old father. His youngest brothers are only four years old."* Dippit answered.

*"Ha, ha, ha. Funny. Do you think my head buttons up the back? Huh, 90-year-old mother. Likely story."* Harry softly punched Dippit on the arm.

Cue Stan's back story...

Stan's mammy, Patricia, was driving to work one morning when she spotted a child, dressed all in green, struggling to cross the three lanes of the busy motorway. She couldn't believe that someone could be so neglectful as to leave a small child like that. She quickly decided that as no one else was helping, or possibly able to help, that she would have to do it. She pulled over onto the hard-shoulder of the motorway and proceeded to get her giant lollipop and her high visibility jacket from the boot of her car.

Risking life, limb and many, many curses from fellow drivers she bravely crossed the lanes to reach the distraught child. As Patricia got closer, she realised that he was dressed in what appeared to be a leprechaun fancy dress outfit and he was becoming increasingly upset.

*"Where's yer mammy? Ya poor wee soul?"* Patricia asked the child and put out her hand.

The child looked up from bellow the brim of his fantastic green felt hat. He then removed his corncob pipe from his pursed lips and was about to speak.

*"You're a man! A bloody idiot, and a bloody man. What do you*

*think yer doing? You'll get yourself killed. Is that what you want? Mmm? Well, is it? Look what you've made me do. I'll be late getting to the school. How will the kiddies get across the road? Come on then, ya big galoot."* Patricia scolded the bearded man.

The man was happy to accept Patricia's help, but thought the incessant hand holding and finger pointing was maybe a bit much. Patricia marched back out onto the motorway. The speeding traffic screeched to a stop at the sight of an angry lollipop lady accompanied by a chastised leprechaun.

Once, on the other side of the road, the embarrassed but grateful man explained that he had gotten a wee bitty tipsy the night before and had fallen off his rainbow into the road. He then asked Patricia what he could do for her in exchange for her help.

*"None of that, now. Just doing my job. No more, no less. Off with you then."* Patricia tried to shoo the grateful man away and get back in her car.

*"How about a share of my pot of gold then? Not all of it, mind you. Just a wee portion. I need it for ma old age and ma aching joints. Hip replacement surgery doesn't come cheap these days. Well, now I've thought about it. No, not ma gold. You've been shouting at me and wiggling that finger around."* The leprechaun corrected himself.

*"What are you blethering on about man? I don't want your gold. Ya eijit. I said away with ye. Off ya go. I'm late."* Patricia began shoo-ing him again. She also did a fair bit of tutting and eye-rolling.

*"Well, I'll give you. Let me think......your first born will have the luck of the Irish. How about that? Will that do you?"* the leprechaun nodded encouragingly.

*"My first born? Away with ye, man. Yer pulling my leg. I've just celebrated ma birthday at the weekend. I'm 60 years old and too old to even think about having children now. And my Sean's 62 years old, so those days have well and truly legged it. We've had forty wonderful years together and never been blessed with little uns, so it won't be happening now. Not now, at all. Ya wee lunatic."* Patricia

had always wanted a wee one to bounce on her knee and sing lullabies to, but she knew it was never to be.

*"Well Patricia I'm not touching yer leg and if you feel that I am I would suggest you get that looked at by a doctor. Not a word of a lie. Your first born will have this gift."* The leprechaun nodded and vaulted onto his mischievous rainbow. It was going on the naughty step. Stat.

Sure enough. Nine months later a bouncing baby boy was delivered to the proud, elderly parents. Two years later and Patricia was pregnant again. That continued until the identical twins: Liam and Patrick appeared. In total, seven boys were born to the astounded and delighted Patricia and Sean.

Back to the present day...

*"So, Harry, that's why Stan repeats himself. No one would believe Patricia's story so they always asked her to repeat it. Stan thought that was how everyone spoke, so it became his habit."* Dippit finished her fanciful tale.

*"Really? That's true?"* Harry was gobsmacked.

*"Do you want me to repeat it?"* Dippit said this with a straight face.

*"Ahhh, I see what you did there Dippit. Funny."* Harry shook her head and gave a tut.

*"So, he's Irish and he has a brother who's a seventh son. That's unusual. Is he lucky too?"* Harry enquired. This story was the dog's bollocks.

*"Funny you should say that. Liam and Patrick, the wee darlings, were raking for sweeties when they found the broken Drill. We had tried again to fix it, but no luck. Well, the twins disappeared for less than ten minutes and then came back. They had fixed it. I kid you not. They had completely fixed it. We now have a working Drill again. I'm not sure how long it will work, but it works. That's the important part."* Dippit beamed and cheekily stole a KitKat from Harry's hidden stash.

# CHAPTER FORTY-FOUR

D evil Keith's room…

Harry, Bub, Devil Keith, Karen, Dr Riel, Dippit, Stan, Sir Andrew and Sir Mark were all sitting round the dress making table in Devil Keith's room, aka the new W. Room. As an aside; Devil Keith believed the W. Room stood for the Wonderful Room. The teams were delighted by the repaired Drill and what it meant to their rescue plans, but they continued to be sceptical about Stan's back story.

*"Seventh son? Really? That's lucky. So, which one is the lucky seventh?"* Devil Keith was dumfounded. Harry noticed his lisp was more pronounced than usual. That meant that he had a big design on the go and had stabbed his tongue, with pins, a lot. An awful lot. In the corner there was a mountain of cloth covered with a blue tarpaulin. Harry hoped that was not another wedding dress. She'd already vetoed four *"creations"* so far that day and this one looked like a doozey; to borrow one of Dippit's favourite words.

Earlier that day…

Wedding outfit 1.0

Devil Keith's creations had started with a white lace thong and pale pink pasties. However, before Harry had said a word, Devil Keith pronounced her to have more cellulite than a bag of spanners and he told her she'd look awful in his wicked design. Harry thought that he meant she looked like a bag of spanners which, come to think of it, was extremely hurtful. Although, she didn't think that spanners truly had cellulite, but maybe in Devil Keith's peculiar universe? She never could tell what went on in that head of his. That particular creation went into the back of the wardrobe. Hopefully never to be seen again.

Wedding outfit 2.0

The second creation was made of metal and looked like a knock off version of Devil Keith's suit of armour. He even provided a posy made entirely of can openers for her to hold. He winked and said that they were for Bub's benefit. Harry did try on the outfit but quickly said no. She then had to cover her cuts, gouges and grazes in plasters and bandages. Where's Brownie Hazel and her first aid certificate when you need her? Harry also insisted on getting an *"emergency"* tetanus jab. Devil Keith still hasn't explained how Harry can no longer, actually, get ill. He felt that ship had already sailed and fell off the edge of the flat-earth.

Wedding outfit 3.0

The third dress was made entirely from lengths of floral wallpaper; complete with lumps of wallpaper paste to add some much needed texture. According to Devil Keith, it would also take the eye away from her truly awful hair. Another hurtful comment to add to the rest, Harry thought. On a positive note; at least most of Devil Keith's tutting had stopped. He had probably been snacking on the left-over paste and could no longer open his mouth wide enough.

Wedding outfit 4.0

The fourth dress was the colour of diarrhoea: as Devil Keith thought Harry was chancing her arm even thinking about wearing a white dress. Cream was also dodgy, according to

Devil Keith. Harry thought he'd probably bought water or fire damaged fabric and was trying to start a money saving trend. Harry was correct. Unfortunately, the tutting had started again.

After those hideous and bizarre options Harry had decided to buy her own wedding dress. So she and Dippit were meeting with Amanda for some advice and a big, big glass of wine. She wasn't sure how she would explain Hell number one, and the adventures that led to the proposal, but she so wanted Amanda at the wedding. It wouldn't be the same without her and her distinctive laugh.

Back to the War Room chat...

*"No idea who's the seventh son. I say no idea. They're both on the go from morning to night so no one can tell. I say, no one can tell. They don't look the same but they're equally fortunate. I say, don't look the same but fortunate. Only one of them has head full of curls but since he didn't have the curls when they were born, we can't work out who was the seventh. I say, work out who was the seventh."* Dippit was sitting on Stan's knee and stroking his hair. Harry couldn't tease her as Bub's hair looked a bit of fright, courtesy of Harry and her need to groom him. Touch him or generally have a whale of a dirty time with him.

*"So back to business. We have to agree on how we get the Knights back and how we help you overthrow that airbag of a King. Harry, quit it. That tickles. It really tickles."* Bub chuckled and wiggled away from her groping hands.

*"Okay Bubbikins. Later?"* Harry whispered but didn't stop.

*"Absolutely, Harry. Ya gorgeous minx. Now, where were we?"* Bub wrinkled his nose and then kissed her nose.

*"We still can't find the collaborator and I'm concerned that if we try to mount an attack, even a covert mission, they'll be forewarned. It would be a suicide mission,"* Karen was bitterly disappointed at their continued lack of progress.

*"Do you think they know, that you know, that they're spying?"* queried Sir Andrew. He said that as he munched through a side

of beef and contemplated the need for a plate of spotted dick with custard. He'd be sorry to leave, not just because of the food, but because he felt a strong bond with the Hell number one team.

*"What if we lull them into a false sense of security? Stop all possible thoughts of attack and just work on the wedding,"* Sir Mark added. He wasn't happy about the situation, but he didn't want to be hasty. This could be messy. Now they had a working Drill they could, theoretically, mount a search and rescue without any additional casualties.

They agreed on the new mission...the wedding.

# CHAPTER FORTY-FIVE

The Brownie camp and the day of the wedding…

"Devil Keith, do *you have the rings?*" Bub nervously asked as he patted down Devil Keith.

"*Yes, I have the rings. Stop asking me. You've already checked twice. And no more pat downs…it's rumpling up my suit.*" Devil Keith groused and straightened his outfit.

"*No, I've asked you seven times and you've chosen to ignore me. Every single time.*" Bub was anxious and exasperated.

"*Keep your kilt on. They're with Neville. Everything else is sorted. Trust me.*" Devil Keith assured the gibbering wreck.

A few weeks before the wedding day…

Devil Keith had gone missing after the War Room decision to concentrate on the wedding. Bub and Harry were initially concerned, but Karen assured them that no "*weird and, or wonderful items*" were missing so they mainly left him to it. They occasionally put their ear to his door, but as they didn't hear any barking and growling they were reassured.

Two weeks later and Devil Keith excitedly called Bub into his room. He proudly gifted Bub with a replica highland outfit from 1743. Devil Keith had been binge watching the series "*Outlander*" and thought Bub would look dashing in the kilt, sporran, and woolly socks. Not as dashing as Devil Keith thought he would look in his outfit, but just dashing enough to set Devil Keith off nicely. Devil Keith called Bub's wedding outfit the "*support outfit.*" Bub just called it brilliant and hugged his talented brother.

Harry had also been called into Devil Keith's room. Devil Keith whisked off the tarpaulin covered mound in the corner, "*ta da!*"

"*Devil Keith, I don't know what to say. I **really** do not know what to say. Do you have a Dalek under that mound of lace and ribbons? Is that an exercise ball propped up under the bustle? I thought you said I couldn't wear white? Plus, I've bought my own dress.*" Harry was confused and concerned.

"*It's not for you, silly. That's my wedding outfit. Duh,*" Devil Keith rolled his eyes and demonstrated that the dress was too small for Harry's rear end.

"*So, you don't consider wearing a veil and a headdress too much? Plus, what could nearly be considered a wedding dress, to your brother's wedding as remotely odd?*" Harry pushed Devil Keith's hands away from her measuring her waist.

"*Harry, Devil Keith you in there? What the fudge is that monstrosity?*" Dippit barged in without knocking. Devil Keith decided to do something about that before it became a habit.

"*Why Dippit, it's my awesome wedding outfit. Stunning, isn't it?*" Devil Keith stroked the fabric and gave it a happy sniff.

"*Stunning, well... yes. I suppose so. Is that a bouquet of oversized cattle prods that the Dalek is holding?*" Dippit rubbed the prods. She so liked new bits of machinery and anything to do with electricity.

"*Yes, I thought it went with the theme.*" Devil Keith made a point of counting the cattle prods in case Dippit acquired one... or all ten of them.

"*Eh, what theme?*" Harry asked. She didn't know there was a theme. A fudging theme?

"*Why, I'm drop dead gorgeous, you silly cookie-bun. You should see what else I have planned.*" Devil Keith winked and put a finger against his pursed lips.

Back to the Brownie camp and the wedding day...

Harry and Bub had decided to opt for a traditional hand-fasting ceremony, so they were walking down the aisle together. Karen had agreed to officiate at the intimate wedding. Harry had tried to find her sisters Willing and Fachance but unfortunately, they were still missing. Harry was becoming increasingly worried about that. God was still recovering from all the fun at the music festival and Gab said that he was far too busy to attend. Devil Keith had asked Nora, but she patiently explained that the Restraining Order included not attending weddings with him. Devil Keith's Falkirk skulking had not been very successful. Dippit was going to be there as a witness, as was Devil Keith. Harry had tried to explain to Amanda, but so far she hadn't had any success. After four attempts and four C.C. reversals, Amanda still thought Harry was pulling her leg about Hell number one's existence.

Dr Riel was staying behind *"to mind the shop"*, but the Knights and Brownies were delighted to be invited.

# CHAPTER FORTY-SIX

T he authors are still going on about the wedding day...

The day of the wedding had arrived. Harry and Dippit agreed to wear simple summer dresses and they would go barefoot. They were so excited and could hardly contain their glee as they used the Drill and stepped into the Brownie clearing.

Harry spotted Bub in his kilt and began to cry. *"You look so handsome. I can't believe you've dressed up. I'm so touched. I hope you've gone traditional under there."*

*"Oh, I have. Or maybe I haven't. You'll have to wait and see."* Bub held out his hand just as Harry was dragged backwards into a bush. The bush was violently shaking, and Harry began screaming.

*"Harry, Harry,"* Bub made to go into the bush, but Dippit held him back. *"Give it a minute Bub."*

*"No, give it a couple of hours. Did you bring the flamethrower?"* shouted Devil Keith from the middle of the bush. Devil Keith had decided against his original wedding outfit as the Faeries had made fun of him. They also had the audacity to throw Brownie Anne's bricks at him. He was so gonna get those oversized bluebottles and when he did, he was going to knock the stuffing out of them or get the Brownies to do it for him. Brownie Hilary and Brownie Mary Jo were quite a scary prospect, he thought.

Instead, Devil Keith was resplendent in a purple suit with sky blue polka dots, pale green embossed cowboy boots and a top hat in a delightfully playful shade of baby pink. He had also managed to snaffle one of Brian's tail feathers whilst saving

Harry. He left that as a surprise, because even Devil Keith knew that Harry might not be too pleased that he had used that opportunity to accessorise. Although, it looked so good together that he was willing to risk the guaranteed bra wire threats and stabbings.

Harry appeared, from the bush, twenty minutes later. She was wearing a full-length cream, chiffon dress. It was delicately embroidered and embellished with seed pearls. Her hair had been tamed, just a little; Devil Keith was good but not that good. She wore a circle of fresh, wildflowers in her red hair and was clutching a small, matching bouquet.

*"Will I do?"* Harry shyly asked.

*"Always,"* Bub smiled and kissed her hand. At that Harry heard a loud bellow of familiar laughter.

*"It's Amanda. You convinced Amanda?"* Harry jumped up and down.

*"I sent in Devil Keith. There was no way she could possibly believe he was from anywhere but Hell, so here she is. Do you know that she calls herself nuts and nuttier; it's bizarre but so sweet? She's more of a 'nuttier' than you described. Great fun but I've had a terrible time hiding her and her boisterous laugh."* Bub kissed Harry's wrist.

Harry and Bub walked hand and hand up the makeshift aisle. Brown Owl Mac rushed out of the trees, *"sorry I'm late. I had a terrible time corralling the Brownies and I've lost Brownie Mary Jo, again."*

Brownie Mary Jo came into the clearing dragging Trevor by the foot. *"I's brings the teddy. Hes needs to comes see yous toos."*

*"Hi, Trevor, didn't you get the invite?"* Bub freed Trevor from the whirlwind's clutches.

*"Yep Bub, but Brownie Mary Jo insisted. The wife's just behind me. She was putting on her hat and locking the door."* Trevor adjusted his tux and made himself comfortable against a tree.

*"Loving your shoes, Trevor."* He was wearing raspberry red,

suede platform heels.

*"They're me daughter Lucy's. Thought they really suited me; gave the outfit a bit of pizzazz. As your Devil Keith would say."* Brownie Mary Jo dressed as a little red fox, sat down beside Trevor. She began telling him what a wedding was all about. *"Thats lady buys thats man with a bits of a washing machines...,"* Harry couldn't wait to hear the rest of that story.

The rest of the adorable Brownies appeared. They were meant to scatter rose petals before the bride and groom, but they were running late. Harry and Bub laughed and beckoned them forward. They formed a rough, pushy queue then tried to solemnly walk up the aisle.

Brownie Hazel was dressed as a fluffy white puppy and instead of flower petals she was throwing plasters and bandages at the guests. A full leg plaster-cast narrowly missed Devil Keith's head and he called over, *"nice try. Ask Brownie Lynette for some throwing lessons."*

*"I's will. Psst. Lady, I's no a real puppy. I's Brownie Hazel. It's a 'prise fors your weddings. I's no need a tree coz I's no need a pee. I's no really a doggys. Maybes later. Oh no, maybes now."* Brownie Hazel ran off to find a convenient tree and fight her way out of her furry costume.

Mac rushed forward, *"spit it out, spit it out."* Mac turned a white and ginger cat upside down and shook the bird feathers from her mouth.

*"Is that Periwinkle? Did Brownie Rachel dye his fur?"* Harry queried.

*"No, that's Brownie Claire."* Devil Keith explained.

*"I's Pusskins today,"* said the dizzy blonde and began dancing up the aisle, none the worse for wear.

Brownie Mary Jo stormed out *"Yous no eat the birdies, nos more"* and bopped Brownie Claire on the nose.

After a bit of a tussle, Brownie Mary Jo and Brownie Claire were tied to their seats with bowers of ivy. They were no longer best friends, but Mac had seen worse and predicated that by nap time they'd be back to being best buddies again.

Brownie Rachel prowled up the aisle dressed as a multi-coloured teddy-bear. *"Grrr. Hi's Teddy Trevor. Grrrrr, grrrr I's likes you nows. I's see you laters. I's love you. Nicest shoes, I's tries them later. Yous need beads, Trevour. I's got lots of beads. Grrrr."*

*"No's you nots Brownie Rachel. I's in charge. Yous be'hav and bes good. We's get yummy cake ifs wes good."* Brownie Hilary was checking the baskets and removing the bricks that Brownie Anne was trying to sneak up the aisle. Plasters were one thing, but the bricks were huge and lethal. Even wee Brownie Hilary knew that.

*"Brownie Hilary, yous nos in charge."* Brownie Rachel had stopped to scratch her fluffy bottom.

*"I's is ands I's Harris t'day."* Brownie Hilary was dressed as a golden Labrador puppy. She was wriggling around and looked like she was also trying to find a tree, hopefully to hide the bricks and not for any other reason.

Brownie Anne and Brownie Arlene held hands as they happily skipped up the aisle dressed as glimmering Faeries, *"we's in 'guise today. Them's Faeries are bad, baddies. Brownie Hilary's is as big, big baddie. Shes has ma bricks. Brownie Arlene's gonna helps get its sorted. Alls sorted fur me, yes."*

Brownie Lisa and Brownie Gillian backflipped up the aisle dressed as pandas, complete with two black eyes.

*"Devil Keith, you made panda outfits? I thought pandas were your nemesis."* Harry went to pat his arm.

*"Well Brownie Lisa and Brownie Gillian so admire the Chinese gymnasts, and all pandas belong to China. Plus, I wanted to make them what they like. So pandas it is."* Devil Keith nodded at the pair and gave them a thumbs up.

*"And..."* Harry rolled her hands to indicate that she wanted more information.

*"And they were gonna throw me around again, so I had to*

*agree. The black eyes aren't anything to do with me. They had been boxing just before the first fitting and they liked the look. So I think they might have done it again today. The burst seams... well they just won't sit still."* Devil Keith checked his top pocket for some emergency safety pins.

*"**Tommy talks,**"* was screamed as Brownie Lynette whooped up the aisle dressed as a native American Indian. She solemnly presented a ribbon covered tomahawk to Bub and Harry. *"Fors yous cake. Stills mines, buts yous cans borrow. I's get back later. Swear. Yous have to gives it back."*

Bub and Harry agreed then quickly hid the lethal axe in Karen's handbag.

Brownie Lesley, Brownie Margaret, and Brownie Jacqui were next and they too had wicker baskets over their arms. They were dressed as alligators due to their love of all things teeth and craft related. Luckily, Brownie Hilary had removed the teeth from their baskets or that would have been messy. Very messy, as many of the teeth still had their bloody roots attached.

*"Thank you for making my wedding ring. It's beautiful."* Brownie Lesley had taken the washers and crafted a delicate wedding ring for Harry.

*"Nos probs buts I's like teeffs better. Yous like teeff? I's make one fur yous."* Brownie Lesley was eyeing up Devil Keith's incisors for her next project. He quickly covered his mouth with both his hands.

*"No, no we're fine. This will do nicely."* Harry patted her on the head and sent her on her way.

Wee Brownie Murphy and Brownie Leanne energetically bounced up the aisle dressed as beautifully embroidered, green frogs.

*"Wee Brownie Murphy, I hear I have you to thank for the gorgeous embroidery and pearls on my wedding dress."* Harry bent down to give them a hug then decided against it.

*"I's gets ma badge."* Wee Brownie Murphy shyly said, wiping

her nose on her sleeve and smudging her green face paint.

"*I's have froggies ands fizzy bits furs you,*" and Brownie Leanne, joyfully, plopped some live frogs and electrically sockets into Harry's bouquet.

"*Yous too. Comes on. Joeys, Chandler. We's be lates.*" Brownie Jill bumped her way up the aisle wearing a turkey that was dressed in a leopard print fur coat. Mac jumped from her seat and began pulling at the turkey before she realised that it wasn't made of flesh and bones. She mouthed "*thank you*" to Devil Keith.

"*Oh, she has another one for later. Don't you worry about that.*" Devil Keith smiled widely.

Brownie Nelli walked up the aisle dressed as a sleek black and brown cat. She was dragging a cow behind her? No, it wasn't a cow, it was a giraffe.

"*I tried to make a giraffe outfit, but due to the length of the neck the head knocked off her centre of gravity. Brownie Nelli offered to help, so Brownie Angela agreed to being pulled along. There's some wheels under there.*" Devil Keith checked that the wheels were still attached and Brownie Angela was not just being dragged across the uneven ground.

"*Makes sense. Well done, Devil Keith. I can't thank you enough for their wonderfully cute and bizarre flower girl outfits. You're a star.*" Harry hugged Devil Keith and gently patted his back.

Brownie Kirsty, Brownie Liz and Brownie Mirka were the last to appear. Brownie Liz and Brownie Kirsty were dressed as two adorable little skunks. As they attempted to negotiate the path they were whispering, giggling, hiccupping, and clutching goblets full of rich red wine. Brownie Mirka was staggering across the makeshift aisle as she attempted to hold the inebriated pair up and prevent them from throwing-up in Mac's rather fetching hat.

"*Devil Keith, why are they dressed as cute little skunks?*" Harry enquired.

*"After their last afternoon drinking session, Mac said they were as 'drunk as skunks' and it kinda stuck."* Devil Keith nodded over to Mac.

*"Okay I get that. So why is Brownie Mirka dressed as a piece of poultry stuffed into tight black leathers?"* Harry checked.

*"Misses Harry. I's got mas bikers badge. I's a biker chicks. Browns Owl says 'Brownie Mirka, yous can't eats the ripe apples, no's more.' Mac shake-ed her pointy finger ats me. So, I's on the bike and I's on the wagon too. Brown Owl where's Brownie Mirka's wagon? I's no have one. Yous get mes as wagon, peas?"* Brownie Mirka began to cry.

*"I'll explain later, come on little one."* Mac led Brownie Mirka away and sat her on her knee for a much-needed cuddle and a breathalyser test.

Neville strutted up the aisle. Gone were all signs of his gang affiliation and in its place were rainbow ribbons, yards of pink lace and shimmering ropes of beads. He and his family were the ring bearers, and they were so proud of their role. The Brownies went wild and surrounded the Hounds of Hell. Neville lapped up the praise and gently prodded Hugo towards the girls.

*"Nows, we gets chances withs the real puppy."* said Brownie Hilary. All thoughts of the wedding and needing a tree gone.

*"Kitty,"* screamed Brownie Nelli and Periwinkle was scooped into her heavily scratched arms. My, those Brownies are strong wee creatures. Bub went to help the little girl as Periwinkle was a *"difficult"* cat. Bub stopped mid stride. Periwinkle proved to be anything but a difficult cat as he cuddled into Brownie Nelli and was purring as she tickled his chin. He gently pawed her face and they bumped noses. Periwinkle was clearly in love with the little bruise.

*"Can we start? Shall I begin?"* smiled Karen, delighted with the wee ones antics but she was keen to get on with the party.

Karen delivered her carefully prepared speech, but Bub and Harry just gazed at each other; oblivious to everyone and everything else around them.

"So, to finish. You promise to always love burnt chicken noodles, and you're going to buy new wallpaper featuring baboons ironing pyjamas. Yes, is that right?" Karen laughingly enquired.

"Yes. I will," Bub and Harry chorused.

"I knew you weren't listening to a word I said. I practised for this **and** I got a certificate. That was a waste of £29.99 and ten minutes of my non-life. Oh well. Bub, just kiss her already. You're hand fastened and legal. Let's party." Karen sighed, smiled, and gratefully slid off her high heels.

Bub took Harry into his arms when two twelve-foot maniacal Crabs scuttled into the clearing. They were deliriously shooting their Kalashnikovs into the air and puffing on their heavily chewed cigars. Everyone screamed and dived for cover. The little Brownies were wedged under the adults, but quickly started squirming so that they could see what all the fuss was about.

The fuss was the evil Pincer James and Pincer Stuart, who rattled up the aisle and threw down a tightly bound scroll. They then scurried back down the aisle, shooting as they went. They stopped, scanned the area, and carefully chose their vulnerable target. They then did their dastardly deed before disappearing back through their portal.

"Those fudgers stubbed out their cigars in my beautiful cake. Those fuckers ruined my **cake**." Harry wailed.

"Yous said as bads word," said Brownie Kat and Brownie Louise; tightly holding hands. They were dressed as bright orange ducklings with a festoon of fluffy feathers on their heads. Where on earth did they come from? Harry wondered.

# CHAPTER FORTY-SEVEN

T he day after the wedding...

They had decided to continue with the wedding despite the interruption; although it was a slightly more subdued affair than had originally been planned. The Brownies weren't at all bothered by the cigars in the wedding cake and gleefully ate around them, whilst slipping large slices of cake to Periwinkle, Neville, and Neville's hellions. Mac had a terrible hangover due to eating some over ripe apples and she had a Brownie clean up to face. She hoped they all wanted their *"clean up the cake badge"*, otherwise she was in for a lot of eating, scrubbing, and barfing.

Devil Keith's room aka the official War Room, although Devil Keith still didn't know about the aka situation...

*"You do know this is my room. My room. For me, alone?"* Devil Keith whined. Devil Keith had Harry's wipe clean board set up on an easel and he was furiously drawing. Harry went to look at his latest design ideas, but he pulled a cloth over the board. *"Harry, it's a secret. No peeking. You might get to see it. If and only if, I think that you're worthy. Dippit, you will definitely get to see the wonder of it as I know you will appreciate it."*

*"Come on just a wee look. Just to keep us amused until everyone else arrives."* Harry coaxed.

*"No, no, no. Amused? What do you mean everyone else arrives?*

*I didn't agree to you pair marching in here, never mind any more of you interlopers. This is my creative space where my dreams become reality. Not some doss house for very distant relatives to hang around in."* Devil Keith huffed at the happy sisters.

*"Devil Keith, you look like you could do with some pilchard tea. I'll keep that nosy witch Harry away from your special project. You can trust me. Remember me? Good old dependable, Dippit."* Dippit's eyelashes were kicking up a storm as she batted them at Devil Keith, whilst making sure that Harry kept her bra wire intact.

*"Ok, but only for a moment. Keep watch. Hit Harry with the baseball bat if she takes one step near this board,"* with those words of warning Devil Keith nipped off for a creative breather.

*"Right, Harry. Don't step. Run. Let's see what he has planned."* Dippit conspiratorially whispered and beckoned Harry over.

Dippit and Harry sneaked the corner of the cloth up and looked at the detailed drawings. Harry tilted her head to the left, then the right. *"Is that a mushroom?"*

*"No Harry. It's a mushroom cloud. As in a nuclear explosion,"* Dippit removed the rest of the cloth.

*"So that makes that drawing in the corner, what, a vat of lava?"* Harry pointed at the corner and turned to Dippit.

*"Yep, I'd say lava. And a lot of it. Harry, is this his plan for dealing with the scroll?"* Dippit carefully searched the rest of the board.

*"Hmm, see that sketch in the corner? The one with a lot of dots of red on and around it. Correct me if I'm wrong, but I'm sure that's a tiny, squashed wing peeking out from under a really big boulder."* Harry squinted again, *"yes, definitely a mangled Faery under there."*

Devil Keith strolled in with his mug of tea and a large slice of Battenberg cake. *"You sneaky little witch. You made Dippit betray my trust. Dippit, you're spending far too much time with that Harry. Dippit, honey, come here and spend the day with me. I'll put you on the straight and narrow. I'll help you kick all those bad habits Harry has plagued you with."*

*"Devil Keith, you are not getting access to my sister. I am not a bad influence. I am not a distant relative. I'm your sister-in-law. Basically, your sister! And lastly, you are a blithering idiot. But I need to know, are you planning on beating up the Faeries?"* Harry distracted him whilst Dippit stole a bite of cake from his hand.

*"Whoa. Mind the marzipan. I had to trade three puffer jackets for that. Anyway. No sister of mine would dress like you. Ah yes, Brownie Anne and I have decided that enough is enough and those winged creatures are getting what's coming to them. Being meanies to Brownie Anne and teasing me about my clothes, they're for it! Nuclear winter and all that. Or a jolly good squashing."* Devil Keith hid the rest of the cake in his secret hidey-hole...aka his cavernous mouth.

*"Good luck, Devil Keith. Sucks to be you."* Harry pinched his nostrils closed and waited on him gasping for breath. Then she stole the rest of his cake. And completely ignoring the salvia and mush, she grabbed a comfortable chair.

Bub, Karen, Stan, and the Knights arrived. They quickly took a seat around the dress making table. There was a feeling of dread emanating from both of the teams.

Dippit tentatively picked up the threatening scroll, *"well, we can't put it off any longer. Do you want me to read it out loud?"* Dippit unrolled the scroll. She immediately turned vivid lime green and fell to the floor.

Stan and Harry rushed to her side as she flashed various shades of green. *"She's been poisoned. Do something. Get Dr Riel. Quickly. Stan don't just stand there. Get help."* Harry grabbed Dippit and began violently shaking her.

Stan gazed at Dippit in total wonder then he started to smile. He scooped her from the floor and cradled her to his chest. He then began hugging and crying, *"I know what this is. I say, I know what this is. Not to worry. No worries, I say."* With that pronouncement he rushed out the door with his unconscious wife draped in his arms.

*"What's going on? Is Dippit alright? Harry, do you want to go*

*after them? Does anyone have a pair of gloves so we can pick this thing up?"* Bub poked the scroll with a knitting needle.

Bub donned thick gloves then carefully picked up the scroll and unwound it. Stan and Dippit ran back in the room. Laughing and crying they announced, *"we're having a baby. The green flushes happened to Stan's mum as well. Patricia and Sean are over the moon! Harry, you're gonna be an aunty. An aunty. Just think. An aunty.*

*"Wow. Brilliant. I can't believe it. That's great news. Oh, an aunty. I can't wait. I'm so, so happy for you both. You're going to be wonderful parents. Are you feeling alright now? Was that a one off?"* Harry was crying, laughing, and producing a great deal of un-ladylike snot.

Stan pushed back Dippit's hair *"Sorry love. I say, sorry love. That's gonna happen a lot. I say, happen a lot. My mammy had it for nearly the whole of her pregnancy. The whole of her pregnancy. I'm sorry Dippit. I say, I'm sorry."*

*"Don't be silly, it's worth it. I can't believe we're gonna be parents. Imagine us with a wee baby,"* and with that Dippit flashed cabbage green and fainted again.

# CHAPTER FORTY-EIGHT

S till in the War Room...

*"So, what does the scroll say?"* Dippit was decidedly less lime coloured and sat cushioned in Stan's arms. Stan kept rubbing her belly and giggling.

*"Dippit we can come back to that another day. Don't you need to rest?"* Bub handed her a soft blanket and his last bar of mint chocolate.

*"Well uncle Bub. No, I'm not ill. I'm having a baby. We all need to know what we're dealing with and make a plan to deal with it. But I'll happily steal your chocolate."* Dippit chortled and took a satisfying bite.

Back to the scroll...

*"Right, so the scroll says:*
*'Dear Hearts, do I see a happy Hell number one before me? Our little scrimmage highlighted a few small deficits in my defences. I am most grateful for the opportunity to correct these minor faults. As such, I have accepted assistance from Hell number eight. These slight errors and those responsible have been dealt with. Fairly and justly: in accordance with my lenient laws.*

*I wish to discuss the immediate return of my misguided Knights and my favourite, royal cat.*

*I feel that a discussion of terms would be of use and as such I propose we meet in Hell number three in four weeks' time.*

*Yours*
*King Adrian*
*The Majestic*
*And The Terribly Fair'*
*Well at least it's not Hell number eight baying for our blood.*
*I was getting worried that a couple of gerbils might have hitched a*
*ride in the scroll."* Bub folded the scroll and lent back in his chair;
relieved that things were manageable. Well, just about.

*"Oh no. Not so fast. Not that. Surely not that. That's the worst*
*possible scenario."* Sir Mark scrambled out of his chair and away
from the scroll.

*"What do you mean, Sir Mark?"* Bub just knew his afternoon
of watching *"The Chase",* followed by re-runs of *"The Waltons"*
was out the window.

Sir Mark and Sir Andrew explained that under the thin
layer of civility King Adrian was furious. He would never have
gone to another Hell for help if he wasn't planning something
truly despicable. He was too conceited to admit to any faults, so
he was just lulling them all into a false sense of security. They
could guarantee that whoever went to meet the King would not
survive the encounter. This scroll was a veiled declaration of
war.

They were also concerned that the King had been able to
create a portal for the Crabs as that meant he had found the
Dimensional Lance. The only way he could have found the Lance
was through the imprisoned Knights. They concluded that the
tortured Knights must have gone through extreme pain and
prolonged starvation if they gave up that information.

*"Sir Mark, so why the four weeks delay?"* Bub also cancelled
his evening entertainment, and he so enjoyed the movie
*"Calamity Jane".*

*"Oh, he wouldn't want the Eurovision Song Contest disturbed.*
*He takes that very seriously. He so looks forward to the nil points*
*UK entry. He thinks it's an absolute hoot that they never get a single*

*point. He also gets a kick outta making everyone else place bets that the British entry will win. There's a rumour that he gained the Kingdom using a similar scheme."* Sir Mark winced as he delivered the bad news.

*"So, we have four weeks to find the collaborator, prepare a plan and make sure we get out of there with our heads still attached? I propose we gather back here in an hour with ideas and weapons. Karen we need to collect the Stills."* Bub was deeply concerned, and he wasn't sure if anyone else had realised that neither Stan nor Dippit could help this time around. The teams were going to need every available minute and their plan had to be fool proof or Devil Keith-proof.

# CHAPTER FORTY-NINE

**B**ack in the War room…

*"Really bad news, I'm afraid. I can't believe it. The Moonshine Stills are missing."* Bub was trying to minimise the impact of the lost Stills. His pacing around the table and running his hands through his hair wasn't helping maintain the illusion of being cool and in control. He couldn't believe how quickly everything was falling apart. He had been relying on the Stills to give the Hell number one teams a bit of an edge.

*"What? Did you double check?"* Harry gave the agitated man a hug.

*"I checked. Then checked again. I can't believe it. They're really gone. Wait. Wait. Give me a minute. Come to think of it… I think the collaborator may have made a mistake. We thought that the spy didn't know about Hitler's bunker, so that meant they had to be a Hell number one resident. A difficult problem to solve, as Karen and Dr Riel found out when they tried to identify the culprit.*

*However, if the spy knew about Stan's Stills, then the first clue was a red herring. The spy must be someone with inside information on the whole Eva/Karen incident. That discounts all of our residents. They were too jacked up on the Greed gases to figure that out.*

*Therefore, we must know and trust the spy. Sir Mark and Sir Andrew if we gave you a list of the people who knew about the Eva incident, do you think it would help you identify who was spreading details of our business in your Hell?"* Bub rubbed his hands together and smiled for the first time on over an hour.

The team looked expectantly at each other then looked

at the Knights. The Knights broke the news that they couldn't help as they had never heard or seen the nefarious tattletale. They had only heard rumours and second-hand accounts of Hell number one. The level of excitement in the room began to fade.

The team decided to talk through the frightening enigma that was a frenemy. Devil Keith, that means a friend who is also an enemy. They started with people who knew about the Moonshine Stills, Hitler's Bunker, Karen/Eva, the multiple Hells and had the knowledge to break the cockroach walking pavement.

The possible culprit...

They agreed that Selena would know about all their plans, but they also agreed that she was sound asleep and wouldn't be waking for many years. If at all. She was quickly discounted. She couldn't be a *"sleeper agent."* Sorry, there seem to be some aftereffects of being near the gargoyles.

The Oracles were a possibility, but Karen had popped into see them and whilst there they had asked her the time. She answered *"10.30 in the morning",* but The Oracles looked mystified by that answer. It turns out they were asking about which century it was. Karen felt that they were sincere in their apparent confusion, and she was deeply concerned about their internal time clock malfunction. They were excluded due to their incompetency, but Bub was tasked with visiting them for a *"chat".* And he was going to try to get them to stop time scavenging objects. That addiction was adding to their confusion and their escalating Nile bill.

Harry and Bub had the knowledge and means but they had nothing to gain from fighting with Hell number three. Although the Knights argued that Bub had a motive as he would have gained his own Hell if the original plan had succeeded. Bub assured them that if he wanted his own Hell then number one would have been a much easier option.

After Devil Keith had a mini strop and then recovered from Bub and Harry's comments about easily taking *"his Hell."* They all agreed that Devil Keith knew all of the necessary information but no one, but no one, thought he was capable of this plot. He fervently argued that he was clever and sly enough to do the dastardly deed. He didn't care that he was implicating himself, but his protestations were to no avail. They had seen his ridiculous wardrobe and heard his rambling piffle for far too long. He was quickly and repeatedly discounted.

Devil Keith, still moaning, decided to invest in some much-needed tee-shirts. He was going to discuss it with Alan, but he felt the, *"It was me all along"* or *"I am the one you want, take me to your leader. Oh, I am your leader,"* or *"Cooee, spy over here,"* should cover it quite nicely.

They also agreed that Karen knew all the necessary information, but she already had Hell number one completely under her control so had no motive to change the leadership model. Devil Keith had another mini strop following that revelation. Devil Keith, how can you consider that a revelation? He rapidly added hats, scarves, and mittens to his list of items requiring a catchy slogan.

Plus, Karen was still recovering from her forced sabbatical in the filing cabinet so didn't have the fortitude or the means to do this deed.

Dr Riel was new to the team, and could be seen as suspicious but he was besotted with Karen so they agreed he wouldn't want to upset their fledging romance. Karen blushed throughout this exchange, but she readily agreed.

It was also agreed that Stan and Dippit had the knowledge but no definite motive. They also didn't want to upset the pregnant couple as they were finding her green flushes really quite disturbing. Plus, Stan was weirdly lucky so if he wanted to run Hell he just needed to poke someone with a screwdriver, and it would be his. This may be the plot line for book four.... only kidding.

Bub looked disappointed but had reached his conclusion. *"That leaves two possible suspects. I know who has my vote. Get ready to shout and get the fudgers attention. He's coming here to answer for his fudging shenanigans. One, two...."*

*"Chick, no Farquhar, no Jonathan. No, Chick, he did it the scoundrel. CHICK. Knew it was him. He didn't have me fooled. No for a single moment."* Devil Keith gabbled and furtively tried to write some betting slips.

*"No Devil Keith. GAB!"* they all shouted at the ceiling.

# CHAPTER FIFTY

S till in the War Room…

Gab appeared. He saluted, and then surveyed the room. He was a tall, slender, effortlessly elegant man with amber eyes flecked with forest green and golden lights. He had an envious mane of thick, slightly wavy black hair. He had it cut into a more suitable short style every day but within an hour or two it grew into glorious, shoulder length tresses. Much to his annoyance.

His deep dimples, and the subsequent flattery he received, were a cause of extreme discomfort so he categorically refused to smile. He managed to stifle a grin, even when shown hilarious cat videos. Weirdo! He had tried to grow a beard to hide the offensive dimples, but the whiskers continuously fell out: leaving his skin silky smooth and open to unsolicited caresses. All of his skin produced a pale golden sheen but there was nothing he could do about that. God had suggested that he buy a truck load of concealer, but he didn't always have the time or the make-up sponges to apply it fully. Instead, he covered himself in from head to foot baggy camouflage gear and donned combat boots.

He wasn't at all vain about his good looks and muscular physique, rather he was embarrassed by the attention and admiration he received. He was always concerned that people wouldn't take him seriously and dismiss him as a merely bit of *"eye candy."*

*"What do you require?"* he politely enquired. His words

were always clipped and precise. He actively disliked small talk and curtailed all conversations when they became remotely personal. In short, he was the opposite of Devil Keith and Harry. He found them eminently puzzling and tremendously exasperating. They vexed him in the extreme.

"*Don't give us attitude. We want an explanation for this,*" Harry threw the scroll at Gab. She had aimed for his head, but the scroll bounced of his firm pecs. Wow. One of the authors needs to cool the fudge down.

Gab read the scroll and carefully placed it onto the table. "*I do not think that I was giving you 'attitude.' Also, I do not think this has anything to do with me.*" He made to leave but Bub put a hand on his arm. "*Time to come clean, mate. Make it a good one.*"

Gab chose a straight back, wooden chair and took a seat at the table. He glanced around the table to ensure that everyone was paying attention. He raised his considerable eyebrows and began to explain. "*I do not intend to repeat myself. So, pay attention and I shall begin. Please leave all intelligent, and not so intelligent questions, and your flimsy excuses to the very end.*"

Everyone shuffled forward, rested their elbows on the table and stared at Gab. Except Devil Keith, he was hemming a green, faux fur muff for Dippit. He thought it could double as a cushion during her fainting spells. He had matched the coloured fur perfectly to her fainting skin tone.

"*Devil Keith, are you quite finished?*" Gab politely enquired.

"*Just about. Just carry on. Ignore me, well try. As if you **can** ignore such a fine specimen of male beauty, huh. I'm an Adonis, afterall.*" Devil Keith patted his chest then checked to see who had fainted.

"*Now for some much-needed clarity. You do not appear to realise just how lucky you are. You do so little work and have very few expectations made of you. It is quite preposterous. For example: Bub, you paint and do small pieces of interior design. No, you are not an architect, but you do have a good eye for overall design. That is your skill set and it appears to be your main focus. Romancing Harry and repeatedly rescuing Devil Keith; that is also taking up a great deal of resources. However, your primary focus should be Hell number one. No distractions. No dabbling, or finger painting is permitted until you acknowledge and undertake your responsibilities."* Gab sagely nodded.

*"I do not finger paint. How fudging dare you..."* Bub spluttered. Harry was gonna get that cheeky Angel.

*"Devil Keith, you basically sew. Do not get me wrong: you are highly proficient at it, but you must admit that...you sew and tack and do other fabric-y things. That is your skill set. It is unlikely that you could manage more than that. Please do not interrupt me whilst I am speaking. Devil Keith, please calm down and stop hemming my trousers together. Take a cleansing breath and reflect on my words. You will be given ample opportunity to pose your side of the argument.*

*Karen, you are obviously the exception in this group of moronic misfits but even you must admit that you are just going through the motions most days. You lack drive and discipline. You are so pleased to write the word Mississippi, with the little horn details, that I know you are looking for more reasons to engage with that particular word. I would like to highlight the following examples: last Tuesday the executive dining room menu listed 'Deconstructed Mississippi Mud Pie.' I am partial to that pudding. So you can imagine my disappointment when I viewed the item on my plate. That dessert was, in fact, just a packet of stale digestive biscuits that had been lingering beside you in the filing cabinet drawer. I know that it must have some sentimental value as it was your only companion whilst you were incarcerated, but even you must admit that it was a bold move to elevate that lowly biscuit to the lofty heights of a mud pie."* Gab tutted at Karen and gave her a pitying look.

*"How do you know about those biscuits? I thought Devil Keith, as my saviour, was the only person who knew."* Karen gave Gab the evil eye.

*"That is of no consequence at this time. What was I saying? Oh yes. Plus, the state of Mississippi has raised an exclusion order*

*against you as their postal workers are finding the sheer quantity of unnecessary memos and threatening letters impacting on their heath. Their osteopaths are inundated with requests for back braces and treatments for lumbago. I know that you have chosen to ignore that situation and persist in your postal worker vendetta.*

*Karen, I can say with absolute certainty that you are not stretched, and you currently lack focus. I believe that you wished to go on their recent missions, but you had to 'mind the shop'. The fact that you **all** refer to Hell number one in that derogatory term tells one that you do not understand the true magnitude of your responsibilities.*

*Please, all of you hold your questions and flimsy excuses until the very end. I have already made that proviso very clear.*

*I was willing to overlook most of your 'shenanigans' and put it down to childish high jinks. That was until the incident with the Kelpies. That was unnecessarily cruel, and Duke is still trying to get over it. Mindfulness is helping but I was, and remain, very displeased with you all."* Gab shook his head and frowned.

Harry skelped Devil Keith on the back of the head, *"ha, you deserve a really good thump."*

*"Harry, save your outrage until the end please. You are not entirely innocent either.*

*Then, not one of you noticing that Karen had been swapped over. That was inexcusable. The accent, people? At the very least you should have questioned that. The change in Karen's personality was another blatant clue. It appears that you were so busy 'fannying about'. Incidentally, that is a terrible term to use in the workplace. It should be struck from your vocabulary. You did not notice a major security issue.*

*Even when the residents were going berserk over unrealistic productivity goals, you still did not take any notice. The walls were moving. Actually moving, people? You have one job...look after Hell number one.*

*Devil Keith, please lower your hand. I do not want to hear about your baby momma situation. Again.*

*Then Devil Keith turns into an unstoppable wild beast. That was unbelievable. I wanted you to manage that, but I had to intercede as I felt that you did not have the necessary skill set. That could have toppled us all. Responsibility, people? Ever heard of that particular word?*

*Devil Keith, is that a new hand up? Put it down immediately.*

*Then we come to the Drill. That was, and still is a major, major breach of protocol. That type of behaviour is why we never told you about the other Hells. You have shown that you cannot be trusted with sensitive information. I was particularly surprised and disappointed in you, Bub. I had previously had some confidence in your ability to 'babysit' this place. The visit to Hell number ten and the subsequent mess you caused. Where do I begin?*

*Devil Keith, I know for a fact that it is a new hand up. I know where to begin, you lunatic. Down and keep it down, or you are going lose it. Make no mistake about that. I have a sword. And it is very big.*

*You upset G.O.D. I mean, really upset her. I could not believe you could do that to her. She goes out of her way to maintain Free Will and you totally abused that privilege. You made her shout. You made her cry. My self-control evaporated. I was furious. I missed my essential daily haircut so that I could comfort her. My haircut, people!*

*I could not take any more. I am ashamed to say that I went to Hell number three for a pint of real ale. They have an astounding selection to choose from. I have to admit that I drank more than I intended, and I spoke out of turn to the innkeeper. This is out of character, and I humbly apologise for that slip in my personal standards.*

*I did not realise that my woes and momentary lack of control would be the catalyst to your latest escapade.*" Gab was genuinely apologising but the team remained absolutely livid with him

"*Escapade? Escapade? My husband was abducted due to your loose lips.*" Gab was now at the top of Harry's list of enemies. Even above H.O.R.S.E.S. Oh, he was in bother now.

"*Harry, please wait until the end. However, when I found out that Hell number three had borrowed Bub I recognised that I had to put some control measures into action. Incidentally, if you had policies and procedures in place that would have been easier to plan and execute.*

*On a more positive note. Harry, you went from being exceedingly disorganised to nearly mounting a successful rescue mission. You should be proud that you nearly rose to the challenge. Although I feel that I should make this crystal clear: they did not do Bub any harm. Harry, please calm down. For goodness sake, he has a double chin due to the excellent food and rest he received."* Gab pointed at the expanding chin.

*"I do not have a double chin and I wish you lot would stop saying that. It's the lighting in here. That's all."* Bub took Harry's hand and stroked it. He then realised that his wedding ring was more than a tad tight, and it was cutting off the circulation to his finger.

*"We can debate your double chin and lighting at another time. Let me continue. So, I realised that things were getting slightly out of hand. So, I broke the cockroach walking pavement as I did not want you being able to access weapons. Incidentally, I paid dearly for that bribe, but I do not want to talk about the cost. It was a little embarrassing. Anyway, back to weapons or should I say serious weapons? Devil Keith, you could not get a tank or a military grade helicopter in Falkirk. I checked first. I knew that you would likely need Stan, so I left Hitler's Bunker intact so that you could get to Falkirk to retrieve him."* Gab may have been looking for positive feedback. And praise. He needed to read the room and check out how perky Harry's boobs are.

*"The Moonshine Stills? What about them?"* Karen said through gritted teeth.

*"They were taken within days of Bub putting them into storage. Dippit did manage to get a few samples, but not enough to cause a major headache. This is yet another example of your incompetency; you only just noticed they were missing. In fact, just this very day. They should be guarded day and night. They are a serious, apocalyptic type of weapon. Stan you can never make another set of those Stills. I cannot stress that enough."* Gab pointed at the guilty looking man.

*"Ok, I say ok. No more Stills, I say no more. Okey dokey, your butterflyness."* Stan took out his notebook and crossed off a few pages of his ideas.

*"Butterflyness? That may be the nicest thing anyone has ever said to me...but I digress. Back to the matter in hand. Thank you, Stan. That is such a relief. Anyway, I thought I had put enough safety measures in place so that even you could not cause any more problems. But I was clearly wrong. You went out with the mission parameters and stole not only the Knights but the King's favourite royal cat. His absolute favourite. I heard that he is livid."* Gab indicated that Stan might want to make a list of rules for the Hell team.

*"Wait a minute. Just you wait a minute, Angel Boy. Why didn't you tell us all about this? Why go to all that trouble when a 30-minute preventative talk would have sorted this all out?"* huffed Harry, as she tried to wrestle Bub's wedding ring off and accidentally punched herself in the face. The little sucker was stuck tight.

*"Why indeed. You do not listen. Not one of you ever actually listens. You are so busy being 'individuals' that you do not fulfil any of your functions as lower-level demons."* Gab responded.

*"Lower-level demons?"* Harry quizzed and looked at the blank faces around the table. This was news to them all.

*"I knew it. I just knew it. Not one of you read the Job Description paperwork before signing it. Did you? Tell me that this incompetence is limited to Hell number one. Sir Mark and Sir Andrew, surely you knew that you were demons?"* Gab looked to the Knights for reassurance.

*"Well, not exactly. We thought we were 'set dressing' or sentient props. I always thought I was a rainbow. Demons? Who would have thought? Eh?"* Sir Mark said this through a mouthful of garibaldi biscuits and a slurp of builders' tea.

*"Stan, you do not have to stay for this. But it might be useful, as at least I know that you will repeat it until it might sink into their*

*thick skulls. Dippit, you do not have to stay either, but I know that Harry will tell you a distorted version anyway. So please stay. Right where do I begin...?"* Gab made a diamond shape with his fingers, placed them under his chin then took a breath.

# CHAPTER FIFTY-ONE

S till in the War Room...

Gab explained that no they were not just "*set dressing*" and yes, they were demons of Hell. All thirteen Hells had a set of twins, who ran that particular Hell. Plus, there were multiple demons working in a complex but unionised shift pattern who administered punishments and/or created the overall atmosphere of their Hell. Karen, Dr Riel, Sir Mark, and Sir Andrew were low level demons. They didn't inflict a great deal of the torture themselves, but they were quite ambivalent about it going on around them. They didn't see any real harm in the residents in Hell number one receiving their "*just desserts*".

As the Hells gradually ascended to Hell number thirteen this changed and the demons became increasingly vicious and influential. This change in demonic role reflected the previous horrors that their residents had plotted, participated in, or inflicted on others. The sins committed whilst the residents were Above equalled the level of malevolence of the demons. A carefully balanced cosmic weights and measures system. Even then there were some residents that had to be split so that their evil deeds could be justly punished in multiple Hells. The splitting had an added benefit as it also reduced the chance of mutiny or a general uprising.

Gab still wasn't sure how Eva was able to transfer so many of Hitler's slices into the one Hell. His current mission was to investigate that and put a containment plan in place. Gab was relieved that the evil, all knowing French Loaf was just an empty crust now: so hopefully that secret was lost for all of time.

The cursed apple pie was still out there, and Gab was dreading the day that it was found and eaten. He was in the process of setting up some detailed risk assessments for that very scenario. Curative custard appeared in a high proportion of the risk assessments.

Those higher-level demons actively executed the torture and punishments; they enjoyed it immensely. They also attempted to leave Hell to possess the living so that they could circumvent Free Will. They were the demons you normally hear about in books and see in movies. The unrepentant baddies of the Horror Channels.

*"But I'm 'the Beelzebub.' Everyone's heard of Beelzebub. I'm famous. I'm named in movies. I'm feared in books. I am an out and out baddie. Surely I must be further up the pecking order than that. Maybe I'm like Stan and just landed on the wrong bus."* Bub waited on the Angel reassuring him.

*"No, I am sorry for all the confusion. You are just plain old Bub. Or Bub Gertrude D'Evil, to be correct."* Gab patted Bub's arm as he gave him the bad news.

*"Gertrude? Gertrude?"* Harry laughed, then quickly cuddled Bub as she realised how devastated he was by the news. He didn't even raise a question after those home truths. This was not going well. Harry was beginning to feel that they would have been better off not knowing any of this. Ignorance is bliss and all that malarkey.

*"I know that you are disappointed and need time to digest all of the information you have received today. But you must take this on board. You have to change. You are all a liability. Talking of liabilities: you need to find out what is wrong with your Oracles and help them fix it. They are all over the place or to be correct...all over the time. This is essential to your future success and happiness. Plus, it would put you in G.O.D.'s good books. You haven't been on her nice list for quite some time."* With his parting warning Gab went to leave. Pleased he had unburdened himself. He was aware

that the team, that he normally sort of tolerated, had received a significant and unpleasant wake-up call.

*"Oh, not so fast Angel Boy. What am I? What is Dippit? We never signed anything. I would have definitely... or probably...or possibly read a Job Description. I am doing a management course, afterall. Plus, I know for a fact that Dippit would have enjoyed reading a contract. She's like that and always has been."* Harry pointed at Dippit and Dippit nodded in agreement.

*"You, Dippit, Willing and Fachance are the four Horsewomen of the Apocalypse."* Gab said this as if he was imparting new information.

*"We know that, duh. Go on. We need more to go on than that. You're obviously stalling. Spill, Angel Boy."* Harry rolled her hands to indicated that she wanted more details.

*"Well, much as it pains me to say."* Gab scratched the back of his neck, *"I am not entirely sure what you are. Some people say you are G.O.D.'s judgements. Harry, you are certainly judgemental enough. Bub, do not start with me. You know this to be entirely correct.*

*Some other people see you as the four elements. All I can say for certain is that you are not entirely human, and you do play a part in the Apocalypse. That is as much as I know. I am finished. Please talk amongst yourselves."* Gab rose and made to leave again.

*"Oh, that's disappointing. Are you sure? I was looking for more details. Dippit, Fachance, Willing and I have human mothers so what is or what was Roger?"* Harry put a restraining hand on Gab's arm.

*"Again, I do not know. He has been around for a great deal of time, but I cannot offer you more than that. Can I go now? I am rather busy. I have other people who need my help. People, who are more likely to listen and act on the excellent advice provided."* Gab tried to sidestep Harry and Bub.

*"Oh no, not so fast, did I say you could leave? Angel Boy. You have work to do here first. You are honour bound to help us out of the problems that you helped to create. Sit back down and you can listen for a change."* Harry was looking forward to passing

a particularly unpleasant task onto Gab's broad, and delicious shoulders.

# CHAPTER FIFTY-TWO

S till in the War Room…

*"Harry, I am not doing it. It is out with my duties and responsibilities. I fear that I do not have the necessary skill set."* Angel Gab was both assertive and slightly whiney. A strange and unpleasant sight.

*"Yes, you fudging well are and you do…Angel Boy."* Harry turned him around and put a tin of tuna in his backpack.

*"No, I do not. Much as you would like this to be the case; you are not the boss of me. I would also like you to desist from calling me 'Angel Boy.' I am a senior Angel and as such I work within the confines of my title and my station."* Gab responded, and tried to see what Harry was up to behind his back.

*"You are doing this and that's final."* Harry added two Mars Bars and Twix to the bag.

*"No, you will do it. I do not have to, and I do not wish to. You cannot make me. I am not Devil Keith."* Gab threw the bag to the floor and would have stomped on it, but the Mars Bars were the innocent party in all of this debacle. However, a Twix was inclined to be a wee touch devious as it could easily swap identities with its chocolate twin.

*"No, you're not Devil Keith but it's your mess. So, yes you are doing it."* Harry shoved the rucksack at Gab.

*"No, it is not. It is not my fault that you went to the wrong Hell…Ginger Girl."* Gab pushed it back.

*"Ginger Girl? Oh, the uptight Gab can be naughty and lose his itty, bitty cool. Oh, and I've been called worse. In fact, I was called worse than that only this morning. By my lovely Bub.*

*No, you have to tell Brownie Nelli that you are taking her kitty back. That's final. It's up to you to break her little heart. She may be just a low-level demon to you, but she loves that feline. We all think Periwinkle is a brute but he is saving Brownie Nelli from being eaten by the tigers and the mountain lions, so you will do this. We'll tell her you did it anyway and trust me: I will make you seem much more villainous if I tell her. In fact, don't do it. I will. I'll go talk with her now. So there."* Harry pulled the rucksack from Gab's arms and Gab pulled it back.

Gab left and two hours later returned. His torn-up combat gear would never see another day's action. Neither would his mangled and semi-digested boots. He was covered in deep scratches and tear stained, shredded clothing. Harry wasn't sure if the tears were Brownie Nelli's, Periwinkle's, or Gab's. However, she was sure that the copious amount of blood belonged to Gab.

*"How did it go?"* Harry innocently enquired.

*"Fmmmss."* Gab huffed.

*"What was that Angel Boy?"* Harry innocently enquired, again.

*"Ginger Girl. I said that I will retrieve him just before you leave to meet the King."* Gab went to the door.

*"Angel Boy, did I say you could leave? You still owe us a debt of honour."* Harry was beginning to really enjoy bossing the uptight Angel around. Devil Keith was currently off the hook and Harry presumed that he was probably endangering himself and others. However, these things sometimes just have to play out.

Harry invited Angel Boy...sorry the authors mean Gab, into the War Room.

# CHAPTER FIFTY-THREE

The strategy...

The teams and Angel Gab all agreed that King Adrian was up to no good and anyone who entered Hell number three was in serious danger. They also agreed that they absolutely had to get the imprisoned Knights out of the dungeon and back to safety. But they weren't going to add Sir Mark and Sir Andrew to the cells. Leaving Periwinkle with King Adrian was absolutely non-negotiable and Gab had the scars to prove it.

*"So Gab, do your flashing thingy and get the Knights outta the dungeons. We also want the Lance so that the King can't create any more portals into here. The Crabs need moving back to Hell number eight. So, chuck them back too. Off you go then. Choppy, choppy."* Devil Keith brushed his hands together and sat back in his chair, very pleased with his take charge attitude and superior planning skills. Plenty of time to get rid of the sour faced interlopers and still have time for a well-deserved nap. Gab was correct; Devil Keith hadn't listened to a word of warning and was still doing his own thing.

*"Devil Keith, I have said this twice already. As Harry is so keen to point out: I am honour bound to assist you. But I cannot just remove the Knights from the dungeon. King Adrian has used his time wisely and he has secured his borders. I cannot flash in or out of the castle. I have to walk back and forth to the woods before I can flash away. Also, it is extremely tiring to flash, so I cannot do that*

*multiple times in a row. With a fully grown adult I can possible flash once or twice at any one time. So basically, I can go in for a pint of ale and possibly do some reconnaissance but no more than that. He has also had his brother making 'counter-Stan tools.' There is no way I can rescue the Knights. One of you will have to go and negotiate surrender. You cannot win this fight. The King knows your strengths and weaknesses. He knows all of your players and he has more horns that you."* Gab couldn't believe that things could get any worse.

*"No way. Just no way. I'm prepared to go in there, but I'm not having the innocent Knights imprisoned and starved. That's what discussing terms or surrender means to that King. I caused the chaos by using the Drill and you caused the extra problems due to your loose lips. We're going in to talk and distract, but not to surrender.*

*Devil Keith, you look bored why don't you go and have a nap in Harry's room so that we can thrash this out?"* Bub was exasperated. They were being stalled in all directions. The team were acting like *"individuals"* and the whole mission was in jeopardy.

*"Okay, I need a little break from all of my marvellous thinking. While I'm gone, no stealing my splendid General's uniform. Wee Brownie Murphy and I have been working on it all day. I know exactly how many medals it has and how shiny the buttons are."* Harry was pleased and surprised that was all Devil Keith had been doing. The last unsupervised episode had resulted in the Stills incident and the one before had led to the Great Fire of London. Although it has to be said; the treacle scones were heartily delicious.

# CHAPTER FIFTY-FOUR

B ack in the War Room…

The teams felt that they couldn't create a viable plan until they had more information. Gab had previously popped over to Hell number three for a quick check-in. He had confirmed that the King was angry and sly, and all of the other things the Knights had accused him of being. A longer search was required so Gab immediately left and returned, ever so slightly tipsy, three hours later. He called a team meeting to de-brief. Sorry to disappoint you, Dippit, but Gab's keeping his boxers on. And you're a married woman!

Gab breaks some bad news…

Although despondent, the team agreed that the recognisance and meeting with the lovely Lady Waddell was worth all of the effort that Gab had exerted. And the beer he had liberally quaffed. The reason for the team's low mood was the discovery of the new *'anti-Stan'* measures that were pervasive and would be difficult to negotiate and defeat.

The anti-Stan measures…

Brian and the other royal Peacocks of Hell were being prescribed hormone replacement therapy patches. This was so they would never again be bothered with pesky male hormones and urges towards fascinator Peahens. Unfortunately for the Peacocks they were spending most of their day eating Mackie's tablet ice cream and chewing on slabs of chocolate fudge. As a consequence their feathers were getting mighty tight on them.

They were also prone to mood swings and had taken a liking to watching rom-coms on a continuous loop. So far, they had worn out five copies of the movie *"Love Story."* And they were currently, and quietly, campaigning for the actress Ali McGraw to become president. However, probably the most dramatic side effect of the patches was the Peacock's development of breasts. A singularly odd occurrence as they were, in no way at all, female or indeed mammals. Plus, the new balconette bras had put quite a dent in the King's tight budget so he couldn't afford a full moat refit.

The Peacocks might not be at full fighting fitness but equally they may actually be worse than usual: one word, hormones! Devil Keith, the sexist idiot, made the authors write this section.

The yodelling polar bears had been given plain earmuffs and a strict *"talking to."* Unfortunately, the *"talking to"* was after the bears applied the earmuffs so no-one was clear on how effective the chat had been. Their fainting couches had been confiscated and they were issued with uncomfortable, wooden upright chairs instead. Gab loved the new chairs. Also, they were all sent on mandatory, *"Unravelling Knitting"* courses and told to be especially wary of anyone who mentioned knit one, purl one, knit one, purl one.

The crocodiles were wearing anti-hypnosis contact lenses. They had tried reading glasses, but they felt that the spectacles didn't suit their face shape. Harry tried to avoid discussing the crocodiles as Bub still hadn't realised that he didn't have to drink the urine laced tea to talk with them. Evidently Hells, with two or more horns, had built in translators. She knew it would eventually click and Bub would be a little, tiny bit miffed at her.

Every demon in Hell number three had been issued with a face mask and small portable fan so that they could avoid or cope with the Deadly Sin juices and gases. Plus, everyone, but everyone, was forced to drink a small cup of triple espresso coffee every 30 minutes just in case they were infected by Sloth's wax and needed a nappy nap.

The services of Hell number eight had been retained so there was the added bonus of having to deal with the pair of Kalashnikov wielding, horrific Crabs. Oh joy! On a positive note, Melvin had been exchanged for the Crabs, so they didn't have both of the bothersome brothers to deal with.

The latest measure was a particularly sore one for our Harry. The King had enticed three Scottish female demons into his Hell. Their sole purpose was to de-sensitise the demons so that they would no longer be seduced by a Scottish accent and the sexy swearing.

The whole of Hell number three was a writhing mix of paranoia, smeared chocolate stains, sexual frustration, multiple toilet breaks, limited communication and hyped-up, star jumping level three demons.

All in all, the Hell number one team felt that they had been cleverly outmanoeuvred by the King and his devious brother.

# CHAPTER FIFTY-FIVE

S till in the War Room...

"So, what is King Adrian's weakness? Please don't say long toenails. Oh sorry, I forgot that Devil Keith had nipped out." Bub waited on a response.

"Vanity. I'm sure that I saw a flash of that particular Deadly Sin cross his gaunt face." Harry was positioned at her wipe clean board and was writing their plan around Devil Keith's murderous sketches.

"Then that is the basis of this course of action." Bub decisively stated.

Twenty minutes later...

The initial plan was discussed, adjusted, and then discussed again. Mainly so that Devil Keith could change into suitable footwear whilst listening to each part of the mission. He had previously commissioned specially designed listening shoes and was chuffed that he'd finally got to wear them.

"Right, we all know the plan." Bub clapped his hands together and reached for a much-needed Bakewell tart.

"How about the reader, shouldn't they be allowed to know what we're doing?" Harry enquired and took a bite out of Bub's tart.

"The reader, Harry? I think you mean the readerS. Plural. I'm sure that we will have a multitude of people wishing to read about me and my acts of extreme heroism. I am a Supreme Being, after all." Yes, Devil Keith had returned from his fourth nappy, nap, of the day. His new shoes clearly weren't working.

*"Ok, one last time,"* sighed Bub, and he put down his cake.

The plan...

The teams and Angel Gab had agreed on a two-pronged attack. To Harry's horror, Bub was going to meet with King Adrian. She protested that it was Devil Keith's responsibility as he was the eldest Devil. As soon as Harry suggested sending Devil Keith, she realised that she didn't want either of them to go. Neither of them to be hurt or captured. However, Bub was adamant. So, he was going with the Knights and Periwinkle to discuss tactics and *"play nice"* with King Adrian. Bub probably had the most difficult and dangerous role, although he felt that he would be sitting on the side-lines during most of the action.

Devil Keith, Harry, Karen, and Angel Gab were going in undercover as team two. They were going for another attempt at guerrilla warfare. However, they hoped that it would be more successful this time as they no longer had a stupid, misguided *"his butterflyness"* spy to contend with. This last sentence should be read in a sarcastic tone and, if at all possible, a Scottish accent.

After much debate they felt that their only means of subterfuge was as part of the evening entertainment. They reasoned that was a key part of the King's vanity and nothing, but nothing, would stop him indulging in a piece of theatre.

*"I am rather good at reciting Shakespeare. Yes, you can count me in. That will settle my debt of honour. Wipe my account quite clean."* Gab nodded and decided to grow out his leg hairs for the doublet and hose costume.

*"Not so fast Angel Boy. We need entertainment where we can all hide our identities, plus there is no way we can learn a Shakespearean play in less than four weeks. Think again."* Harry intervened in Gab's daydream.

*"Ahem. What about Stan and me? I noticed that you've totally missed us out of the entire mission."* Dippit cleared her throat. Preparing for a battle.

*"Dippit, you can't go. You've fainted six times since we started*

*this conversation. Stan needs to look after you, so he can't come either. We're going to leave Dr Riel here too. We thought that between the three of you, this Hell was in safe hands."* Bub had hoped that Stan had already told Dippit about this tricky issue.

*"Stan did you know about this? I'm not ill. I'm having a baby. They need us. They need intelligence and luck to pull this off. It's a suicide mission without us."* Dippit stamped her foot then flashed green and fainted again.

Stan did know about that part of the plan, and he totally supported it. He wasn't risking his Dippit. A fact that he had repeated, repeated, repeated, and repeated again. However, he did have a possible solution to their problem.

*"Dippit. Bub and I, we already discussed it. Discussed it and agreed. What about Liam and Patrick? I say, Liam and Patrick? They can help. I say, help. My little brothers. I say, little brothers."* Stan rubbed some warmth into Dippit's cold hands.

*"Two little four-year-old boys? Bub, you agreed to this? I'm not comfortable with that. It's not safe. We'd be better taking the Brownies rather than two wee human boys. At least the Brownies can bounce back...some quite literally."* Harry was shaking her head at the addition to the plan.

*"Harry, it's not really a risk. Those two are amazingly clever and they can make the most unusual things. They might make this less suicidal and more likely to succeed."* Bub had gone through the same worries until Stan assured him that the boys were their only solution. Stan's mammy had also supported the idea.

Back to the plan...

*"So, the entertainment?"* Sir Mark prompted.

*"A pantomime."* Sir Andrew said this round a mouthful of tofu and alfa alpha sprouts.

*"What?"* Harry questioned.

*"A pantomime. Sir Derek and Sir Ougie put one on last year. 'Cinderella.' It was a hoot. It held everyone's attention so if we do the same, then in theory, we would be able slip in and slip away*

*unscathed. It would be perfect. The characters dress up and wear heavy make-up. There are virtually no lines to learn. The ones you do need can either be learned or written on bits of paper and stuck to the props. If worse comes to the worse, you can just make up the lines. To be honest I think that's what they did last year. No two performances were ever remotely alike.*

*The costumes and stage sets are already there. Needs a little bit of alteration that's all. Devil Keith or Wee Brownie Murphy could do that for us. It's a perfect disguise."* Sir Andrew smiled tentatively and waited on the response to his idea.

Harry grabbed him and kissed him, *"you, Sir Andrew, are a fudging genius."*

*"You can easily smuggle weapons in via the costume trunks and you can smuggle the wee ones in that way too. Safely."* Sir Mark also, earned himself a kiss.

Bub also received a kiss because, well he is Bub Gertrude D'Evil.

# CHAPTER FIFTY-SIX

The War Room, about a week later...

"*No. I am not comfortable doing it and you cannot make me. I am not Devil Keith. I cannot be bullied. I am an Angel of the first water.*" Angel Gab shouted and stomped his foot.

"*Yes, you are and yes, I can bully you. Angel Boy.*" Harry shouted.

"*No. I'm not and you cannot. Ginger Girl.*" Angel Gab shouted back and slapped his hands against the tabletop.

"*Look Angel Boy, you are. And that's final.*" Harry shouted back and stuck her fingers in her ears.

A version of this conversation/argument had been happening for over a week now. They had all agreed to putting on the pantomime "*Cinderella,*" well Gab had his reservations and expressed them frequently. However, despite his misgivings he had collected the costumes from Lady Waddell's excellent Sign Language School. The fittings and assigning of roles had, and continued to, pose some challenges. Hence the aforementioned argument.

The roles...

It was agreed that Harry was going to be Cinderella. She initially objected as she didn't want to kiss Devil Keith. Even the thought of it was yucky. She had also said she couldn't sing well enough to carry off the part. She expected everyone to rally around and contradict her. There was silence until Devil Keith helpfully pointed out it never usually stopped her singing.

Actually, her singing talent was frequently used to clear the pubs at closing time. Devil Keith was, purely accidentally, punched in the throat. Repeatedly.

Devil Keith was delighted to be Prince Charming as he felt he had been born to play that part and he frequently referred to himself as charming, so he reckoned that it was merely the pinnacle of method acting. Although he categorically refused to kiss Cinderella Harry. He thought she was gross and had wanted either Nora or Karen to play the part. Harry was most relieved about the avoidance of the revolting kiss, but try as she might Karen refused to be cast as Cinderella. Karen requested the part of the Wicked Stepmother. She so wanted to be a baddie for a change. A true fiend: as befitted a demon of her stature. She kept practicing her surprisingly good, evil laugh and pretended to stroke a pussy.

The two ugly stepsisters, Anastasia and Drizella, were going to be played by the Knight triplets or the triplet Knights. No one was sure what to call them. Sir Mark assured them that the boys had been the understudies the previous year, so they knew their parts well. Plus, they were a major distraction when walking never mind when they were decked out in corsets, stockings, garters, ribbons, and ruffles. Gab had sneaked back into the castle the day before and the boys had agreed to help with the plan.

That left the role of the Faery Godmother for Angel Gab. He was not pleased as it was an undignified role and he argued that it wouldn't meet his particular skill set. He frequently tried to get Devil Keith to swap parts with him. Devil Keith said he would swap, but only if Gab gifted him with one of his wings. Devil Keith wanted to add the Angel wing to a pale blue bowler hat. Devil Keith felt that the hat needed a dignified boost. Gab promptly left to evaluate his options (AKA in the huff), but he quickly realised that his fate was sealed. He was the Faery Godmother, and his seldom used wings would be useful in that role. The wings just needed a small darn as Gab had caught them on a rusty nail that was protruding from the oak bar in his favourite Medieval Inn. He was not drinking a double gin and tonic, and eating a family sized bag of cheesy Whotsits at the time. No way. He was also not hiding from Ginger Girl at the time. No way.

Plus the wings needed a good airing and iron beforehand so they'd be no use to Devil Keith. Bub thought it was hilarious, and said that it was just what Gab needed to develop a bit of flexibility and release his true inner child. Angel Gab may have tripped up Bub and blamed his boisterous wings.

Devil Keith had been releasing his inner child and was delighted with the results. His and Wee Brownie Murphy's complex brief was to produce outfits that:

- were embellished enough to captivate the audience and hold their attention. No matter how badly the play was going. They also had to hide the fact that the costumes had been previously used. This was in case King Adrian linked them with Lady Waddell and her lucrative self-storage business. They didn't want to risk her as she had been a true ally, and she had promised them unlimited raspberry jam sandwiches between acts.

- were light enough so that everyone could run. When required.

- were loose enough that everyone could fight. When required.

- were wide enough and had multiple pockets to hide all necessary items such as weapons and pies. When required.

Devil Keith produced clothing that he was sure would strike wonder into the heart of the masses for years to come. He was right and they did strike the masses. Harry was speechless and couldn't stop patting Devil Keith on the back and smiling.

The boy did good.

# CHAPTER FIFTY-SEVEN

The four weeks were up and the UK did, indeed, get nil points…

The team looked at their paltry stack of weapons. Swords, clubs, baseball bats and machetes rested beside the two packets of Fornication and Greed. Angel Gab steadfastly refused to give them any more packets just in case they did a *"Devil Keith"* and completely destroyed Hell number three. They still had access to Sloth's wax, but they feared that it was now ineffectual due to the demon's frequent caffeine shots. They had their utility belts and Harry was trying to cheer up the team by teaching the cheeky wee belts some new tricks.

Stan had spoken with his little brothers and explained the adversary they faced. Liam and Patrick weren't fazed by it and stuck their totty heads together in order to come up with some solutions. The boys had created a few possible items of protection but they point blank refused to hand them over to Stan. They had correctly guessed that Stan would refuse to allow them to go if he had their inventions. The authors did say that the boys were clever.

*"Any last-minute suggestions?"* Harry looked hopeful.

*"Have you tried finding Willing? She is the Horsewoman of War so she would be a real asset and she could take my place as the Faery Godmother."* Angel Gab also looked hopeful.

*"Nope. No luck with finding Willing. Fachance is missing too.*

*I'm getting really worried about them. They've been missing for ages. I even asked Stan to try to locate them, but he wasn't successful. A rarity in itself. Oh yeah nice try, Angel Boy. I heard you learning your lines. You're just pretending to hate your part. I heard you giving it a bit of gusto last night."* Harry gave Angel Boy a nudge and a wink.

*"I can assure you that I was only looking out for the mission. I have been learning my lines. Not because I want to act, but because it is key to the overall success of the search and rescue. No more, no less. I am dedicated and I have impeccable discipline."* Gab assertively stated.

*"Except when there's beer around."* Harry gave him another nudge and grinned.

*"Humm. Yes Ginger Girl, it appears so."* Gab ruefully answered.

*"Can you ask G.O.D. to help? That would be brilliant."* Harry enquired and crossed her fingers.

*"No Harry, I would rather that we kept her out of this, and it is highly unlikely that she would wish to interfere in inter-Hell politics. We have to go with what we currently have planned."* Angel Gab went off to do some packing.

What they have planned....

They agreed that on the night of the prison break Mr Hamhands would give the dungeon key to the first member of the team he encountered. Lady Waddell said that he was concerned that he would be caught with the key, so he was going to delay collecting it from the cooks for as long as possible. The locks were changed regularly so pre-dropping the key at Lady Waddell's school was not an option. Also, the key was likely to be food related and by all accounts Mr Hamhands is a comfort eater so he may very well eat it by mistake. Hence the need for a delayed pick up and a quick handover to the team.

Angel Gab, as the Faery Godmother, would provide a long introduction to the pantomime then leave the stage. Gab and one of the twins, probably Patrick, would then go to the dungeons and use the key to free the Knights. The skirts of Gab's costume had large pockets so that he could store, then provide costumes for the freed Knights. Once disguised, the Knights, Angel Gab and little Patrick would go to the woods. If challenged, Gab could make the excuse that he'd forgotten a prop. Gab would then flash as many of the Knights away as possible. The rest would make their way to the boundary between Hell two and Hell three where they would use the Drill. If they ran into problems, then Patrick would have a means of neutralising the Crabs. The twins still wouldn't say what it was. They all hoped that Patrick would hand over the device before they entered the woods so that he could be flashed out of danger first. Gab would then return to the castle so he could continue his Faery Godmother role.

Whilst Gab did his long introduction Harry would take Liam and find the Dimensional Lance. As she was playing the part of Cinderella she'd be dressed to look like a palace maid so she shouldn't be challenged. The twins were going to wear rat onesies so that they could store additional provisions in their pockets and again, they had the means of neutralising any curious Crabs. Harry would use the Lance to send little Liam back to Hell number one. Harry refused to go with Liam as she wanted to make sure the rest of the teams got away first.

Karen, playing the part of the Wicked Stepmother, and the triplets had the most difficult roles. They took the stage directly after Gab's lengthy monologue. They needed to keep the crowd entertained until Gab and Harry returned from their respective missions. Devil Keith had an essential role as the look out. Bub wasn't clear what Devil Keith was to look for, but Devil Keith was assured that it was essential.

Bub had to keep his eye on Periwinkle so that they could get the cat back to Brownie Nelli. He hoped that Periwinkle would chase one of the twins whilst they were wearing their rat onesie, as that would get the cat backstage and he'd hopefully stay there until rescued. Bub also had to keep King Adrian distracted as the team weren't entirely convinced that the pantomime could adequately do that.

That left Bub, Gab, Karen, Harry, Devil Keith, and Periwinkle in the Banqueting Hall at the end of the night. Gab broke the bad news that he probably would have used up all of his flashing abilities by then. Their plan from that point was vague as it hinged on Harry retrieving the Dimensional Lance, them getting out of the castle and then having the time to use the Lance or the Drill to escape via a portal. Having both the Lance and the Drill would give them two portals, so that would double their escape potential.

*"Right then. Stan, can you collect your brothers? Gab, can you go fight with a cat and an angry Brownie? We're leaving."* Bub was anxious but the four weeks were up. They literally had to face their demons.

# CHAPTER FIFTY-EIGHT

I n the War room…

"*Harry, I want to go. Sitting waiting… no that's not for me. You know it's not. It's gonna be more stressful for me… just waiting and getting fat. So much worse. I won't rest, and you can't make me. I'll get into more trouble here. I promise. I really will. You can bet on it. Please let me go.*" Dippit whinged.

"*Dippit, I can't risk you. I love you and I want to keep you safe. We can't find Will and Fachance. And that's got me up to high dough. I'm not risking another sister, so I'm not letting you come with us. So, give us a hug and eat some more toast with marmite. This is it… we're going. You're staying. Please, no more arguing.*" Harry hugged the distraught Dippit and pushed her into Stan's arms, "*take good care of her. She's precious.*"

Bub hugged Harry, picked up his rucksack and placed the InterDimensional Drill against the wall. The portal appeared and the two teams entered Hell number three. Once in the Hell Bub quietly passed the Drill to Karen and winked. Bub had made Karen promise that no matter what happened to him they were to get back home. Get his Harry home.

Alpha team consisted of Bub, the Knights, and a mightily disgruntled Periwinkle. Beta team consisted of Angel Gab, Harry, Devil Keith, and Karen. Bub's team deliberately made their presence known so that the Beta team could sneak by and hide until the coast was clear. Lady Waddell had offered to hide Beta team at her school as she was thoroughly fed up with the King attacking the minor demons and removing their tongues.

Afterall, she **did** only have two hands and a limited supply of ruby red lipstick.

*"Ahhh, Dear Hearts. You received my tiny invitation and decided to visit little old me, haw, haw, haw. It was so delightful having my Dimensional Lance back in its rightful hands. It opened up so many evil possibilities. Did you like the Crabs and their little wedding crash? I didn't know what to get you. Ohh, so wonderful to see my naughty Knights and my majestic cat again. Haw, haw, haw."* Bub was correct to be cautious. The King was waiting on them, but luckily he hadn't noticed or had the opportunity to stop the other team. King Adrian's vanity was truly astonishing. Apparently, the King viewed himself as invincible so he hadn't planned for a Hell number one covert mission. He just presumed that Bub would bend to his will and silently surrender.

*"Yes, well I thought I'd better. Did you know that the Crabs stubbed out their cigars in my wedding cake?"* Bub was furious with the conceited clown.

*"Ah, yes. A minor communication issue, Dear Hearts. All sorted out now. Let's hurry. One has such a delightfully fun evening planned. Tally ho my walking luggage. Haw, haw, haw."* The King giggled behind his feathers hat and was hoisted onto his docile crocodile.

Team Alpha mounted their huge crocodiles and rode off to the castle. Harry and her team did not envy them their mounts and their evening of *"fun."* She would rather risk the forest, so with that thought the team turned and viewed the long trek ahead.

*"Well people, let's shake a tail feather,"* she quietly encouraged them.

Team Alpha

King Adrian went to great pains to point out all of the upgrades in Hell number three. During the journey he frequently told Bub how grateful he was for the opportunity to test his skills against Bub's mediocre Hell. He made wild promises and bets that no other Hell could meet his high standards. Bub was more bored than impressed, but he allowed King Adrian to witter on in case he could glean more useful information. They still hadn't finalised the full escape plan.

Na hour later...

King Adrian had lied. There was no entertainment or dinner organised for that evening. King Adrian felt that they would need their beauty sleep following their long journey. Bub tried to tell him that it was a relatively short journey, but King Adrian rudely talked over and around him. Bub let him have his way. He had expected this type of underhanded tactic and had previously filled his pockets with snacks and treats, plus tins of cat food. Bub wasn't risking Periwinkle becoming hungry then hangry. No siree. The sweets and cat food were ignored but, as expected, his weapons had been quickly removed. This *"decluttering of naughty weapons"*, was accompanied by a great deal of head shaking, finger waving, sighing and tisking from the well-fed guards. The King had realised that he had to bribe some of his demons with food in order to keep the peace.

Brian, the disgraced Peacock, made a desperate play for Bub's chocolate buttons but he was told off by one of the portly guards. Brian went off down the corridor: sobbing and muttering about his sensitive nipples and swollen belly. The Peacock was still adjusting to the hormone replacement treatment and Bub was glad of that reprieve.

Sir Andrew and Sir Mark were led away on the pretence of having to change into more suitable armour. Bub noticed that the route the Knights took would take them directly to the deepest dungeons. However, there was nothing any of them could do about that now. Bub reluctantly retired to his bedroom with Periwinkle and readied for bed. It was then that he realised that his room was directly adjacent to the entertaining gargoyles. Bub groaned as he realised that *"beauty sleep"* was also off the menu. He sent a virtual hug to his Harry, and hunkered down for a long, cold night of terrible entertainment. The King was trying to break his spirit and break him.

Team Beta

Harry, Gab, Devil Keith, and Karen slid and sloshed through Hell number three. Carefully avoiding the rusting bear traps, dank marshes, quicksand pits and rushing rivers. Deep in thought, they contemplated the plan and how they could possibly deal with any unforeseen circumstances. They we soaked through, but realised that they were probably having an easier time than the other team. Following Gab, they quickly found Lady Waddell's Sign Language School and self-storage business. It was tucked in just below the west wall of the castle.

They were warmly greeted by an attractive silver haired lady who had sparkling blue eyes, was wearing ruby red lipstick and sported a wicked, infectious grin.

*"I'm Lady Waddell, at your service. But we don't stand on ceremony here. Come on in. Come in. My you're like drowned rats. Here's some warm towels to try yourself with. Let me take your coats and get you something warm in your bellies."* Lady Waddell said all of this whilst collecting their wet coats, putting on a pot of vegetable soup, slicing cheese, peeling an apple, reapplying her bright red lipstick, and producing a running commentary in perfectly executed sign language. *"Wow, now there's a lady who knows how to multi-task,"* thought Harry, as she was roughly bundled into a cosy towel.

They sat down to eat a hot meal and Lady Waddell explained that she had booked them into the following night's entertainment programme. The twins were currently having a much-needed nap as they had been playing with Glen and Warren, her grandsons, all day. Angel Gab thought it best that the wee lads were flashed into Hell number three slightly earlier in the day. The costumes were already aired, ironed and on padded clothes hangers. Gab had dropped the adjusted outfits off earlier that day too. *"Yep, multi-tasking and anally retentive, glad she's on our side,*" thought Harry.

They all bedded down, and Harry sent Bub a virtual hug... and a quick grope.

# CHAPTER FIFTY-NINE

T he castle in Hell number three...

Bub was exceedingly grumpy. He missed his Harry. Plus, there was no decent food, not a moment of peace, and a lumpy bed to boot. He wished someone would buy Kerri a fudging cat and arrange an intervention order for her. That gal sure could drink. And giggle. And fall off castle walls. Lum M., Pip and M'Key could also use some new material and a swift skelp around the head. This was not at all like his last luxurious visit to Hell number three. He felt that he'd best not complain as he did still have a very small double chin. No matter what light he was in.

Bub hadn't been able to sleep so he'd spent much of the night talking to Periwinkle. Explaining why he loved Harry and what he wanted for their future. Bub was convinced that Periwinkle could understand him but then he dismissed that notion as he hadn't consumed the special, urine infused tea. Periwinkle thought Bub should *"man up"* and give it a rest, but the cat did so like the salmon roulade that Bub had packed for him, so he sort of patiently listened. He'd let Bub twitter on like an idiot as he ate the salmon and chewed through the eight pounds of freeze-dried spaghetti bolognaise. Then he'd settled down for a fart laden sleep.

Bub's morning consisted of no breakfast and yet more of King Adrian's boasting and veiled threats. Bub tried to discuss the terms of the treaty, but King Adrian stated that he preferred to talk on a full stomach. At that Bub gave up and let his mind drift.

"*Oh, I say Dear Hearts. Have you met Mr Hamhands? A cheery wee chappie. Not too bright I'm afraid. Haw, haw, haw.*" King Adrian shoved the man-table at Bub. The King then brutally kicked Mr Hamhands to the ground. Bub picked up Mr Hamhands and helped to brush him down. Bub felt something solid pressed into the palm of his hand. As predicted, the cook had used hardened pastry to copy the dungeon key. Sir Andrew and Lady Waddell had assured Bub, that despite being anxious, Mr Hamhands would help them. Bub was relieved that the first part of their plan was now in place, and he pocketed the precious key.

"*Ten hours until dinner, Dear Hearts. My loyal and un-bribeable Knight will keep you amused, haw, haw, haw.*" The King was replaced by an equally repulsive and boastful prison guard.

Beta team...

Harry and her team. Ok, stop huffing you silly cookie-bun. Devil Keith and his team were well rested and full of delicious, homemade strawberry pancakes. Harry hoped that Bub was safe, comfortable, and remained free from the dungeon. She wasn't convinced that King Adrian would honour any of his promises. She kept that fear to herself, but her anxiety was noted by the full team.

"*Off to the castle for an adventure.*" Harry said and crossed her fingers under the laden table.

# CHAPTER SIXTY

B eta team are at the castle...

Later that day and Harry and Devil Keith's team arrived at the castle's moat. They were wearing their bulky costumes, in full stage make-up and carrying a set of large trunks and wicker baskets. Lady Waddell had arranged to have the scenery delivered and installed earlier in the day. Yep, anally attentive and a wee bit wonderful to boot.

After a perfunctory search, the team crossed into the castle and were taken to the Banqueting Hall. Karen had heard about the castle, but nothing could prepare her for the vanity of the King. She felt that he needed a more productive hobby than modelling and he urgently needed some curtains. Lots of thick curtains... and some y-fronts would be good too.

The start of the night's entertainment...

Bub had learned from Harry's visit to Hell number three so when the food touched the Banqueting table, he touched the food. Wow, did he touch that food. It went everywhere; across the table, all over the floor, up the walls and through his hair. Chest and head. Two largish rats raced out and picked up his leftovers. They also picked up the pastry key and they were chased away by the plump Periwinkle. "*So far so good,*" thought the delighted, but nervous Bub.

Harry looked through the thick stage curtains. Bub looked fantastic in his black tuxedo, gleaming white shirt, and stolen black cufflinks. Devil Keith really was a marvel with pins and needles. She was relieved that Bub was on show in the audience, and not in a dank prison cell.

Cue lights…

As soon as the lights dimmed Harry and Liam left to find the Dimensional Lance. As Liam passed Mr Hamhands, he took one of Mr Hamhands' large hands and gently pulled. Mr Hamhands happily left the boisterous hall and the random kicks he frequently received.

*"Oh, Mr Hamhands. It's lovely to see you again. I didn't expect you to come with us."* Harry was surprised to see the little man-table as she thought he had already played his part in their plan.

*"I think he's so sad. They were being mean to him. Harry, can he come with us?"* Liam shyly asked and tucked his other hand into Harry's.

*"Of course, Liam. Mr Hamhands, if you want to come you're most welcome. We're looking for the Dimensional Lance. Any ideas where it could be?"* Harry gently coaxed the bullied wee guy.

Angel Gab had given them rough directions but if Mr Hamhands helped them they would be quicker, and time was crucial to their plan. Mr Hamhands smiled, nodded, and pointed to the right hand corridor. After checking a few doors and with Mr Hamhands help they found the room containing the Lance. It was on a pedestal in the middle of the room: locked in large crystal box. The lock was full of whirring gears and howled when anyone went near it.

The small team weren't prepared for the lock and the safeguards, but they tried anyway. It was a long and noisy twenty minutes, to be sure.

*"I'm sorry Harry, I can't get near it. I can't open that. We have to leave it."* Liam whispered, whilst wiping away a tear drop. He was so looking forward to the adventure and it was all going wrong.

*"That's all right, honey. Getting the Lance was important but not as important as you and Patrick making a device to deal with the*

cruel Crabs. You've done so well, wee one. Don't be upset. We'll sort all this later. We need to go back to the play. Remember, Bub has the Drill. We just need to adjust our plan a little." Harry dried his tears with the end of her ragged, soot-stained dress.

"What about Mr Hamhands. Do you have a key, sir?" said the little voice.

Mr Hamhands made some hand signals, but Harry and Liam couldn't understand him. He stamped his disproportionately large foot. Harry just noticed that his other foot was disproportionately petite. Harry and little Liam turned back to the door and made to leave the room.

"Sorry little Liam. Lady Harry, I don't have a key..." the crystal box exploded and the cogs went flying through the air. Mr Hamhands had the most piercing, high pitched squeak that Harry and Liam had ever heard.

A cowering Liam and Harry took a few steps back. Liam covered his ringing ears and Harry rapidly grabbed the Dimensional Lance. Harry had made such a quick recovery as she was used to blocking out Devil Keith's incessant screams and whines and wailing.

"Time to send you home, ma wee one," whispered Harry as she pressed the Lance against the wall and dialled up the correct Hell. Liam handed over a small bundle, then stepped through into Hell number one. He felt he had enough adventures for just now and wanted his mammy. Being brave was scary.

Mr Hamhands stopped Harry and pointed at the portal. "Do you want to go too?"

Mr Hamhands vigorously nodded, and then he too stepped through the portal.

Harry jubilantly rushed back to the Banqueting Hall with the Lance in her apron pocket.

# CHAPTER SIXTY-ONE

The pantomime begins...

A bright white spotlight picked out a slightly anxious Angel Gab. He was wearing a stunning silver dress adorned with clear crystals and dripping with pale blue feathers. His real wings had been heavily disguised with glued-on, paper feathers and they were draped in yards of silver tinsel.

He had been convinced to grow out his black wavy hair so it was artfully piled on his head; secured with glittering clips, a jewelled tiara and a full can of sparkly hairspray.

Gab's make-up was thickly applied but he was looking surprisingly attractive. All in all, he made a truly beautiful Faery. He took a steadying breath...

*"Ahem. Once upon a time. In a kingdom far, far away there lived a poor servant girl with her wicked Stepmother and two ugly stepsisters. The poor servant should have had a life of luxury and love but..."*

*"Oh, Dear Hearts. Bub, what a lovely bit of totty. Don't you agree? Rosie, the chamber maid, can have the night off. That Faery, she's the one for me. I'll be unwrapping that tinsel tonight whether she wants it or not. Although, why wouldn't she? Haw, haw, haw."* King Adrian arrogantly strutted onto the stage and roughly grabbed Gab by the arm. He began dragging the extremely reluctant Faery towards his golden monstrosity of a throne.

*"King Adrian, I don't think she's too keen on being pulled along. She's just here to do a job. She'll likely get in trouble if she doesn't finish her set, and it'll knock off the rest of the play. Ruin*

*everyone's night."* Bub was trying to reason with the King, but he was being completely ignored. Without Gab's long introductory monologue, how were they going to be able to give Harry enough time to find the Lance then return to the Banqueting Hall for her cue?

*"Oh, it won't ruin my night. Not at all, haw, haw, haw. Come here you gorgeous shiny creature. Don't be shy, Dear Hearts. Oops, you are a big, big girl. These wings are amazing. So realistic and so utterly, delightfully useful. We can hide behind them whilst we become better acquainted. Haw, haw, haw."* King Adrian pulled the scrambling Gab onto his scrawny knees and tried to steal a kiss. There was an ominous crack then a brittle crunch, but King Adrian appeared oblivious to his fractured, porous thigh bones.

*"Sire, I am in the middle of a performance. I can't just leave the stage. No matter how attractive and powerful you are. No matter how honoured I am to be selected by such a dazzling gentleman. You are a gentleman after all? Can you please let me finish? I don't want to disappoint the audience."* Gab was trying to look coy and engaging whilst edging away from the King's roaming hands. A complex and uncomfortable process.

*"Dear Hearts. Nonsense. Don't you worry that empty little head of yours. Haw, haw, haw. I'll happily share you with the audience when I'm done with you. They're used to my damaged scraps. Haw, haw, haw."* King Adrian had taken to leering down Gab's padded cleavage and putting his bony hand on Gab's knee. Then Gab's knee, then up his clenched thighs.

Gab began fussing with his gown, in order to access the hidden pockets sewn into his wide skirt. He knew he couldn't get away from the King and his invasive hands, but he also knew the rest of the plan had to go ahead. He managed to pull out the Knight's disguises and began shoving then into Bub's hands. Bub kicked the clothing under the table and into the waiting hands of a larger than average rat.

*"Oh, Dear Hearts, you are keen. I thought you were shy and would put up more of a fight. I so enjoy it when they fight. And*

*cry. And vomit. Wait, we'll rip that all off later. I don't want to share you, not just yet, haw, haw, haw. Wait until my brother sees you. He won't want Rosie either. Bub, I'm sure you too would like to become acquainted with this ravishing beauty. You can wait your turn though, Dear Hearts. I don't recall your bilious wife Harry being quite so fair of face so this will be a rare treat for you. Oops. Haw, haw, haw.*" The King pulled the wriggling Faery firmly into his arms and leaned in for a wet, sloppy kiss.

Bub was seething, but he was powerless to stop the lecherous pig. If it had been his Harry in the King's lap, then the King would have been wearing his own rib cage as a hat by now.

How were they going to release the trapped Knights? The plan was rapidly unravelling...

# CHAPTER SIXTY-TWO

S till in the Banqueting Hall...

A concerned Karen was looking out through the stage curtains onto an empty stage. They had timed Gab's essential and long introduction so that Harry had time to search for the Lance then return for her act. Then Cinderella and Prince Charming's cliched performance would allow Gab enough time to get to the dungeons and release the Knights. Karen as the Wicked Stepmother and the triplets weren't due to appear on the stage for at least another twenty minutes. However, the audience were getting restless as there was no pantomime happening and the King was keeping Gab all for himself. She caught Bub's pained look and decided it was time for a change of plan.

*"Devil Keith, no need for a look-out any longer. You've done a stellar job. You've been promoted, so you're now on dungeon duty. Patrick, honey, did you get all the disguises from the Faery?"* Karen smiled and hoped Keith bought her lie.

*"Yes,"* said the little curly mopped boy. Peering up at Karen, who looked like a spectacular baddie. Patrick's eyes were like saucers as he pulled out the disguises and handed them over.

*"Right Patrick, this is your bit of the plan. Gab's busy so you're in charge. Now, can you take care of Devil Keith for me? You and Devil Keith are heading to the dungeon to get the Knights. Take Periwinkle with you. Now both of you get in the wicker basket. No Devil Keith, not you. You stay out of the basket.*

*Devil Keith, off to the dungeon with you and don't forget the disguises. The show must go on, or at least until Harry gets back.*

*Patrick, don't forget to take whatever it is you made to deal with the Crabs with you. Good luck sweetie."* Karen patted his cute curls and helped him into the container.

Devil Keith slipped out of the hall carrying a very heavy wicker basket in his straining arms. He took two laboured steps when he was stopped by a pair of slightly tipsy Knights.

*"What you up to? Skulking about the corridors? Up to no good, are you? We should search you. What have you got in the basket? Got any food? We're starving,"* said the swaying Knight. Trying to focus and failing miserably.

*"Just a cat and a rat. Taking them to the dungeon, where they belong,"* Devil Keith gulped and reached for the baseball bat hidden in his Prince Charming armour.

*"Gives a look then. We're so bored and could do with a wee daunder to the dungeons. Have a look at those traitorous Knights and laugh at them."* The Knights pulled the lid from the basket and quickly stepped away. All signs of alcohol wiped from their sodden system.

*"It's Periwinkle. Eh, sorry we didn't mean to disturb you, Royal Favourite. Go right ahead and eat the rat. Not that you need our permission. Please eat anything you wish, but hopefully not us. Oh, majestic cat. Please, take a flagon or two of wine. I'll just carefully slide them into your basket. There you go. That rat looks a bit tough. The wine will help it go down a treat."* The Knights carefully added the wine to the basket, avoiding any possible contact with teeth or claws. They were bowing and scraping as they scurried away from the ferocious cat.

Devil Keith also investigated the basket and realised that Periwinkle had Patrick's tail and hind leg in his rather guilty looking mouth.

*"Please don't eat him, we need him. Brownie Nelli might like to play with him. Remember Brownie Nelli? Brownie Nelli loves you so much. Plus, Stan and Dippit will kill me if I bring Patrick back with bits and pieces missing,"* Devil Keith pleaded, but made no

attempt to put his hand near the cat. Periwinkle spat Patrick out and began grooming his rather large ears. The cat was willing to bide his time until he could warm up some milk chocolate. Rats were so much better with a touch of chocolate and smattering of strychnine smeared on them.

A long trek later...

Devil Keith dragged the heavy basket the last few steps to the rotten cell door. This was no luxurious prison cell this time. He used the pastry key to open the door and he was shocked by the sight that met his eyes. Sir Andrew and Sir Mark were covered in raw cigar burns and they had a multitude of new bruises covering their bodies. Their lips were burst open and roughly torn. Sir Mark was holding his side and gasping for breath as he nursed several broken ribs and a collapsed lung. Sir Andrew was chained to the slime encrusted wall and was trying to push his humerus back into its socket. The remaining Knights were painfully thin, filthy, and covered in weeping dove bites. They looked over at the open cell door and cowered away from Devil Keith. They were covering their shorn heads and moaning pleas for mercy.

In the corner of the rancid cell two small mounds were covered in patched woollen blankets. There were no movements, only gut-wrenching smells emitting from the pitiful heaps.

"It's Devil Keith. I'm here to set you free." Devil Keith gently whispered. He slowly entered the cell with his hands raised in front of him. He quietly squatted down beside the two flea infested blankets. "I'm here to rescue the Knights. If you're able, you can come too."

A small, husk like hand pushed away the thin blanket. Devil Keith fell backwards onto his bottom. Willing and Fachance, Harry's sisters, were hunched under the course covers. They were dirty, bruised and covered in itchy red flea bites. Their skin was stretched over their bones and their lips were dry and cracked. They had been starved and severely beaten. Fachance appeared to have some important pieces missing.

*"That fucking King has gone too far. Harry will kill him for sure. Then I'll kill him. Then Bub will kill him, and Harry will kill him again. Just to make sure. What happened? How long have you been here? Sorry for the swearing. You're safe now."* Devil Keith ended his rant with a whisper and an awkward pat. It was difficult finding any part of the sisters that would be able to cope with the gentlest of physical contact.

*"Devil Keith, just get us out. Then we can explain."* Willing quietly rasped then coughed. She was using the last of her limited energy to lift her head and attempt a weak smile. Fachance was utterly silent. Devil Keith had never witnessed her in that state and it frightened him. A lot.

Devil Keith and wee Patrick shared out the peasant disguises and carefully helped the beaten prisoners to change their clothing. Even getting them out of the cell was an ordeal as each movement brought forth hisses of fresh pain. They then had a long and difficult walk ahead of them. Devil Keith decided that if he could get them a few yards into the forest he would have to risk using the Drill against a tree. It was just pure luck that Karen had left the Drill just lying around in that impenetrable locked box. Luckier still that Devil Keith had decided to use the box to stand on so that he could be the best lookout ever. Luckier, luckier still that Devil Keith repeatedly ate all of Harry's groceries and plumped up ever so slightly. And lastly, that he had conveniently fell through the locked box and located the Drill. Devil Keith then stole the Drill as he fancied re-visiting Hell eight so that he could have a go on the mysterious Dodgems.

Back to the Knights plight...

After a few minutes it became clear that they couldn't walk through dungeons then the castle and the forest. They could barely walk at all. Plus, Devil Keith had to get back to the pantomime before he was missed. Karen had made him repeat that, as if a Supreme Being would forget such an insignificant instruction. *"Now what was it she said?"* Thought, Devil Keith.

The plan was dissolving before their very eyes, thought a sad wee Patrick. His wispy curls drooping into his big brown eyes.

# CHAPTER SIXTY-
# THREE

T he Banqueting Hall and a surprisingly happy audience...
Karen and the triplets had stepped into the vacuum
caused by the lack of Gab and his speech. They had been
on the stage for a full twenty minutes. Bub couldn't believe how
well they were doing. The King and the audience were transfixed
by their unusual performance. Karen had delivered all of her
lines perfectly and the audience fervently joined in with loud
boos, shouts, and hissing. Her laugh was truly evil and set the
tone for an excellent play. Unfortunately, with all possible lines
used up Karen had realised that they still needed to spin out
their act until Harry and Devil Keith reappeared. In response to
the problem she had started to tap dance across the wide stage.
She was surprisingly nimble and very flexible. Bub was seriously
impressed.

Sir Muckle, Sir Alan and Sir Fergus were behaving
themselves, at the moment. There had been a couple of sticky
moments when they were enthusiastically playing the spoons,
but Karen stared them into submission.

Despite the King being entertained by the play, Gab
continued to have to fight off the King's hands. and his other
scrawny, hairy bits. It was exhausting, frustrating and Gab was
rapidly losing his legendary cool. Gab had a slight respite when
the King called for Sir Spaghetti De Legs to aid him.

Sir Spaghetti De Legs reluctantly and unsteadily walked

across to the giggling King. The King leaned over the side of his throne, and using a hatchet he calmly hacked through the Knight's lengthy right thigh, from buttock to knee. The King then viciously yanked out Sir Spaghetti's warm femur. The King made a dainty slice in his own withered thigh, dusted out some thin bone fragments and pushed in the Knight's new bone.

"*Ah, a fresh leg bone, Dear Hearts. A little burst of calcium for little old me. How delightful. Sir Spaghetti Legs I will shortly be requiring your left femur and possibly a tibia or two. It all depends on how feisty this hefty handful is. Wait here until I call for you. Haw, haw, haw.*" The ruptured Knight slid down the side of the throne and bled over the marble floor. No one raised an eyebrow, so Bub knew that this was an all-too-common occurrence in Hell number three.

Bub looked up and realised that Karen was fast running out of steam, but there was still no sign of Harry or Devil Keith. Bub was about to propose a toast to the King when Karen slyly tripped up an innocent Sir Muckle of Nursingerton. Down the triplets clattered; a fleshy confusion of gangly limbs and rampant testosterone.

The fighting started as soon as the bamboozled Knights hit the stage floor. Sir Fergus of D'Fries stuck a concealed spoon into Sir Alan de Aloha's left eyeball. Sir Muckle of Nursingerton rabidly bit the tip off Sir Fergus's pinkie finger then made a show of spitting it out onto the stage. Sir Alan landed a blow that, by the sound of the crunch, broke most of Sir Fergus's sternum and ribcage. Sir Muckle laughed and Sir Fergus grabbed him by the throat and squeezed until the young guys eyes were bulging out of their sockets.

The audience were on their feet. Clapping loudly, stamping and placing extraordinary bets as to the outcome of the fight and the fate of the triplets. The King dumped a startled Gab to the floor, jumped to his feet and started making his own bets. The room was a baying pack of hounds: keen for blood, tissues, and carnage. Someone up the back may have requested a hat instead.

The bloody, squealing Knights began rolling around the floor. The gross ball of flesh gathered momentum and began heading for the scenery. Smash! The scenery wobbled... then teetered.. then collapsed under the onslaught of head butts, hair pulling and noisy slaps.

Bub jumped to his feet...

# CHAPTER SIXTY-FOUR

**D**evil Keith's quest continues...

Devil Keith and tiny Patrick managed to drag the torn Knights and Harry's beaten sisters through the dismal dungeon. They had to stop every few seconds, but finally they emerged at the drawbridge over the moat. Patrick had suggested that they cover themselves in the flagon of alcohol as it would hide their stumbling and fatigue.

*"You'll also need this,"* Patrick handed over a small, wrapped bundle and weakly smiled.

The massive Crabs crashed from their secret hiding spot and ran, full pelt, at the shocked team. Devil Keith panicked and tried to hide the package behind his back.

*"So, what do we have here then? Can't walk straight? Had a bit too much of the old falling down juice, eh? Oh, you smell ripe. Had a good night then? Glad to hear it,"* Pincer Stuart had removed his heavily chewed cigar stub. He was laughing and putting them at their ease. He slipped his machine gun from his shoulder and placed it on the ground.

The exhausted team made to walk off. *"Hold up. What do you have in your hand? Eh? Hand it over NOW!"* the tone had changed, and the threat of violence was blatantly obvious. Devil Keith wondered if the look-out position was still vacant. That sounded like a much better option.

Devil Keith stopped. He looked at the snarling Crabs but quickly realised that he couldn't fight them both whilst keeping the damaged Knights and sisters safe. The subdued polar bears were taking far too much interest in the team and there was a floating log with teeth heading their way too. No, he couldn't fight the Crabs, the bears and a crocodile. Devil Keith reluctantly handed over the small, wrapped bundle.

*"Holding out on us were you? It's good to share. Good for your heath I mean, ha, ha, ha,"* and with that Pincer Jim opened the small bundle.

*"Oy, Pincer Stuart look what we have here. A couple of cigars and a box of matches, eh? Now what were you going to do with them?"* The Crab sneered.

*"Smoke them?"* Devil Keith tentatively asked. He looked at little Patrick. The team had placed all their faith in being able to bribe the Crabs? That wasn't what they expected. They thought, despite enlisting two four-year-olds, that the Crab solution would involve something painful. Or rough, or at the very least…unpleasant. This was an anti-climax and the mood fell accordingly.

The beleaguered team slowly walked into the woods, with the Crab's cruel laughter their marching tune. Once clear of the Crabs, Devil Keith put the Drill against a tree. The light appeared and they helped the Knights, Periwinkle, Willing and Fachance through the portal.

*"It will work. I pinkie promise,"* whispered Patrick as he too left to go home. Devil Keith passed them the Drill and trudged back to the Banqueting Hall. Just before entering the hall, he stopped and slapped his forehead. *"Why did I give them the Drill?"* He thought.

The plan was failing…

# CHAPTER SIXTY-FIVE

The Banqueting Hall in chaos…

Bub was on his knees sifting through the broken scenery. He hoped that Harry and Devil Keith hadn't made it back in time. He would rather suffer the consequences than have them both lying hurt under the debris. He lifted a large section of the scenery and he spotted a beaten Karen underneath it. She was dazed and there was blood dripping from a deep head wound, but luckily she was alive. Bub propped her up then started searching again

The King pointed at another area of the buckled stage. *"Pick that up and find those three wastrels, Dear Hearts. A night or two with the gargoyles is required to cool their heels. Then an eternity in the dungeons. Haw, haw, haw."*

Sir Fergus had lost most of his magnificent orange beard and his head currently looked like a shiny bowling ball. The maniacal hair pulling was at a high-school girl level of extreme violence. Sir Muckle's head was decidedly floppy as his vertebrae had been pounded and crushed during the vicious choking episode. Sir Alan had a spoon in one eye and the heel from a glass slipper wedged in the other eye. They all had protruding bones, torn nostrils, and the odd missing ear lobe.

*"Well, well, Dear Hearts. Where are the rest of the cast? Off, a wandering? I'd bet. My castle is so fascinating. Haw, haw, haw."* The King smirked and giggled.

*"We're over here,"* and with that Harry and Devil Keith picked themselves up off the floor. They were covered in dust,

limping, and coughing but there was no evidence of blood or guts. Bub went to leap over the debris to get to Harry and give her a hug, but Gab held him back.

*"Not now, we may have gotten away with it. I think the King still thinks that I'm an actress."* whispered Gab.

*"Well, the entertainment has been well and truly ruined. I expected at least one fatality to lighten the mood, haw, haw, haw. I won't be honouring any of my bets. I think it was all a fix. The person who requested a hat...see me later.*

*I also think it's about time that you lot left, Dear Hearts. Bub, you returned my cat and the naughty Knights. I can't be bothered discussing terms with you just now. Please leave, but be prepared to accept and respond to my next summons. We are not finished yet. Not by a long shot. Haw, haw, haw.*

*I'll see you all out. I don't want to risk one of you ruffians trying to steal my glorious paintings. Off we go now, Dear Heats. Pick up that dreadfully, untalented Wicked Stepmother. I will be billing you all for the cleaning of the floors. Blood is so hard to get out of marble. Haw, haw, haw."* The King did a fair bit of kicking and slapping as he guided his guests out of his Banqueting Hall.

# CHAPTER SIXTY-SIX

F reedom...

The pantomime actors, the triplets and Bub were pushed and shoved out of the castle. They couldn't believe that they had made it over the moat. They were going home. It was over and everyone was safe.

*"Dear Hearts, just one tiny thing. I think you know this little chap. He's been ever so helpful. Telling all sorts of 'tales out of school,' as the saying goes. Prince Charming or should I say Devil Keith, what a terrible disguise. You really shouldn't have tried to ruin his fashion label? You already had his coat for your eyebrows. You greedy, greedy little piggy. Oink, oink, little piggy. Haw, haw, haw."* The King pulled Chick, the mouse, from a side pocket in his robe then roughly pushed him into a small, metal cage. The Hell number one team gasped.

*"You have outlived your usefulness, Dear Hearts. Goodbye tattle tale. Ha, haw, haw."* The King threw the cage into the cavernous mouth of the nearest yodelling polar bear.

*"Enjoy the tiny morsel, my pet. Oh, I can see by your faces that you had no idea that he was nipping back and forth with all that scintillating information. It was such a shame, and quite frankly a surprise, when Devil Keith worked out that he was the collaborator, Dear Hearts. My huffy little spy. He moved into the castle after that and I've had to put up with Chick's whinging since that oaf's discovery. Such a bore. Knights, now. Haw, haw, haw."* The King screamed into the night air.

At least four dozen hostile Knights broke cover and

surrounded the unsuspecting team. The Knights withdrew enormous swords, powerful maces, razor sharp spears, and colossal clubs, just waiting for the order to attack and maim.

*"It's so satisfying to give hope then snatch it all away, don't you think? Now, what will we do with you? Let's start with Harry, the talentless Faery Godmother. Bub, I could see you squirming all through the entertainment. It was so deliciously naughty having her on my knee and you helpless to defend her, Dear Hearts. My loyal crocodile, bring her over here. Haw, haw, haw."* The King nodded his head, and the moat crocodile used his heavy tail to knock the stunned Faery Godmother into the King's waiting arms. The King grabbed the Faery Godmother by the throat and dangled her off the ground. The King was enjoying pushing his torn, grubby fingernails into the Faery's tightly stretched neck and jaw.

Bub realised that Gab was right. The King only knew part of the plan. He probably didn't know about the Lance, and he definitely didn't know that Gab was the Faery Godmother and an Angel to boot.

*"I can't believe how good your disguise is, Harry. You've gone from a ratty little urchin to this truly magical creature. Your fake wings are superb. I may commission my very own set, Dear Hearts. I'm so glad that I get to keep you with me forever. Then share you... repeatedly, Dear Hearts. You'll make such a lovely prize for the winner of the talent competition, haw, haw, haw. My brother will be so happy to take what's left of you off my hands. There's a box, in his magic show, just dying to be occupied.*

*Oh, you must realise that your sisters are positively plain compared to you, my lovely big girl. Plus, they do complain... an awful lot. They want to be fed every day. The greedy vultures! Haw, haw, haw."* The King bent double with glee and mirth.

Harry was puzzled. She looked over at Bub and Bub subtly shrugged his shoulders. Harry's sisters, how di...? All at once, Bub and Harry realised that the evil King had kidnapped their Willing and Fachance.

*"Oh, poor little Bub. You didn't know? Did I forget to say? Yes, I have them residing in the luxury that they so richly deserve, Dear Hearts. Now where was I? Let me think, what do I have before me? I have my majestic cat back and all four Horsewomen of the Apocalypse at my disposal. And dispose of them I shall. To be honest Harry, I can't believe you let your pregnant sister join your suicide mission and you gave her the starring role as Cinderella, too. How were you going to hide that? Tut, tut. The delectable Stan has obviously left that disgusting breeder to her own devices. Good for him.*

*My naughty, traitorous Knights are back and languishing in the deepest dungeon, Dear Hearts. I also have both of the Hell number one twins all of a twitter. Plus, I have the real power behind your Hell. The bounteous Karen, or do you want to be called the talentless Wicked Stepmother? Haw, haw, haw. Oh, and you lot: the moronic triplets. You're welcome to share Hell number one's fate. In fact I insist. Double haw, haw, haw."* The jolly King was ecstatically counting off his prisoners on his bony fingers.

Harry was momentarily puzzled until she realised that the King still thought Dippit was Cinderella. Gab's identity remained a mystery to the King. They still had a small chance. She hoped that Angel Boy was well and truly annoyed by the King's wandering hands, and that he was willing to act on that anger.

*"Search them whilst I explore this delight again, Dear Hearts. I want their Drill to add to my Lance. Don't spare the pregnant one either. Treat her as roughly as the rest. Afterall, we don't want any more of those lowly demon-type things birthed. Haw, haw, haw."* The King roughly pushed his hands under Gab's ruffled skirts and began cruelly prodding and poking.

*"That's what the King wanted to do to his Harry,"* Bub's brain bellowed. Bub threw back his head and he roared. Then he roared again. His skin became mottled as it infused with blood and pus. He exploded. He sprinted at the King with the speed and focus of a juggernaut. He was powering across the drawbridge and he started swinging at the frightened King. Viciously punching,

kicking, and repeatedly slapping the cowering creature. The King wasn't prepared for the volume of pure rage focused on his spiteful personage. Not prepared at all. Bub jumped up and grabbed the King by his skinny shoulders then furiously head butted him. The noise: a loud, rupturing crack was nauseating for the witnesses to hear never mind the King to feel. The King looked like he had been hit in the forehead with a pickaxe. His skull burst open to reveal a small sticky grey brain hiding beneath. Before the King could fully react to the cranial explosion Bub grabbed him by the hair. Ripping the hair out by the roots and making Sir Fergus's hair pulling episode look like an Indian Head Massage. The King was dizzily flailing around and screeching for help.

Meanwhile, Angel Gab did a quick risk assessment. He spread his beautiful wings and flew high into the air; avoiding the freight train that was a furious Bub. He ripped off the confining dress then turned and sharply dived into the trifle moat. He bypassed the shocked polar bears and within seconds he was violently wrestling with the enormous crocodile. He needed to burn off some of his anger, plus that big "bag wannabee" had it coming. "Knocking him around and letting that disgusting King have another grope." Gab's brain kept repeating this as he did a half nelson hold on the repulsive reptile.

The Hell number one team and the triplets leapt into action. Although grossly outnumbered, they were giving it their all. Slaps, kicks, knees and elbows collided with steel armour and flying polar bear fur, but that didn't stop the determined but exhausted team. They still had Fachance and Willing to save from the King's clutches. Let the blood splatter and fall. They were giving it their absolute all. Wow, and time for a tiny bit of excellent poetry too.

"Pincer Stuart and Pincer Jim. Help me, I command you," the King screeched. He had clearly lost his sense of humour and most of his brain's frontal lobe. He needed reinforcements and fast.

*"No, no, no. Not those two evil beings,"* thought Harry. She tried to pull her bundle out of her pocket. She still wasn't sure what she was to do with it, but she trusted her wee Liam to come up with the goods.

The Crabs came wondering out of their hiding place. Blissfully ignorant of the carnage going on around the drawbridge. *"It's all good man. Take a chill pill or better yet. A wee draw on this."* The Crabs began laughing as they nudged each other and puffed on their newly acquired cigars. They then pulled a couple of the larger polar bears into a full body hug and roughly knuckle rubbed the bear's furry heads.

*"They're stoned. The Crabs are completely stoned."* Harry laughed, abandoning her search for the other bundle. Those clever little boys did it. No wonder they didn't want to tell anyone what they were up to. Oh, their mammy is gonna ground them for sure.

The Crabs released the semi-bald bears then began awkwardly, and unsteadily, sauntering over to the distraught King. Bub stopped beating on the King and pulled out a packet of cheesy balls. He threw it at the jolly guys. *"For the munchies boys. Enjoy."*

*"Cheers mate,"* the Crabs caught the snacks and crashed against a large tree. Laughing, munching their treats, and lighting another cigar: the fight hadn't even started for them, and it wasn't likely to either.

Harry looked around. The Hell number one team were being pushed back into the castle by the King's Knights. They could, maybe, manage a few more minutes but the team were hurt and exhausted. They might have to accept their fate and surrender. Harry thought that at least she'd get to see two of her sisters again and their vulnerable Dippit was safely tucked away at home.

***"Tommy talks,"*** an axe came hurtling through the air and sliced an unsuspecting Knight between his eyes. Another six axes followed in quick succession.

"*Yous hurts mys kitty,*" Brownie Nelli charged at a Knight, picked him up by the scruff of his neck and threw him to a hungry polar bear. Then she threw another and yet another. Clearing a path to the suddenly revitalised team.

"*Has somes of mines bricks, yous baddies.*" Brownie Anne squealed. Several missiles sailed through the air and dazed the nearest Knights. The Knights fell and the polar bears received a second course of tenderised dinner. The poor polar bears were getting really quite full up by then.

Brownie Gillian and Brownie Lisa somersaulted and cartwheeled onto the bridge, knocking down Knights as they went. A few well-placed Karate chops and some very brutal Chinese burns saw off the rest of the Knights.

"*Not fair. Not fair,*" screamed the stunned, bitter King. Bub used the Brownie distraction to knock the battered King into the trifle filled moat. The King shouted on the polar bears for help, but the polar bears were still wearing their earmuffs, so they were puzzled by the King's panicked movements and left him be.

"*I should have invested more coins in Lady Waddell's excellent Sign Language School,*" really should have been the King's final thought. In fact, his thought was, "*why is this jelly so thick and why didn't I wear any underpants today. It's getting everywhere, ughhhhhh,*"

# CHAPTER SIXTY-SEVEN

Post-fight tidy up...

The remaining Knights were covered in runny honey. They were securely tied up against a tree and left for the marauding polar bears to chew on. Mmm, breakfast with added iron.

Devil Keith explained the sisters' situation to Harry before she had the opportunity to tear the castle apart and mount a second rescue operation. Whew! That would have been a wee shade messy. Devil Keith then received a disturbingly enormous number of hugs for his rescue efforts. Devil Keith was appalled by Harry's affection and subtly asked her if she thought he was Bub. Or to be accurate he told her to get off him and keep her overgrown armpit hair from his person as he was a Supreme Being then there was some twaddle about squirrels, etc.

Harry laughingly assured him that she knew who he was. Devil Keith was in complete awe of his heroic brother as even the thought of a Harry hug was vomit inducing and to think, Bub regularly *"took one for the team."*

*"What a guy,"* a struggling Devil Keith mumbled into Harry's tangled hair.

The teams, the triplets and the Brownies all happily left Hell number three. Bub dropped the Brownies off in Hell number two and thanked Mac for all their help.

"*Devil Keith accidentally gave the Knights your Drill, so they immediately sent Periwinkle back here. Incidentally, please stop using so much duct tape to bind his paws. He's not that scary. So Periwinkle told the Brownies that you lot were in trouble. Well, Brownie Nelli just took off. One of their badges is a Dimensional Badge so they went for it. It surely was a sight to behold. I didn't know that they could do that,*" Mac was tucking the tired wee monsters into their blankies for a well-deserved nappy, nap.

"*Wait. Periwinkle can speak? Without folks needing to use pee infused tea?*" Bub enquired with a raised eyebrow.

"*Bub, all the animals can speak and we can understand them. It's to do with a Hell having a second horn. Didn't you know? It was in my pamphlet.*" Mac patted his arm.

"*I spoke with Trevor, but it just didn't click. Oh, that minx,*" Bub laughed; and thought about a suitable punishment for his Harry.

Back in Hell number one…

A smiling Bub returned to Hell number one. A frail Fachance and Willing were laying on the sofa. They were trying to sip water as Dr Riel slowly checked them over. Harry and Dippit were crying, wiping snot, and hugging their sisters. Generally getting in the road.

"*We'll tell you about it later. Need to sleep just now,*" and with that Willing drifted off into a nightmare laden sleep.

"*Well, I think that's the last we've seen of the King. We have his Lance so he can't visit here and the Crabs kinda like us. I think.*" Devil Keith smiled, brushed his palms together and started to wander off to his room.

"*Dream on, Devil Keithie boy. This isn't over. You still have to sort out Hell number one, recalibrate The Oracles and fix your horrendous love life,*" whispered the authors.

# THE DEVIL'S A...

**The Devil's A Courting**

**The Devil's A Fighting**

**The Devil's A Hunting**

**The Devil's A Learning**

Printed in Great Britain
by Amazon